"Perhaps," he said suddenly, "that would be the answer."

"Answer to what?"

"The answer to what we should do about this inconvenient attraction I feel for you."

"I…I don't understand you."

"Oh, yes, you do."

He closed the distance she'd put between them and murmured into her ear again. The heat of his breath slid all the way down her spine.

"We should become lovers, Lydia. And lay the past to rest in your bed."

He straightened and gave her a slow, sultry perusal.

"Just send me word. Whenever you are ready I will be more than happy to oblige."

* * *

Reforming the Viscount
Harlequin® Historical #1140—June 2013

Author Note

The house in which I've set this story was inspired by Sezincote, the home of a genuine "nabob." He had gone out to India as a young man, risen through the ranks of the East India Company Army and returned to England in his later years a very wealthy man. When he designed the mansion where he intended to spend his retirement, he provided his architect with sketches he'd drawn of Mogul architecture, which he wanted incorporated in his home.

In 1807 the Prince Regent, whilst staying with the Marquess of Hertford at Ragley Hall, heard about this unique house and drove over to take a look. He was so impressed that he promptly decided his Royal Pavilion at Brighton should have domes and minarets, too…only more of them! In one of the main reception rooms of Sezincote there is still a painting of the Prince Regent tooling his curricle up the drive.

There are reminders of India throughout the grounds, too. Statues of Brahmin bulls adorn the parapets of the bridge that takes visitors over the stream that winds through the gardens. And instead of having a classical Greek temple, which is a feature of so many stately homes of England, there really is a temple to Suraya, the Hindu goddess of the sun.

REFORMING the Viscount

ANNIE BURROWS

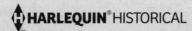

HARLEQUIN® HISTORICAL

Recycling programs
for this product may
not exist in your area.

ISBN-13: 978-0-373-29740-5

REFORMING THE VISCOUNT

Copyright © 2013 by Annie Burrows

This edition published by arrangement with Harlequin Books S.A.

For questions and comments about the quality of this book, please contact us at CustomerService@Harlequin.com.

® and TM are trademarks of Harlequin Enterprises Limited or its corporate affiliates. Trademarks indicated with ® are registered in the United States Patent and Trademark Office, the Canadian Trade Marks Office and in other countries.

Printed in U.S.A.

**Did you know that these novels are also
available as ebooks? Visit www.Harlequin.com.**

To all the scientists and doctors who've discovered medicines to cure us, vaccinations to protect us and treatments to help us through diseases that used to kill and maim the most vulnerable members of society.

ANNIE BURROWS

has been making up stories for her own amusement since she first went to school. As soon as she got the hang of using a pencil she began to write them down. Her love of books meant she had to do a degree in English literature. And her love of writing meant she could never take on a job where she didn't have time to jot down notes when inspiration for a new plot struck her. She still wants the heroines of her stories to wear beautiful floaty dresses and triumph over all that life can throw at them. But when she got married she discovered that finding a hero is an essential ingredient to arriving at "happy ever after."

Chapter One

'Who is that man you are staring at?'

Rose's question snapped Lydia straight out of her state of heart-fluttering, dry-mouthed, weak-kneed tumult.

'I was not *staring* at anyone.'

She'd managed to remember she was supposed to be setting an example for her stepdaughter, and behaved with as much circumspection as she'd ever been able to achieve at the age of eighteen. She'd watched him surreptitiously, in a series of thirsty little glances, knowing that gazing at him directly, with her heart in her eyes, would be *fatal*.

Though not only for herself, this time round. Poor Rose had enough to contend with, during her first Season, without the behaviour of her stepmama adding fuel to the fire. So far, people were treating her as though she was a perfectly respectable widow. To her face, at least. But a woman's reputation was a fragile thing, and she knew—oh, yes, she knew—that there must be talk. How could there not be?

'Yes, but you do know him, don't you? The handsome one. The man over there, talking to Lord Chepstow and his friends.'

'Oh, him,' said Lydia airily, striving to conceal how guilty she felt at having been caught out. Sometimes, Rose reminded her of her own chaperon, Mrs Westerly. Both of them noticed everything.

'Do not waste your time in that direction,' the eagle-eyed woman had warned her, when she'd noticed her doing exactly what she was doing tonight. *'The entire family is at point-non plus. Yet again. They have a habit of marrying heiresses to pull them out of the mire. Not that this particular Hemingford is showing any signs of wishing to give up his bachelor lifestyle just yet. But you mark my words, when the time comes, he will do as his forebears have always done.'*

'Yes, I do know him, slightly,' she admitted. 'That is the Honourable...' honourable? Hah! Not so as you'd notice '...Nicholas Hemingford.'

'Oh, do tell me all about him.'

'There isn't much to tell,' said Lydia, blushing at the outright lie.

For she'd fallen head-over-heels in love with him. In spite of his reputation. In spite of her chaperon's dire warnings. Like a moth to a flame, she'd been completely unable to withstand the pull of that lop-sided, slightly self-deprecating smile of his, never mind the mischievous twinkle in his blue, blue eyes.

She hadn't stood a chance when he'd decided, for his own typically eccentric reasons, to turn the full force of his charm upon her.

She mocked her younger self for feeling as though he'd thrown her a lifeline, for it had turned out to be no more than a gossamer thread of wishful thinking.

Which had snapped the moment she had to put it to the test.

'I danced with him once or twice during my own Season,' she told Rose, striving to make it sound as though it had been a trivial matter.

'And you have never forgotten him,' observed Rose with typical astuteness.

'No.' She sighed. And then, because if she didn't give Rose the impression she was being open with her, she would never let the matter drop until she'd wrung the very last ounce of the truth from her, she admitted, 'He is not the kind of person one forgets. He is so…unique.'

'Really? In what way?'

'Well, for one thing, he was an incorrigible flirt,' she said tartly. 'I used to watch him regularly reducing the prettiest girls in the room into giggling, blushing confusion, then saunter away while they all sighed after his retreating back. Usually straight over to the plainest, most unprepossessing of the wallflowers drooping on the sidelines, where he would make her evening by leading her into a set of country dances.'

'Well…that was kind of him.'

When Lydia frowned, Rose added, 'Wasn't it?'

'I do not think kindness forms part of his character,' she said repressively. 'It just amused him to set female hearts a-flutter. His real interest was always gambling. No doubt what he is doing now,' she said, indicating the group of men who had all subtly shifted position to include him in their number, 'is arranging to meet them in the card room later.'

'But…' Rose was frowning '…if he only danced with the wallflowers, how is it—?'

'I was quite ill, if you recall, by the time I met your father. My chaperon insisted I attend every event to which I'd received an invitation, in the hope I would somehow make a conquest. Which wore me down. So I was not in looks.'

What an understatement! Mrs Westerly had insisted she apply rouge to disguise her pallor and rice powder to conceal the shadows under her eyes. It had made her resemble a walking corpse. Or so the charmed circle surrounding that Season's reigning beauty had sniggered, as she'd walked past.

The night she'd tumbled so hopelessly in love with Nicholas Hemingford, she *had* been, indisputably, the most desperately unhappy female in the place. Her Season had started out badly and gone steadily downhill. And after overhearing the cutting comments about her appearance, she'd started to try to edge her way out of the ballroom, desperate for some respite from the heat, the crush, the overwhelming sense of failure. Otherwise he might never have noticed her.

Just as he had not noticed her tonight. He was sauntering away from the group of men now, heading unerringly for the furthest corner of the ballroom, where a rather plump young lady was sitting somewhat apart from the others, looking a bit forlorn.

Oh lord, he was doing it again.

The plump girl's face lit up when he bowed over her hand. Lydia knew just how that girl felt as he escorted her across the room to the set which was starting to form. She would hardly be able to believe that a man as handsome as Mr Hemingford had actually asked her to dance without any coercion from the matrons who sometimes prompted the younger men to do their duty by the girls who lacked partners. Her heart would be fluttering, her soul brimming with gratitude. Pray God this one didn't mistake his casual fit of knight-errantry for anything meaningful and get it broken.

'Why do you suppose,' said Rose thoughtfully, 'he only dances with plain girls?'

'Well, he would tell you,' she replied, 'that everyone deserves to enjoy themselves when they attend a ball, no matter what. He would say that he hated having to look at long faces, and if nobody else would do anything about it, then he would.'

'But you don't think that was true?'

'Oh, no.' She laughed a little bitterly. 'Once, he actually admitted that there was no point in asking any of the eligible females on the premises to dance, because their chaperons would not have granted him permission. He was considered too dangerous.'

'Dangerous?' Rose's eyes widened. 'And was he?'

'Oh, yes.' To the peace of mind of lonely, desperately unhappy females, anyway.

She inhaled sharply. Then breathed out slowly.

There was no point in getting angry about the way he'd made her yearn for the impossible. Nor the careless way he'd tempted her into believing it was within her grasp. It had all happened what felt like a lifetime ago.

Except that seeing him again made it feel as though it had only been yesterday.

At her first sight of him, she'd reacted exactly as she had done when she'd been an impressionable girl of Rose's age. And she could hardly tear her eyes away from him as he led the plump girl on to the floor.

Though there was some consolation in noticing she was not the only female tracking his progress across the ballroom with fascination.

For there was something about the way he moved that always drew admiring glances. While some men could manage to look impressive only when standing perfectly still, striking a pose, Nicholas Hemingford brought a kind of languid grace to the steps which had the effect of making her insides turn to molten toffee.

When the gentlemen lined up, facing her, he ended up standing practically opposite her. And though she didn't want to, she simply couldn't help taking the opportunity, while his attention was all on his partner, to take a good long look at him.

Oh, but he was just as handsome as ever. His light brown hair was cut slightly shorter nowadays, but other than that, he'd hardly changed at all. Just as fit and trim, and elegantly dressed as ever.

Typical! Why couldn't he have run to fat, or developed the raddled complexion of so many of his contemporaries? But, no—he'd managed to carry on with his dissipated lifestyle and emerged unscathed. Just as he'd always done.

She snapped open her fan and waved it vigorously before her heated cheeks. It gave her something to occupy her hands, instead of clenching them into fists and pounding them into the nearest hard surface.

The movement must have caught his eye, for his head jerked up and for a moment or two he looked straight at her.

Her heart pounded against her ribs. She lifted her chin and stared right back at him.

Yes, Nicholas, it's me. Look. I survived. And now I'm back. And what have you to say for yourself?

To her shock, and fury, his gaze slid right past her without so much as a flicker of recognition.

'It did not look as though he remembered you, Mama Lyddy,' said Rose, unwittingly touching on the bruise he'd just inflicted.

'No. Well,' she bit out, 'why should he? It has been eight years since he last saw me. And I was only one of a large crowd of insignificant females he favoured with his attentions.'

All these years, in spite of everything, she'd hugged her memories of him to herself in secret. But it looked as though he'd forgotten all about her.

Because she hadn't really meant anything to him, had she?

'Is something the matter?'

'It is a little lowering,' she admitted, 'to be so completely unmemorable.'

It was worse than that. Until now, she'd harboured a faint hope that he might have meant what he'd said, even if only for those few heady moments when he'd held her in his arms. The words he'd murmured into her ears that had made her feel as though she was clasped in a lover's embrace…when the reality was that he'd only caught her up because she'd almost fainted. And he'd been nearest to her when it happened. Anyone would have been chivalrous enough to carry her into the shade. And yet, for those few minutes it had taken to carry her into the cool interior of the house, it had felt as though he was transporting her to heaven. Feeling his arms round her, being so close she could inhale his unique scent as she burrowed her face into his shoulder, hearing him say the words she'd never believed a man like him could say—words of yearning, and possibility, that had made her heart soar with hope…

Not that hope had lasted all that long.

The moment he'd put her down, he'd backed away, his face a picture of regret.

And he'd never come near her again.

The band struck up, the gentlemen bowed to their

partners, and Lydia delved into her reticule for a handkerchief.

'Mama Lyddy?'

Rose was looking at her with concern.

Lydia blew her nose rather crossly, since if there was one thing she hated it was letting her emotions get the better of her. 'That is what comes of dwelling on memories of my own Season.'

'They do not look as though they were very happy memories,' Rose observed.

Lydia grimaced. 'They were not.'

Rose sighed and glanced up at her half-brother, who was standing behind their chairs, glowering at the entire assembly.

'Was it worse than this?'

'Oh, Rose, are you not enjoying yourself?'

'How can I,' she muttered mutinously, 'when Robert is being so impossible?'

Since the orchestra was going at full pelt and they were muttering to each other behind their fans, Lydia did not think Robert would overhear, even though she suspected Rose half-hoped he would.

'I am sure he is only trying to be protective…'

'Well, I wish he wouldn't. I don't see why he would not let me dance with Lord Abergele.'

Nor had Lydia, not really. Though since she'd got into the habit of playing peacemaker between the siblings, she said, 'I expect he had his reasons…'

Rose turned to her, muttering crossly, 'He probably thinks he is just a fortune hunter.'

'Oh? Well, then…'

'But I don't care! It's not as if I have come to town to get a husband, only to find my feet in society. And how am I ever going to do that if he will keep every man who shows an interest in me at arm's length? Lord Abergele has a sister, who has the kind of connections that would be most useful. Now that he's offended the brother, I have no hope of making a friend of her either.'

And what was worse, now that he'd turned down a perfectly respectable dance partner on her behalf, Rose couldn't dance with anyone else this evening.

'I will have a word with him,' said Lydia. Not that it would do much good. He was far too much like his father, firmly believing he knew best, and expecting his family to fall in with his wishes without question.

And, yes, she conceded that it must be particularly hard for him to listen to her opinion, because she was four years younger than him. She could understand why he'd taken to treating her as though she was another of his younger sisters, rather than with the respect he should have accorded a stepmama, but it didn't make it any less annoying.

Particularly when he stood over them both, as he was doing tonight, like some kind of guard dog, his hackles rising when anyone he considered unsuitable came anywhere near his beautiful sister. Signalling to the entire world that he did not quite trust her to keep Rose safe.

At the exact moment she firmed her lips with pique, and flicked her fan shut, the line of gentlemen stepped forwards in unison, and Hemingford's eyes lit on her, briefly.

He did not smile this time, either, but he did grant her a slight nod of his head.

So he'd finally dredged up a memory that hadn't troubled him for years, had he?

Or perhaps he had recognised her before, but it had been his guilty conscience that made his eyes slide away from her. Just as he'd slid out of the room, and out of her life, after uttering the statement he'd so clearly regretted the moment it had left his lips.

'Oh, he does remember you after all.'

Rose was looking, not at him, but at her, with a perplexed expression. And she realised she was trembling. She'd become so angry at the casual way he'd broken her heart that she was physically quivering with it.

What was happening to her? For years she'd managed to preserve an outward semblance of serenity no matter what she'd been thinking. In fact, the last time she'd got so worked up she couldn't control her physical reaction had been her wedding day.

Her knees had been shaking so badly she'd started to worry she might not make it all the way down the aisle. But even so, she'd managed to lift her chin and force a smile to her lips, determined that nobody should guess how scared she was. Particularly not her husband. Colonel Morgan had frowned when he'd taken her hand to slip the ring on her finger, feeling her tremors. He hadn't liked the notion she might be afraid of him, of what she'd agreed to. So as she'd spoken her vows, she'd made secret ones of her own. That she was never, ever, going to let her feelings get the better of her again. She would keep a mask of calm acceptance firmly in place at all times.

And until tonight, she'd been able to do so.

Before she could pull herself together sufficiently to form some plausible excuse, Robert leaned down and growled into her ear, 'I quite forgot that you knew him.'

Oh, lord, that was all she needed. Now she was going to have to convince Robert, too, that he had merely been an acquaintance. If he should guess she had been in love with him, and was, to judge by her remarkable reactions just now, still far too susceptible to him, he would no doubt redouble his guard-doggy role towards her, as well as Rose. It was bad enough that he was already undermining her role as chaperon, with his heavy-handed vetting of all Rose's potential admirers. She simply could not hand him the opportunity to accuse her of setting a bad example for Rose to follow. That would be the end of ever getting him to listen to her point of view.

In an automatic gesture of self-defence, she parried his query with a thrust of her own.

'You have a short memory, then. It was he who introduced you to me, in the first place. Do you not recall? He brought me to one of those picnics you used to hold at Westdene.'

'But I thought you said you only danced with him once or twice,' put in Rose.

'Did I?' She had to wave her fan quite swiftly to cool the heat that rushed to her cheeks. 'Well, it hardly amounted to much more than that, really.'

Although he had been what her chaperon described as 'particular in his attentions,' after that first dance. They'd both been surprised by the number of times he'd called upon her, and sought her out as a dance partner, even though she'd blushed and stumbled her way inelegantly through set after set of country dances. He had not been put off by her stammer, or her apparent stupidity, not like the other men who'd shown an initial interest in her. If anything, he had redoubled his efforts to put her at ease. And gradually, she'd found herself unfurling in his company.

To the extent that one afternoon, as they'd been walking in the park, she'd let slip that she couldn't understand why he bothered with her.

'If that is a hint you wish me to leave you be,' he'd

warned her with mock severity, 'then you are going to have to stop looking so pleased when I come to call.'

She'd blushed harder and studied her feet for several paces, before plucking up the courage to answer.

'I d-do not want you to leave me be. I-I like your company.'

'That is just as well,' he said cheerfully, 'because I have no intention of leaving you be until I have coaxed one genuine smile from your lips.'

'B-but, why? I m-mean, what can it m-matter to you? M-Mrs Westerly s-says you aren't interested in m-m—'

'No! Do not say that word in my presence,' he'd cried in mock horror. 'There is more to life than…' he'd looked round as though checking to see if anyone might overhear, before bending to whisper in her ear '…matrimony. We can enjoy a walk in the park on a sunny afternoon, or a dance together, just for its own sake, can we not?'

'The sun is not shining today,' she had remarked with sinking spirits, as they'd halted in front of a patch of equally depressed-looking daffodils which were straining their golden trumpets in the direction the sun would have been shining from, had it been able to penetrate the heavy layers of cloud. In spite of Mrs Westerly warning her not to read too much into the way he'd taken her up, her foolish heart had dared to think that perhaps he was not such a lost cause as everyone thought.

'But we can still enjoy each other's company, can we not,' he'd said, 'without expecting it to lead to wedding bells?'

She associated the scent of daffodils with the death of her romantic hopes to this very day.

'We can,' she'd said, forcing a smile to her lips,

though she had not been able to look up into his face. If a light friendship was all he was prepared to offer, she would do nothing to scare him off, for sharing the occasional few minutes with this wickedly witty and dashingly handsome young man had become the only bright spot in her otherwise gloomy existence.

'B-besides, everyone knows you aren't in the market for a wife. And even if you were, you wouldn't look twice at someone like me. You know I have no dowry, I suppose?'

'Of course I do. The tabbies make sure everyone knows every newcomer's net worth within five minutes of their entering any ballroom. It makes no difference to how I feel about you.'

Well, it wouldn't since he didn't see her as a potential wife.

'And yet,' he'd said, tucking her arm into his and setting out along the path again, 'you still…light up whenever I ask you to dance.'

'Well, you do dance divinely,' she'd admitted. 'And Mrs Westerly says—' She'd broken off, biting down on her lower lip.

'Go on. Tell me what Mrs Westerly says. I promise that however bad it may be, it won't surprise me. Chaperons normally give their charges dire warnings about me.'

'Well, she says that it is no bad thing to spend time with you, because you make me smile. Which makes me look more attractive to *eligible* men.'

'Aha! So that is why she doesn't forbid me to pollute her drawing room with my presence.'

She'd nodded, lulled into a sense of…something almost like companionship as they'd strolled along, arm in arm. Which could be the only thing to account for her blurting, 'Not that it does any good, in the long term. Because the moment I try to talk to anyone eligible, I start blushing and stammering so much they take me for a perfect ninny. And if there is one thing a man does not want, that is to take a ninny to wife. Not unless she is a great heiress, or has a very grand title.'

At that point, Nicholas had given her a quizzical look and observed, 'But today you have stopped stammering altogether.'

'Why, yes, so I have.'

'It is because you aren't striving to impress me. You know I am completely ineligible.'

Was that what it had been? Or was it just that she'd finally given up all hope of anything more than friendship?

'I dare say your chaperon has warned you,' he'd said airily, 'that there is a good deal of bad blood in my family. The first Rothersthorpe was little better than a pirate, you know, although Good Queen Bess rewarded him for his efforts against the Spanish with the title.'

'Oh, yes. Everyone knows that. But what she primarily objects to is…your lack of money. Mrs Westerly warned me that is why you invite me to go for walks with you, rather than taking me for a drive around the park.'

'Did she? The old b—besom,' he'd said. 'Though of course it's true. I haven't a feather to fly with.'

'Perhaps,' she'd said with just a touch of asperity, 'if you did not place wagers on such ridiculous things…'

'Such as?'

'Well, I did hear there was one between a goose and a mouse.'

He'd let out a surprised bark of laughter. 'Who told

you about that? Not that it isn't true. But at least I backed the mouse. Won a packet,' he'd finished smugly.

'And on what did you subsequently lose that packet?' she'd snapped. 'The turn of a card?'

'No! I am an extremely proficient card player,' he'd said, raising his chin just a little, which showed she'd touched him on the raw. But after only a few leisurely paces, his lips curving into a smile, he'd darted her a look of pure mischief and confessed, 'It was a horse.'

She'd pursed her lips.

'You are right,' he'd sighed, in mock despair. 'I am incorrigible. Money flows through my hands like water. Cannot keep a hold on it for longer than five minutes. And yet,' he'd said, giving her a quizzical look, 'you never appear to think that coming for walks with me is a waste of time. Even when there are no potential suitors about to witness you smiling and managing to string whole sentences together without stammering.'

Her heart had thundered so hard in her chest it had been almost painful. If he guessed how she truly felt, would he take fright, and disappear from her life?

But even so, she'd found herself blurting, 'You make me laugh when sometimes I think there is nothing left to so much as smile about.'

For a moment it had almost overwhelmed her. All of it. She'd had to lower her head and press her lips together to stop them trembling, and blink rapidly to disperse the burgeoning tears.

He'd patted her hand and said, 'I shall consider it my duty to make you smile, then, whenever our paths cross.'

He already did that. Whenever she was dancing with him, or taking supper, or walking along like this, with her hand on his arm, gazing up into his laughing blue eyes, it was as though the sun had broken through the dark clouds that habitually hung over her.

But then he'd brought those clouds rolling back, by adding, 'Life is too short to ruin it by worrying about what might or might not happen, Miss Franklin. We should just enjoy each day we are given and let the future take care of itself.'

And she'd had to bite back a sharp retort. It was all very well for him to say such things. He had no idea! He had a roof over his head. A regular allowance—even if he did complain it was a beggarly amount. A secure place in society, because of his rank.

And, most importantly, he did not have to marry, not unless he really, really wanted to.

Was he married now?

She watched him smile down at the plump girl as they went into a right-handed star.

She had no idea. She'd deliberately avoided finding out anything about him since she'd married Colonel Morgan. Things had been difficult enough. If she'd read the announcement of his betrothal to some other woman, and known that *she'd* managed to impress him enough to renounce his hedonistic lifestyle, she would have wanted to curl up and die.

Which would not have been fair to her husband. To whom she owed so much.

No—to repay all Colonel Morgan's generosity by breaking her heart over another man—that would have been unforgivable.

'So…he is a friend of yours then, Robert?' Rose was looking from her to her brother, a perplexed frown creasing her brow.

'Not any longer,' Robert growled. 'I did not mention it, but…' He shifted uncomfortably. 'Well, if you must know, we had a bit of a falling out. I have not spoken to Rothersthorpe since a short while after you married our father,' he said to Lydia, though it was Rose who was questioning him. 'I did not tell you about it, because, well, because…'

Rothersthorpe?

He'd come into his father's title, then. Her insides hollowed out at the thought they'd drifted so far apart she did not even know that much about his life.

Though it had been what she'd wanted.

It had.

'But Mama Lyddy called him Mr Humming…something.'

'Hemingford,' Robert corrected her. 'That is his family name. Now that his father has died, he has of course inherited the title. He is Viscount Rothersthorpe now. I would have thought you would have known that, Mama Lyddy.'

'No.' She'd taken such pains to avoid seeing his name in the *Weekly Messenger* that she had missed even that.

When you made your bed, you had to lie in it. And it had been hard enough to accustom herself to Colonel Morgan as a husband as it was. Letting anyone suspect she had married one man, whilst mourning the inconstancy of another, would have done nobody any good.

And it would do nobody any good to so much as hint at the truth now, either.

'Heavens, Robert, surely you know I have never been one to pore over the society news? I left that world behind when I married your father.'

'But you have been talking about him,' Robert persisted. 'Neither of you can take your eyes off him.'

Oh dear. He was not going to let it drop. Now he was like a guard dog with a bone.

'I was trying to warn Rose to be on her guard. I don't want *her* taken in by his handsome face and superficial charm.'

He gave her one of those penetrating looks that put her so very much in mind of his father. He had the same steely-grey eyes, the same hooked nose and eyebrows that could only be described as formidable. Of all Colonel Morgan's children, he was the one who resembled him, in looks at least, the most.

He reminded her of him all the more when he looked down that beak of a nose and said, 'You need not worry. I am more than capable of protecting her from undesirables.'

Both Lydia and Rose turned their backs on him, snapped open their fans and began to ply them vigorously.

Men! They were all so…impossible!

Especially the handsome charmers like Rothersthorpe, as she must think of him nowadays. Because, even though she was angry with him, she was still achingly aware of exactly where he was, at any given moment.

She refused to look at him, yet she knew when he returned the plump young lady to her chaperon. And she sensed him turn and begin to saunter straight across the room to where they were sitting.

Her heart skipped a beat when she realised he was coming straight towards her.

That he was going to speak to her.

Well, his first words had better be an apology for letting her down, just when she'd needed him the most.

He came to a halt not three feet before her chair, a sardonic smile hovering about his lips.

And it took all her will-power not to get up and slap

it right off his face. She had to remind herself, quite sternly, that this was a public ballroom and she must not cause a scene that would rebound on Rose.

She took a deep breath and snapped her fan shut.

She could be polite and dignified. She could, even though her heart was pounding, her mouth had gone dry and her knees were trembling.

She wasn't an impressionable eighteen-year-old any longer, but a mature woman, and she refused to blush and stammer, or go weak at the knees, just because a handsome man was deigning to pay her a little attention.

Chapter Two

'Good to see you, Morgan,' said Rothersthorpe, his gaze sliding right past her as if she was not there.

After a moment's struggle, she acknowledged that it was probably just as well he had not spoken to her first. Apart from the fact that it wasn't the done thing, she still wasn't fully in control of her temper. Only think how dreadful it would be if he'd said, 'Good evening, Lydia', as though nothing was wrong, and she'd let all this bottled-up hurt and anger burst forth like a cork flying from a shaken bottle.

As it was, she felt Robert's hand go to the back of her chair. And when she turned to look up at him, she saw her stepson glaring at him too. He'd placed his other hand on the back of Rose's chair and taken up such an aggressive posture that not even Rothersthorpe could fail to read the warning signs.

Oh, no. It looked as though there was going to be some kind of scene after all.

But at least it would not be of her making.

Not that Lord Rothersthorpe looked in the least bit daunted.

'It has been a long time,' he persisted. 'Too long,' he said with a rueful smile and thrust out his hand.

Lydia's heart thundered in her breast while Robert stood quite still, looking at that outstretched hand. It was only when Robert finally took it, saying, 'Yes, yes, it has', that she realised she had been holding her breath. It slid from her in a wave of guilty disappointment. She hadn't wanted Rose's evening ruined by a scene, she really hadn't. But a part of her would still very much have liked to see Rothersthorpe flattened by her stepson's deadly right hook.

'I cannot believe our paths have not crossed in all this time,' Robert was saying as though he truly *liked* Rothersthorpe. When she'd been relying on him to dismiss him, the way he'd dismissed one penniless peer after another, during the few weeks Rose had been attending balls.

'I do not spend much time in town these days,' replied Lord Rothersthorpe. 'And when I do come up, it is not to attend events such as this.' He looked around the glittering ballroom with what, on another man's face, she would have described as a sneer.

'I have made a point of avoiding the company of most of the set I ran with at one time,' he drawled. 'A man has to develop standards at some point in his life.'

Standards? He had always laughed at people who claimed to have standards.

What on earth could have happened to make him sneer at his younger self?

And now that he was standing so close, she could see that there were subtle changes to his appearance which she had not noticed from a distance. Time had, of course, etched lines on his face. But they were not the ones she might have expected. Instead of seeing creases fanning out from his eyes, as though he laughed long and often, there were grooves bracketing his mouth, which made him look both hard and sober.

'So, the rumours about you,' said Robert, 'are all true, then? You have reformed?'

Lord Rothersthorpe smiled. In one way, it did remind her of the way he'd used to smile, for one corner of his mouth tilted upwards more than the other. But although he'd moved his mouth in the exact same way, it was somehow as though he was merely going through the motions.

'Not entirely,' he said. 'I still enjoy the company of pretty young ladies.' He looked down at Rose in a way that made Lydia's hackles rise. Had there been just the tiniest stress on the word *young?* And where had all his charm disappeared to? When she'd been a girl and Nicholas Hemingford had spoken such words, she would have defied any girl it was aimed at not to have melted right off her chair.

But this man, Lord Rothersthorpe, well, she couldn't quite explain why, but he did not sound charming at all.

And when he said, 'Will you not introduce me to your lovely companion?' the expression on his face put Lydia in mind of a…of a…well, yes, of a pirate intent on plunder.

Her fear crystallised when Rose smiled back up at him, for Rose did not appear to find anything about him the least bit sinister. But then what girl, fresh from her schoolroom, could fail to be anything but fascinated when he turned those smiling blue eyes upon her so intently?

A painful sensation struck her midriff. Rose was as deaf to warnings as she'd been herself at that age.

She couldn't see the danger. And nor, apparently, could Robert, because he was performing the introduction.

'This is my half-sister, Miss Rose Morgan,' said Robert. 'It is entirely on her account we have all uprooted ourselves and come to town this spring.'

'Enchanted,' said Rothersthorpe, bowing low over her hand. 'London society will be all the better for having such a beauty adorn its ballrooms.'

'And this is my stepmother, Mrs Morgan,' continued Robert, while Lord Rothersthorpe continued to gaze at Rose. 'Though, of course, you already know her.'

Rothersthorpe turned his head. The expression of admiration which he'd bestowed upon Rose vanished without trace.

'I would hardly claim to know her,' he replied, making her a curt bow. 'Our paths crossed, briefly, almost a decade ago. I seem to recall that you came to town for the sole purpose of catching a husband?'

There was a distinct note of accusation in his voice, which was monstrously unfair. She could have snatched at those rambling words and held him to account for them. Instead, when he'd made it so obvious he regretted them the moment they'd left his lips, she'd let him escape.

'You know very well that I did,' she therefore replied. In fact, she'd told him quite plainly that if she didn't find a husband before the end of the Season she was going to be in a pickle. And he'd brushed her concerns aside by making a jest about things never being so bad as you feared when the time came to face them.

'And since,' he said with a hard smile, 'in those days, I was virtually penniless, that naturally meant you did not waste much of your time upon me.'

It had not been like that. Why was he twisting it
to make it sound as though *she'd* been in the wrong?

'Not when you made it so very clear that you did not
wish to get married, my lord,' she retorted, confusion
temporarily diluting her annoyance. 'No woman with
an ounce of self-respect would wish to be accused of
setting her cap at a man so clearly averse to the notion
of getting *leg-shackled.*'

'*Touché.*' He raised his hands to acknowledge the hit.
'It is true to say I was young and enjoying my freedom
far too much to sacrifice it. However, now,' he said,
turning his attention back to Rose once more, his expression softening, 'I have matured to the point where
the prospect of matrimony no longer terrifies me. On
the contrary, now that I am a respectable man of means,
marrying is not only the next logical step for me to take,
but one which I find most desirable.'

Lydia felt as though he'd slapped her. The prospect
of marriage back then *had* terrified him. She'd seen it
on his face, understood it from the way he'd vanished
without trace after uttering what she might have inter-
preted as a proposal, if she hadn't known him better.

Mrs Westerly's words rang in her ears, for the second time that night. *'You mark my words, when the time
comes, he will marry an heiress...'*

An heiress. She looked at the predatory way he was
examining Rose. Rose, who was not only incredibly
wealthy, but extremely pretty too.

Had it been only this evening, before setting out,
that she'd decided she'd never been in better looks? Oh,
she'd dismissed Rose's comment that she looked like a
fairy princess as the nonsense it was. She was too cur-
vaceous nowadays to warrant that description. Not that
she minded. She'd been positively scrawny when she'd

been Rose's age. Worn down by cares that the Colonel had lifted from her shoulders. From the moment she'd married him, her health had begun to improve. And bearing and feeding a child had even bequeathed her a bosom of which she was positively proud.

She was better at picking out clothing that suited her, too. The pastels Mrs Westerly had told her to wear for her own début had always made her look completely washed out. White-blonde hair, greyish-blue eyes and milk-white skin could really make a girl look, according to the acid-tongued reigning beauty that year, like a streak of pump water.

So she'd been pleased with the ensemble she was wearing tonight. The rich blue of her underskirt brought out the colour in her eyes, though it was the gauzy overskirt, sprinkled with spangles, that had caused Rose to make the comment about fairy princesses. She'd even decided not to worry that the neckline was a touch too daring, that there was nothing wrong with revealing what she now regarded as her best feature. Besides, the pearls that nestled between her generous breasts had always boosted her confidence. Colonel Morgan had given them to her on her wedding day, telling her she was a pearl beyond price. If he'd only said it on that occasion, she might have dismissed the words as idle flattery. But he'd kept on saying it, right up to the day he'd died. Even when he'd taken to giving her diamonds, these pearls remained her favourite. Because they made her feel…valued.

But now she felt as though she'd become invisible because Lord Rothersthorpe had eyes only for Rose.

'But I am being remiss,' he said, turning towards her with an obvious effort. 'I really ought to offer my condolences on your loss. Although…' he paused, his eyes scanning her outfit slowly, before returning to her face '…you are so clearly out of mourning that I wonder if it is indelicate of me to remind you of Colonel Morgan's demise at all.'

It felt just as though he'd honed sarcasm into a sharp blade and thrust it between her ribs. The others might have missed it, but she'd seen the barely concealed contempt with which he'd assessed the finery with which she'd been so pleased, not half an hour since. And it all became too much.

'Do you think I ought to go about in blacks for ever?' She felt Rose flinch, though she was too angry to tear her gaze from Lord Rothersthorpe's sardonic eyes.

'And if it was indelicate to remind me of my husband's demise,' she continued, in spite of Robert clamping the hand that had rested on the back of her chair firmly on her shoulder, 'why did you do just that?'

'Naturally,' put in Robert, while Lydia was floundering under the horrible feeling that Lord Rothersthorpe was deliberately trying to hurt her, 'we had to delay Rose's come-out until we were out of full mourning.'

'I beg your pardon,' Lord Rothersthorpe said mechanically, 'if I have caused any offence.'

But he didn't look the least bit sorry. On the contrary, she'd seen a flare of something like satisfaction flicker through his eyes when he'd goaded her into lashing out at him. And just to prove how insincere his apology to her had been, when he turned to Rose, his face showed nothing but compassion. 'The death of a parent is always a difficult milestone in one's life.'

A parent, but not a husband, was what he meant.

'I trust it would not be inappropriate for me to ask if you would care to dance? Is it too soon for you to think of it?'

'Not at all,' said Rose, leaping to her feet.

'Oh, but, Rose,' said Lydia, 'you really ought not…'

Lord Rothersthorpe turned to her and smiled. Mockingly.

'If you remember me at all, Mrs Morgan, surely you recall that I never pay the slightest attention to anything a girl's chaperon might have to say?'

Oh, but that twisted the knife in the wound he'd already inflicted. To refer to her as a *chaperon*…

She knew his opinions of chaperons, all too well. He'd never had a good word to say about any of them and now he was calling her one, to her face.

And it was no good reminding herself that a chaperon was exactly what she was. She knew what he meant.

Her eyes stung as the last vestige of hope that she might ever have meant anything to him at all curled up and blackened, like a sheet of paper tossed on to an open flame.

'Rose,' said Robert sharply, 'you cannot dance. You know you cannot.'

'I know no such thing,' she retorted. 'My brother has some dreadfully stuffy notions about the suitability of dance partners,' she said to Lord Rothersthorpe. 'If he had his way, I would never dance with anyone. But he cannot object to you, since you are clearly a good friend of his.'

'That is not the reason for my objection and you know it,' growled Robert. 'Lord Rothersthorpe, I hope you will forgive my sister for being so outspoken—'

'Of course,' he cut in smoothly. 'It is far better than blushing and stammering out some nonsense, like so many of the débutantes one comes across.'

Lydia flinched. It was as though he was deliberately

distancing himself from all he'd once claimed to find appealing about her.

The only good thing to come of her reaction was the fact that Rose noticed it. Her eyes flicked from Lydia to Lord Rothersthorpe, and for a moment, she looked as though she was regretting her defiant outburst.

But then Robert, fatally, said, 'Rose, I am warning you...'

At which she stiffened her spine, shot her brother a rebellious look and laid her arm on Lord Rothersthorpe's sleeve.

Short of leaping over the chairs, and forcing her back into her seat, there was nothing Robert could do.

With one last hard smile, Lord Rothersthorpe bore Rose away with him.

And Lydia felt as though a chasm had opened up inside her. A cold, aching void, into which all her cherished memories of this man tumbled. And shattered.

Lord Rothersthorpe hadn't known he had it in him to dissemble so convincingly. He hadn't known he could smile and perform all the steps of the dance in the correct sequence, and even flirt with his partner as though he was enjoying himself, when his gut was roiling with acid rancour.

But then, a gentleman simply couldn't give way to the savagery that had welled up in him when he'd seen Lydia sitting there draped in the silks and satins she'd got from marrying that disgusting old man. A gentleman couldn't walk up to a woman he had not seen for eight years and twist on the obscenely opulent ropes of pearls she had round her neck until they choked her.

Especially since no jury in the land would believe he had any reasonable excuse for feeling so murderous, if there was such a thing as a reasonable excuse for committing murder.

But then what man would feel *reasonable* when a woman betrayed him by marrying another man without even having the decency to reject his proposal first?

And not just any man, but one old enough to have been her father?

He snorted in disgust, causing Miss Morgan to raise her brows in surprise.

'Slight cold,' he excused himself. 'Beg pardon.'

Father? Grandfather, more like. Much-married grandfather, too, according to Robert when he'd broken the news. 'He's already worn out three women with his filthy temper and his unreasonable demands,' Robert had slurred, his voice thick with alcohol and revulsion. 'Each of them younger and more unsuitable than the last. Can you imagine how I feel,' he'd said, downing yet another glass of brandy in one gulp, 'having to call a chit of a girl, scarce out of the schoolroom, "Mother"?'

He hadn't cared a jot what Robert thought about having a stepmother who was younger than he was. It wasn't as if they'd ever been close friends. They'd fallen in with each other because they were much of an age and enjoyed the same pastimes, that was all. Besides, he was having too much trouble coping with the sensation of having been punched, hard, in the gut.

Lydia, married?

'She cannot have married him,' he'd just about managed to gasp. 'She wouldn't.' Fearing he might actually be going to cast up his accounts as he imagined her giving herself willingly to that stick-thin, papery-skinned old man he'd glimpsed striding about the grounds on the fateful day he'd taken her to the picnic Robert had thrown at Westdene, he'd shakily reached for the brandy decanter himself. 'I only took her there two weeks ago. And I...' asked her to think about marrying *him*.

'Well, we're not talking about a love match, are we?' Robert had splashed a measure of brandy into a glass and passed it to him, when his own hands had failed to accomplish the task himself. 'My father likes young women. The younger the better, apparently. And he's so rich that he has no trouble getting them to marry him.'

The words had eaten into him like acid scoring into a printer's plate.

This was her answer, then. The Colonel had money and he didn't, that was what it boiled down to. She was just like all the rest.

Though at least all those eligible débutantes who'd turned their pretty noses up at him because of his reputation, and the state of his finances, had been honest. Only Lydia had fooled him into dropping his guard. Into making him...*hope*.

'If your reaction means what I think it does,' Robert had said, looking at him with such concern he knew he must have turned white, 'then let me tell you, my friend, you've had a lucky escape. She's obviously mercenary to the core. God, but I pity my sisters, having that harpy foisted on them.'

The remainder of that encounter had vanished into the red mist that had risen up and swamped him. He knew he'd said some pretty harsh things about elderly men preying on females barely out of the schoolroom, but he could not recall which of them had thrown the first punch.

It could well have been Robert. A man can say what he likes about his own parent, but he won't tolerate hearing it from another's lips.

Family was family, after all.

Which brought him neatly back to this dark-haired, wilful beauty, with whom he was dancing right now. One of Robert's half-sisters from one of those wives Colonel Morgan had worn out with his unreasonable demands and filthy temper while he'd been clawing his way up the rungs of the Company army ladder. Not his first, or she would be Robert's full sister. But did it really matter which of them it was? All that concerned him was that Lydia had been his fourth wife. He ground his teeth. His fourth.

Of course, he'd known Lydia had come to town to find herself a husband. It was why they all came, year after year, all these well-bred girls in their uniform white dresses. But he'd started to think she shrank from the prospect. He'd seen the way that dragon of a chaperon was always breathing down her neck, and how the longer the Season went on, the more she'd wilted under the constant pressure to bring some man up to scratch.

She'd started to look so fragile she'd put him in mind of a dandelion clock. All that silvery-haired trembling beauty, being held together only by a tremendous effort of will. One hard knock was all it would take to scatter her to the four winds.

Or so he'd thought.

He snorted again. When he thought of how hard she'd made him work to get her to speak without stammering and blushing…or when he recalled the sense of triumph she'd aroused when she'd shyly confided that he could take her mind off her woes just by being there…or worse—that surge of protectiveness that had swept through him that day when she'd just about fainted, and he'd caught her in his arms, and carried her into the house.

'God, how I wish I had the right to take you away

from that dragon,' he'd bitten out as she'd turned her face into his chest with a moan. 'I would never force you to do anything you didn't want,' he'd said, wishing he could drop a kiss into the curls that had been tickling his chin. 'You're so delicate,' he'd said, 'you should have someone to look after you. I wish it could be me.'

And before he'd gone three more paces, he'd loved the way she felt in his arms so much he'd found himself casting caution to the winds.

'And why shouldn't it be me? I've got to get married some day. I've got a duty to my family to preserve the name, if nothing else. And you know, I don't think it would be such a dreadful chore, if it was to a girl like you. You make me feel as though I'm worth something, even though I haven't two brass farthings to rub together.'

She hadn't said a word in reply. She hadn't thrown her arms round his neck and said that marrying him would make her the happiest girl on earth. Even though he knew she was determined to marry *someone.* She'd confided in him, just the once, that she dreaded what would happen if it came to the end of the Season without her getting even one proposal.

So the look on her face, as he'd lain her down on the sofa, had filled him with foreboding.

It could have been the result of the headache that had felled her, of course, but he'd been so worried she was about to frame the words of refusal that he'd cut her short.

'Don't say a word,' he'd said, backing away hastily. He could see he was going to have to prove he could support her, even if it wasn't in very much style. He'd noticed that his rather cavalier attitude towards paying bills had perturbed her. And she'd expressed open disapproval of his tendency to make rather reckless wagers. He was going to have to prove that for once in his life he was in deadly earnest. In short, he was going to have to raise enough money to at least pay for a ring, and a licence, and the vicar. 'Just think about it,' he'd said as he backed out of the room.

He'd thought she would at least have done that, while he was off fleecing every drunk too cross-eyed to see what cards he held in his hands. But no. By the time Robert caught up with him at Newmarket, she'd already worked her wiles on that…jumped-up clerk! She'd coldly, ruthlessly assessed what the Colonel could give her and then…sold herself to him without a qualm. She must have a core of steel to have survived marriage to a man who had gone out to India with nothing but the clothes he'd stood up in, and burning ambition, but who'd returned to England with wealth beyond most men's wildest dreams.

And nobody was ever going to convince him that a man could amass such a fortune, so quickly, by honest means.

'I beg your pardon?'

Rose Morgan was giving him an odd look. 'What was that you said?'

It was only then he realised he'd been getting so worked up he'd begun muttering under his breath.

'I'm thinking of a poem,' he came back smoothly. 'Something along the lines of…*Your beauty surpasses my wildest dreams, I mean to have you by any means…*'

Miss Morgan giggled and blushed. 'You really should not repeat that kind of verse to me. If Robert ever found out, he would be simply furious.'

But she did not look displeased. She simpered and looked up at him from under those long, dark lashes of hers, with just the hint of a smile hovering round her lips.

Had Lydia coached her to look at men like that? Miss Morgan must definitely have practised often, to have perfected a look that conveyed so neatly both maidenly modesty, spiced with a clear dash of willingness to accept his suit, should he choose to further her acquaintance.

Well, if anyone knew how to get her young charge to bag herself a husband, no matter what obstacles society's high sticklers might throw in her way, Lydia was the woman. Lydia had not appeared to have anything going for her when she'd come to town for her own Season. Not only had she been of a naturally timid disposition—or so he'd thought—but she'd also lacked the means to make the most of what assets she had. He had sometimes overheard other girls mocking her for having no more than two evening dresses, which she'd made over, in various ways, time after time. He had not minded. On the contrary, he'd admired her ingenuity, for he knew what it was like to always be juggling his own finances.

But she'd clearly minded more than he'd guessed. She'd been determined to marry money, no matter what kind of man would provide it for her. And being wealthy certainly looked as though it had suited her. Just look at her, sitting on the chaperons' bench, fanning herself indolently while she watched Rose dancing with, he made no bones about admitting, just about the most eligible bachelor in the room.

Yes, she'd positively thrived on having married money. There was a sleek, contented look about her, like a cat that had been at the cream. He had always known she had the potential to become a beauty, but she'd had to paint on a facsimile of the roses that bloomed naturally in her cheeks now. She'd entirely lost those gauche mannerisms that had so appealed to him, too. And her gawky, coltish figure was now hidden beneath distinctly feminine curves.

She was no longer that frail, pale waif, who'd made him feel she needed some big strong man to come dashing to her rescue. The girl who'd so cunningly made him feel as though he could *be* that man. She was a self-assured, healthy, wealthy widow. A woman who'd got exactly what she'd set out to achieve in life.

In fact, to her way of thinking Colonel Morgan's age might have been a positive advantage. She certainly had not had to put up with his *filthy temper* or his *unreasonable demands* for very long. She'd been a widow now for almost two years.

'Typical,' he muttered. The very year he'd finally decided that he was ready to dip his toe into matrimonial waters, some malign fate had brought her up to town as well.

Dammit, how could he search for a bride, when the mere sight of her provoked him so much that he'd started muttering imprecations under his breath while he was dancing with just about the prettiest girl in the room? He'd thought he'd got over his disillusion. His disappointment. His mistrust of everything a woman said. But then he'd seen her sitting there, pretending she had not seen him. Or worse, she simply hadn't recognised him. The thought he might have been such an insignificant feature of her life that she did not even remember him had made him so boiling mad, he'd had to march across the ballroom and challenge her. Hurt her. And the only way he could think of to do it was to make her think he was only interested in her stepdaughter—when nothing could be further from the truth. He'd scarcely been aware of her, throughout this entire set.

Damn her, but Lydia had even ruined *this* for him, too. He'd used to enjoy dancing for its own sake. What could be more pleasant than indulging in vigorous exercise alongside an appreciative female? And then being able to return her to her seat, and walk away, and select another one, without risk of censure?

But he was not enjoying dancing with Rose Morgan. Not with his head full of Lydia. Not knowing that the moment would come when he would have to return the girl to her seat and stand within strangling distance of her all-too-alluring stepmother once more. And make polite conversation, when what he wanted was to demand an explanation.

It was hard to know whether he was angrier with her for being here, or himself for reacting to her in such an illogical, irrational...uncontrollable way.

His face set, he steeled himself to escort Rose across the floor. Why the hell should he let her make him feel in the least bit uncomfortable? He had as much right to be here as she did. More. He belonged in society, had been born to a position of rank and privilege. And what was more, he'd really made something of himself. People no longer assumed he would never amount to anything, because of the family he'd come from. They'd seen him turn his fortunes around by dint of hard work and resourcefulness. He'd become famous for being the first Hemingford for generations who hadn't resorted to charming an heiress into marriage to pull the family out of debt. He'd come back to town knowing that, at last, he could marry any woman he damn well chose.

And he was not going to let her return to society spoil his plans.

* * *

'This is all your fault,' Lydia had said to Robert, as Rothersthorpe led Rose on to the dance floor. 'You might have known that being so strict with her would drive her to some act of rebellion.'

'Well, I don't regret sending Lord Abergele to the rightabout,' he retorted. 'Not when everyone knows his pockets are to let.'

'What does that have to say to anything? Rose has no intention of marrying the first man she dances with. She has come to town to find her feet socially and *enjoy* herself. She was the very first one to declare she would not think her Season a disaster if she did not find a man who truly loved her, whom she could love in return. She knows it won't be easy to find a man like that, on just one trip to town. But you are making it impossible. How is she going to get to know any man well enough to know if she could possibly fall in love with him, if you won't let any of them get anywhere near her?'

She'd never raised her voice to him before and he clearly didn't know how to take it.

'I'm only trying to protect her,' he protested, looking for all the world like a man who had gone to pick an apple and accidentally put his hand in a wasp's nest. 'She is so innocent...'

'But she is not a fool. You should let her associate with all sorts of men, Robert, and let her judge for herself. Do you really think she is the sort to be taken in by a handsome face and a lot of flummery?'

'You never know.' He sighed. 'You hear about it all the time. And Rose is not only extremely wealthy, but extraordinarily pretty, too.'

He pulled out the chair behind which he was standing, so that he could squeeze through, and sit next to Lydia.

'The only danger, so far as I can see,' she said, 'comes from you keeping her on too tight a leash. I wouldn't put it past her to start a flirtation with the most unsuitable man she can find just to teach you a lesson.' She looked pointedly at Rose as she skipped down the set with a hard-faced Lord Rothersthorpe.

'I suppose it could have been worse.' Robert sighed. 'If she had to choose someone to be her rebellion, then at least it is a man to whom I cannot object for himself.'

'I should have thought he was exactly the sort of man you would object to. You have been at pains to shield Rose from so very many other penniless peers.'

Robert shot her a quick frown. 'Rothersthorpe is not penniless. I won't say that he's wealthy, exactly, but he has prospects.'

'Prospects? What do you mean, prospects?'

'Well, it is some kind of uncle, or cousin, or something. I'm not sure of the exact details. But it is well known that some elderly bachelor related to him has decided to make him his heir, since he has no other. Rothersthorpe stands to inherit mills and mines and what-have-you from him. Because of the way he turned his own estates around.'

'He did what?'

'I know. Hard to believe of the young scapegrace we knew back then, isn't it? But apparently, when his father died, Rothersthorpe worked like the very devil to bring his holdings back from the verge of bankruptcy.'

Hard to believe? Impossible to believe! He'd been hopeless with money. And as for *working,* at any level, let alone like a devil…no, she just could not credit it.

'Rose could do a lot worse,' he said thoughtfully,

his eyes following the couple as they conversed whilst passing each other in the set.

'Y-you mean, you seriously think that Rose, and Lord Rothersthorpe…'

'I don't see why not. You heard what he said. He's obviously come to town to look for a bride.'

Rose and Lord Rothersthorpe. Her head began to spin. It couldn't be…

And yet they did make an extraordinarily handsome couple—him with his fair athleticism, and her with all her dark, spirited beauty.

'I've seen it before with men of his class,' Robert continued. 'All of a sudden, they abandon their wild ways, make themselves a list of the qualities they want from a wife and come up to town to find a woman who has them. At least if Rothersthorpe does start to court her in earnest, we can rest assured that he wants her for herself. He has no pressing need of her fortune.'

Robert might as well have slapped her repeatedly in the face as deliver all those salient facts in such a blunt manner.

Eight years ago, Rothersthorpe had been so terrified of the prospect of matrimony that he'd fled at the mere mention of something that might have put him in danger of getting leg-shackled. But during the years they'd been apart, he'd turned his fortunes around through dint of hard work. And now he'd come to town to crown his achievements by acquiring a wife to preserve his proud lineage.

She did not need to ask Robert what Lord Rothersthorpe would require of a wife. Her own chaperon, Mrs Westerly, had told her often enough. Men of rank wanted an ornament to grace their house. And a substantial portion to swell their coffers. They also wanted a woman in the full bloom of health, so that they could be fairly sure of getting heirs and spares.

But, above all, they wanted a virgin.

She forced herself to watch Rose and Lord Rothersthorpe, as they circled one another on the dance floor, though their delight in each other was making her feel so old, and unwanted, and unattractive. And second-hand, to boot. She knew that she was not completely worthless in the scheme of things, but now her value was more like that of a chipped vase. One that had been removed from the best rooms and put to utilitarian purpose in the kitchens.

And she would just have to accept it.

They had all come to town, after all, to see if Rose could find a man who would *want her for herself.*

If it had been anyone but Rothersthorpe showing an interest in her, anyone but he who'd broken through Robert's defences, she would be thrilled. He was exactly the kind of man they had hoped she would find.

She should be smiling with approval as they twirled round the ballroom with their arms round each other's waists.

It was what everyone would expect from her.

So she smiled. And waved her fan indolently before her cheeks, as though everything was as it should be. Whilst inside…

She'd got out of the habit of pretending to be content with her lot, that was the trouble. Since Colonel Morgan's death, she hadn't *had* to pretend quite so often.

Well, she'd have to get back in the habit, that was all. She wasn't going to let anything spoil Rose's Season. Rose needed her to stand up to Robert and be her friend and advisor, not start acting like a silly, jealous schoolgirl.

She pulled on her social armour, rather in the same way she would have reached for a fire screen to shield herself from the heat of a blazing fire. And after a while, her smile began to feel less forced. Her manner towards Robert became more natural as she obliged him to chat of this and that.

Mrs Westerly would have been proud of her. She was elegant and poised. It might only be on the outside, but at least nobody, looking at her, would ever guess she felt as though she had been fatally wounded.

Chapter Three

'Mama Lyddy, can you show me how to press flowers?'

Lydia looked up from her perusal of the meagre stock of invitations spread upon the desk. There were only two events they might attend tonight. A musical evening at Lord and Lady Chepstow's, or a sort of rout party at the Lutterworths'.

She knew Robert would want her to persuade Rose to attend the musical evening. They did not receive many such invitations from persons of rank. Society hostesses were not warming to Rose. With all her money, and her exotic beauty, she was a distinct threat to the chances of their own daughters. And Robert would keep discouraging the ones who had sons who would definitely have benefited from a match with the daughter of a nabob.

Not that Rose looked at all downcast. In fact, she was smiling broadly as she waved her corsage from the night before.

'I want to do what you did,' she said. 'I want to keep a scrapbook of my Season. And so I simply must preserve a bloom from the corsage I wore on the night I danced with my very first aristocrat.'

As Rose smiled dreamily, Lydia wondered how many scrapbooks had been filled with flowers hopelessly smitten young girls had preserved as mementoes of an encounter with Lord Rothersthorpe.

'Of course, it is not as if I have a posy from an admirer, yet,' Rose continued. 'Not like you.' She plumped herself down on a stool at Lydia's side. 'Oh, won't you tell me all about the man who sent you those violets you have in your own scrapbook? You must have had very strong feelings for whoever gave them to you. For you sighed and went all misty-eyed when you turned over that page.'

Had she? Oh, lord, she'd tried so hard not to reveal her weakness for Lord Rothersthorpe, as she must now think of him. While Rose's father had still been alive, she'd deliberately suppressed all thoughts of him, not wanting to be disloyal. And even once he'd died, well… it would still have been a form of betrayal to wish things had been other than they were. Colonel Morgan had been very good to her, in his way.

'It was a silly infatuation, nothing more,' she said. And last night had proved just how silly.

'But you just said you were infatuated with him. So you must have—'

'I did as I was told,' she interrupted. 'It was my duenna who insisted I create that scrapbook I showed you. I think she thought it would give me gainful employment during slack hours when she didn't know quite what to do with me.' She rubbed at a tension spot she could feel forming in the very centre of her forehead. She really, really did not want Rose badgering her about anything that might lead to her discovering that, once, Lord Rothersthorpe had got to the brink of proposing to her, before coming to his senses. He'd made it so obvious, last night, that he'd considered he'd had a lucky escape that she couldn't bear to let anyone discover how deeply her feelings for him had run.

'I really don't even know why I kept the silly thing all these years. Or why I dragged it out to show you when we were discussing your Season. I was utterly miserable the whole time.'

'Not the whole time, surely?' Rose leant her elbow on the desk and rested her chin on her cupped palm. 'Or you would not have spent three whole minutes staring at that arrangement of dried violets with that faraway look in your eyes.'

'Three whole minutes?' She shifted in her seat, taking care to avoid Rose's inquisitive stare. 'You are surely exaggerating.'

'Oh, but it was.'

'I was probably thinking of something quite different. A…a shopping list. Or wondering how soon we would be able to discover who are the best modistes this year. I am so out of touch.'

'You are trying to hide something!' Rose grinned impishly. 'Were you in love with someone, before you married Papa? Did you have an admirer? Oh, how romantic! Won't you tell me?'

Sometimes, she did not know quite how to handle Rose. She was so perceptive it was no easy matter to fob her off.

'He did not send me this posy because he wished to become my suitor. He sent it out of sympathy because I had been ill, that was all.' Though now she wasn't looking at everything Rothersthorpe did through blinkers, she recalled that she'd been ill several times and he'd only sent her a posy once.

At the time, she'd been elated by the note that had accompanied it, which told her that he'd missed her at the ball she had told him she was to attend and how he hoped she would recover speedily so he could dance with her again.

And then almost crushed by his awkwardness the next time they'd met. The way he'd attempted to brush aside the whole incident, making up some tale about a ragged flower seller and a win on the horses, and what was a fellow to do?

And he'd looked so worried he might have raised false hopes by sending her those flowers, she'd felt obliged to reassure him.

'You should take care,' she'd said playfully, 'not to make a habit of sending poorly young ladies flowers in that fashion, or one day one of them might get the wrong idea. And then where would you be?'

His relief had been so palpable it had cut her to the quick.

Had he ever done anything but hurt her?

'It was ridiculously sentimental of me to preserve the entire thing,' right down to the ribbon, she finally admitted, to herself as much as Rose. 'But then it was the only posy I received my entire Season. From any man. For whatever reason. But I repeat, there was never any chance of anything romantic developing between us,' she said, with just a touch of asperity creeping into her voice as she recalled his words from the night before. 'The romantic thing was the way your father came to my rescue…'

'Pooh,' said Rose scornfully. 'There was never a man less romantic than Papa. He treated you as though you were one of his platoon most of the time. Barking orders at you and practically expecting you to salute…'

'Rose, you will not speak with such disrespect of your papa. He was a good man. A decent man. He gave me a home and—'

'And made you work hard for your keep,' Rose persisted.

'He gave me a home and a family,' Lydia continued firmly. 'And I grew very fond of him. I know he had a bit of a temper, but you yourself know that his bark was always worse than his bite. For heaven's sake, he'd been in the army all his life. Of course he was prone to *barking orders,* as you put it. It was just his way. And what is more, young lady, it was you who taught me exactly how little he truly was to be feared. I was not in your house five minutes before I saw you had him wrapped round your little finger, you and your sister both. The way you used to just sit there, waiting until he'd finished his tirade, and then tilt your heads to one side and smile up at him in the full knowledge that he was helpless to refuse you two anything. And he expected *me* to teach you and Marigold how to behave!' She flung up her hands in mock horror, causing Rose to giggle.

'Well, I could never teach either of you anything about how to wrap poor unsuspecting males around your fingers, but if you really want to begin a scrapbook,' she said, turning to the corsage Rose had tossed on to the desk, 'I *can* teach you how to preserve flowers.'

'I think you are trying to steer me away from the subject of your own posy,' Rose observed astutely.

'Yes, because it is painful for me to think about it,' she admitted. 'I…well, I did become rather too attached to him.'

'Oh,' said Rose, immediately contrite. 'I would not hurt you for the world. And if he really was your first love, and then you had to marry Papa instead…oh…I am sorry. Forgive me?'

'I never said he was my first love,' she protested, blushing.

'I will not mention him again,' said Rose, filling Lydia with relief. 'Though I should love to know who it was. And if he is married now…'

Lydia winced. She might have known that Rose's idea of not mentioning the donor of her posy of violets would be to launch immediately into a volley of questions.

'The first thing we need to do,' said Lydia, firmly changing the subject, 'is to separate the bunch, so that we can press each flower individually. Although it might be better to select just one bloom, or we will need a dozen scrapbooks. You will have many occasions you may want to commemorate in a similar way.'

'Do you think so?'

'Of course you will. I dare say you already have a pile of tickets and programmes from various events we have attended already.'

'That's true.'

'But before we start, I am mindful that in a very short while we are likely to have a room full of callers—' one of whom was bound to be Lord Rotherthorpe, since a man should always call upon his partners from the previous night's entertainment '—and we have not yet discussed which event you would like to attend this evening.'

Rose beamed at her. 'That is what I love about you, Mama Lyddy. You never try to dictate to me.'

'What would be the point?' Lydia pursed her lips. 'I

learned long ago that it is far too much like hard work to attempt to cross you. Besides, I never felt I was old enough to tell you what to do. I feel more like…an older sister, than a mother to you.' At least, she had until last night, when for the first time Lord Rothersthorpe's cutting comments had made her feel every inch the chaperon.

Although she would not, absolutely not be the kind of chaperon he so despised. She was not, and never would be, a dragon, pushing her charge into situations that would make her miserable.

'I shall, of course, give you my advice, but that is all. You must make up your own mind.'

'I only wish I could. About where I want to go tonight, I mean. I…I think,' she said, with a slight blush, 'that I shall be able to tell you later, though.'

'Oh?' It was not like Rose to be so indecisive, but then she'd never come under the influence of a practised charmer like Rothersthorpe before. If she knew anything about Rose, she was not going to declare her intentions about where to go tonight until she'd discovered where he meant to go. She took a penknife and sliced through the ribbon which had held Rose's corsage together with jerky finality.

'Well, there is no rush,' she said to Rose as she pulled the corsage apart. 'It would just be preferable to warn Robert, one way or the other. He has not your love of spontaneity.'

They spent the next few minutes selecting the best blooms for preservation, finding sheets of blotting paper and dragging the heaviest books down from the shelves.

By the time the doorknocker heralded the arrival of their first morning caller, not only Lydia's writing desk, but also the marble-topped console table under the window were strewn with all the paraphernalia associated with their activity.

Rose glanced at the mess they'd made, then at the door with alarm.

'Do not be afraid to let your admirers see you employed in some genteel pursuit, Rose. My own chaperon told me that men like to imagine their future wives being gainfully employed.' Though what was gainful about pressing flowers, or, in her own case, creating acres of decorative embroidery, she could not think.

Surely it would be better to demonstrate an ability to plan a menu for twenty guests at a moment's notice, or deal with the personal problems of servants in such a way that the household continued to run smoothly? In her experience, that was what her husband had valued about her.

If Colonel Morgan had thought all she did all day was sit around pressing flowers, he would have been most annoyed.

Still, they were not talking about her, but about Rose. And she was determined to prove to Lord Rothersthorpe that their relationship was a good one. The kind of chaperon he'd implied she was would never let her charge enjoy herself so much that the room got strewn with flowers and books like this, would she? She would have her sitting on a chair looking like a waxwork dummy. Only rather more rigid.

Though the effect was spoiled, somewhat, when he didn't come with the first wave of gentlemen. Mr Crimmer and Mr Bentley, who were sons of wealthy businessmen, grinned at one another when they realised they were first and, making straight for Rose, they pulled up seats as close to her as they dared.

She would greet him as graciously as she received any of the others, of course. And no matter what he said, or did, she was not going to lash out as she'd done the night before. She'd spent many hours, when she should have been asleep, reliving the few minutes when he'd dumped her on Colonel Morgan's sofa, then fled for the hills. And come to the conclusion that if he could look upon it as a lucky escape, then so could she.

Next to arrive were the two naval officers whose names she could never recall. She really ought to, they were here so often. The trouble was that in almost identical uniforms, and with their blue eyes, fair hair and hard jaws, there was little to tell them apart.

Although when pressed, Robert declared he couldn't recall the names of half the fellows who cluttered up his house these days, either. 'Never knew I had so many friends, until I produced an attractive sister,' he'd snarled.

In the light of his usually overprotective attitude towards Rose, she was a little surprised he had not come in the moment the clock struck eleven, to keep a watchful eye on proceedings. He always grumbled that though he could not actually bar any of these fellows from his house, he could at least let them know he would not permit any of them to take liberties with his sister.

Was it too much to hope he'd taken her words last night to heart?

Or had it been the way Rose had deliberately caused a stir by dancing, when Robert's earlier refusal had meant she should not have done so?

Well, whatever had caused him to stay away, Lydia could only be glad. The atmosphere was a lot less fraught than usual. Mr Crimmer and Mr Bentley were genially competing to be the one from whom she accepted her scissors, or a withered bloom.

But in spite of the atmosphere that prevailed over the others, every time the doorknocker sounded, she felt herself winding up a little tighter.

The room was feeling somewhat crowded when a young lawyer and Lord Abergele came in one after the other. She had to admire Lord Abergele's persistence. In spite of Robert's continual discouragement, he kept on coming right back for yet another rebuff. She supposed he had hopes that his handsome face, and the speaking looks he gave Rose from those limpid green eyes, would soften her to the extent she would defy her brother. He might well succeed. There was nothing Rose liked more than a challenge.

And she was certainly rising to the challenge of having a room full of suitors vying for her attention. Rose managed them all with a dexterity that filled Lydia with admiration. If she felt a preference for any of them, she was taking such care not to show it that not even Lydia could attempt a guess.

Until Lord Rothersthorpe walked in.

Rose's face lit up, then she actually stood up, crossed the room and held out her hand.

She hadn't minded when the others paused only to shake her hand and utter the briefest of commonplaces, before making for Rose. But when he virtually ignored her, it really hurt.

She felt completely in tune with the men who glowered at Rothersthorpe as he bowed over Rose's extended hand, though at least they had the freedom to leave when they couldn't bear watching the pair admiring each other any longer.

As they began to drift away, in varying attitudes of

despondency, it was left entirely to Lydia to bid them farewell, since Rose was engrossed in showing Lord Rothersthorpe what she had been doing with her corsage.

She supposed she ought to reprimand Rose for such lack of manners, but she was still striving to prove she was not a repressive ogress. Besides which, she knew exactly the effect Lord Rothersthorpe could have on a female. She had stretched her own chaperon's tolerance to the limits, in order to snatch a few moments with him in private, even if it was only the limited privacy of the corner of a crowded room.

She could even excuse Lord Abergele for furtively stuffing the slice of cake he'd been eating into his pocket before shaking her hand in farewell. Lord Rothersthorpe had such an unsettling effect that there was no telling what madness he could provoke.

When the others had all gone, Lydia chose a chair as far from Rose's work table as she could, sat down and smoothed out her skirts with hands that were not quite steady.

She was not eavesdropping. Absolutely not. It was just that it was quite impossible not to hear every word they were saying, now that they were the only ones left. She had no choice but to sit and listen to him flirting gently with her charge.

If he had *wanted* to humiliate her, he could not have chosen a better method.

'Lord Chepstow? Yes, he is a friend of mine,' Lord Rothersthorpe was saying. 'And, yes, I do have an invitation to his musical evening.'

Just as she suspected. Rose was determined to find out where Lord Rothersthorpe was going, before making her own plans for the evening.

Her insides tightened and twisted into a knot as she watched the animation in Rose's face. However would she cope if these two made a match of it?

She would just have to, that was all. It wasn't as if she'd ever dared hope she might become…something, to him. This was nothing new. It was just…well, it was quite a different thing, knowing she had no chance, in her head, and seeing him courting another woman, right before her eyes.

Oh, why had their paths had to cross now, like this? Why could he not have been safely married to someone else?

If he really began to court Rose in earnest, whatever was she going to do?

Nothing. Nothing, of course.

She loved Rose. She wanted Rose to be happy.

So she would just have to stamp down hard on these pangs of jealousy, whenever they took hold of her.

He had *never* been hers. She had long since accepted that fact. She had. Once she'd married Colonel Morgan, she'd made a point of counting her blessings, daily, and refusing to allow herself to hanker after the impossible. In that way, she'd gradually schooled herself to be content with her lot.

Only now it was looking as though it might not have been impossible. If only Lord Rothersthorpe had changed into this pillar of society sooner…if only he'd cared enough for her to have become this man that people now admired…

But he hadn't. That was what she had to remember. He hadn't turned his fortunes around because he'd wanted to provide her with a home and security. On the contrary, his feelings for her had been so fleeting that he was standing here today, flirting with Rose whilst discounting her very presence in the room.

'But no,' he was saying with a laugh that sent a bitter pang shafting right through her. Once upon a time he had exerted himself to amuse her, as he was now attempting to amuse Rose.

Though it was utterly ludicrous to feel as though he was deliberately attempting to gouge her heart out of her chest with a teaspoon.

'I shall not be attending the Chepstows' musicale. It is Wednesday. Almack's beckons.'

Rose's face fell as dramatically as did her own stomach. In her own case it was because his determination to attend Almack's meant that he really was serious about finding a wife.

She'd known it, deep down. His behaviour last night had told her, even before Robert had started to talk about how men of his class always settled down, eventually. He had not gone to the card room at all. And when he'd danced, he had done so with an eligible girl, not just one of the wallflowers.

Though in Rose's case, the despondency was because of the impossibility of gaining vouchers.

'As if I would want to attend such a stuffy club,' said Rose with a toss of her head. 'From what I hear, it is all rules and regulations, and people looking down their noses at everyone.'

'Yet that is where a gentleman has to go when he is searching for a bride,' he said to her with a meaningful look

'Well, if a man wants to marry me,' replied Rose mutinously, 'he will have to come looking for me where I am.'

Lord Rothersthorpe finally turned towards Lydia and deigned to speak.

'You have your hands full with your spirited young charge, do you not, Mrs Morgan?'

The words might have sounded as though he was expressing sympathy, but she could not forget what he'd said the night before, about preferring a girl who spoke her mind to one who became easily tongue-tied. Besides, there was a challenging glitter in his eyes which she was beginning to recognise. It gave her the distinct impression he had only brought her into the conversation in order to taunt her.

'On the contrary,' she said firmly. 'I am in complete agreement with her. Rose has no need to go hunting for a husband. Any man who wishes to marry her must do her the courtesy of demonstrating that he values her enough to court her properly.'

'Strange,' he said, with a lift of one eyebrow. 'Your attitude towards marriage appears to have undergone a complete reversal since you were having your own Season.'

How could he fling that in her face? How could he mock her for letting him treat her so contemptibly? Oh, how she wished she'd had the strength to turn him from her door when he'd come calling in those days. Instead of letting him…toy with her.

'It is not my attitude that is in question here,' she said coldly, looking him straight in the eyes. 'But the attitude of any man who would aspire to the hand of my stepdaughter.'

He bowed his head. 'I stand corrected,' he said. Then he turned back to Rose. 'And accept my apologies if I implied that you are not worthy of pursuit. When I spoke of your spirit, it was entirely from admiration,

I do assure you. I dislike the kind of girls who put on die-away airs to make men feel they need a champion. A man needs a partner when he chooses a wife, not a woman so feeble she could never be anything but an encumbrance.'

Well, he could not have made his feelings plainer if he had walked up to her and slapped her face. He despised her for having been so weak and vulnerable, when he'd known her, did he? It was just as well she hadn't told Mrs Westerly what he'd said as he'd carried her into the house, then, or she would have clapped him in matrimonial irons so fast he wouldn't have known what hit him. And he would have been stuck with her and all her...*encumbrances.* If he was being this determined to let her know he regretted having almost proposed to her, then it was a good job she hadn't taken him seriously.

Not for the first time, she thanked God Colonel Morgan had seen fit to marry her. He had never, ever looked upon her as an encumbrance. Oh, Rose might have said he made her work hard for her keep, but at least he made her feel as though she *could* play a valuable role within his household.

Lord Rothersthorpe had done himself no favours with Rose, either, to judge from the way she was looking at him as though she had never seen him before. The way *she* had felt last night, when she'd first begun to suspect she had been mistaken about his nature. Rose might be a little outspoken, but she was also a tender-hearted girl. She was bound to recoil from a man who could speak so callously of people who had some form of disadvantage.

Thank heaven Rose had spotted that in him now. *She* would not waste years pining for a man who turned out not to have been worth a single one of the tears she'd shed over him.

And even though he would still be out somewhere looking for a suitable wife, at least she wouldn't have to watch him do it. She thought she could probably handle the news of his marriage to anyone, so long as it wasn't Rose. It would have been extremely painful to have watched them making a life together, having children together, growing old together, when he had so neatly wriggled out of having to do any such thing with her.

As Rose made an appropriate reply, she deliberately looked away. And it was then Lydia noticed her hands had clenched until they'd formed fists.

Well, now she could unclench them. Rose had seen through him. Whoever Lord Rothersthorpe decided to marry, it was highly unlikely to be Rose. So she wouldn't have to purchase Rose's trousseau and write out invitations, and organise the wedding breakfast, all the while feeling as though she was being torn apart inside.

Before she had much time to wonder why she still felt as though Lord Rothersthorpe's marriage was an issue that would cause her such grief, when she'd just decided he was not worth a single one of the tears she'd shed after he'd demonstrated that she didn't mean enough to him to give up his bachelor freedoms for, the door burst open and Robert strode in.

'Thought you had better see this, Mama Lyddy,' he said, waving a letter he was clutching in his hand. 'Oh,' he said, coming to a halt when he spied Rothersthorpe. 'I thought all Rose's admirers had left.'

'All but me,' he replied, crossing the room with his hand extended.

Robert folded the letter swiftly before accepting his

hand. 'Have you had tea?' Robert glanced at the detritus left behind by the pack of Rose's younger suitors.

'I do beg your pardon,' said Lydia, aghast to discover that she'd spent the entire duration of his visit flailing around in a morass of negative emotions which had apparently robbed her of the ability to act as a competent hostess. 'I shall ring for some more. If you are staying?'

'Please do not trouble yourself *now,*' he replied sarcastically. 'I can see your stepson has some pressing business he wishes to discuss with you.'

'Yes,' said Robert, looking rather taken aback by Lord Rothersthorpe's rudeness. 'Very pressing business, as a matter of fact.'

'And I have still to call upon Miss Hill.'

Of course. His other dance partner from the night before.

She did not miss the way Rose's lips tightened in displeasure at his announcement that this had been a mere duty call.

Oh dear. That was two marks against him.

So it came as no surprise when, the moment he'd left, Rose informed her that she rather thought she would as soon go to the Lutterworths' soirée, as anywhere.

The one place where they were certain *not* to encounter Lord Rothersthorpe, even if he did decide to take Rose's hint and abandon his plans to attend Almack's. Now that he was in the market, he would have so many invitations to choose from that he would be spoilt for choice. And he'd become so very top-lofty nowadays, to judge from their two brief meetings, that he would not deign to enter the house of a family that had made their fortune from pickles.

'I am sorry,' said Robert, 'but I really do think you

should read this.' He pulled out the folded letter from the pocket where he'd tucked it earlier. 'It is from Marigold.'

'Oh. Is there some problem at Westdene?'

'It is Cissy, I'm afraid.'

'No!' She snatched the letter from him with a trembling hand.

'I did not want to worry you about her before,' Robert confessed. 'But all the reports I have received suggest she is growing worse by the day.'

Lydia sank down on to a chair to read the letter. Rose came up behind her, so she could read over her shoulder.

'Robert,' said Rose with a soft gasp, when she came to the middle of the page. 'How could you have kept this from us?'

'Because I thought she would improve! I thought at first, when Mrs Broome wrote that she was not doing very well, that it was only to be expected, but that after a reasonable period of time, she would settle down. And I did not want to worry you. I did not want any shadow to fall over your Season, Rose.'

He paced to the console table and began to fiddle with the flowers scattered across its surface.

'Things have not always been between us as they should. I regret that now, and I wanted to…to make it up to you. I wanted this time in London to be perfect…'

'And to think I was grateful for the way you took charge of the more tedious aspects of organising this trip to town,' Lydia breathed. She'd actually told him that she could not have picked a finer house than this one he'd rented for them, nor staffed it with more suitable servants. She'd appreciated the fact that he'd seen to the provision of carriages and horses, and been incredibly impressed when he'd even managed, through the amazingly wide circle of acquaintances he had, to arrange for Rose to have a court presentation. And all the time, he'd been keeping…this from her.

She looked down at the letter which she'd crushed between her fingers.

'But no more. This has gone too far. We must return to Westdene,' she said, getting to her feet and moving towards the door. 'And I am sorry, Rose, but this means the end of your Season—'

'Not necessarily,' put in Robert.

'Of course it does,' cried Rose. 'Lydia has to go to Cissy. And I cannot stay in town without a proper chaperon. And anyway, how could you think I would *want* to stay here now I know what it has cost Cissy?'

'I didn't, of course. It is just that I think I have found a way to deal with this problem without curtailing your Season completely.'

'Cissy is not a problem,' said Rose indignantly. 'She is a darling!'

Lydia looked at the way brother and sister were squaring up to each other and sighed. They'd come so far in the months since their father's death. The Colonel had been hopeless at demonstrating his feelings for his children when they'd been little. It had left Robert resentful at being sent away to school in England while he'd kept the girls with him, and them feeling second-best. They only saw that he'd been educated as an English gentleman, while they'd had ayahs and tutors. It had taken some time to explain that the Colonel had been afraid Robert might succumb to some tropical infection, as his English mother had done. That he was trying to protect him, rather than rejecting him. And that, conversely, he couldn't bear to be parted from all his children.

She could not let all their newly established rapport

disintegrate, just because Lord Rothersthorpe had put her out of countenance. For that was what it boiled down to. She had been angry before Robert had even entered the room.

'I think we should both try to calm down and hear what Robert has to say,' she said wearily. 'There is no sense in us all falling out with each other.'

While she sank into the nearest chair, Rose flounced on to another and folded her arms.

'It was meeting Lord Rothersthorpe that put me in mind of a solution, funnily enough,' Robert began. 'It made me recall how I used to treat the house, before Lydia married Father. How I used to invite parties of friends to row up and picnic in the grounds. And how popular those outings used to be.'

'You mean, even though we will be staying at West-dene, we could still write and invite people down for the day?' Rose sat up straighter. 'Yes, that would work. What do you think, Mama Lyddy?'

Lydia flushed and looked down at her feet. It had been on one of those picnics that Lord Rothersthorpe had raised her hopes, for those few brief, exhilarating minutes. Robert surely was not going to suggest she organise another? It would mean reliving the pain of rejection all over again.

Fortunately, before she could draw breath to voice her reluctance, Robert spoke again.

'That was not quite what I had in mind. I rather thought we might have a fully fledged house party. Mama Lyddy accused me of not letting you get to know any of these young men who claim to have been smitten by you. So I thought, if you have them about you all day, we will soon discover what they are really made of.'

Rose let out a shriek of delight, leapt to her feet and flung her arms round Robert's neck.

'Robert, you are brilliant! It is just the thing. I need only invite—' she broke off with a blush '—the people I really like. And we *will* soon see what they are really made of, by the way they react to Cissy.'

'Ah,' said Robert with a frown. 'I had not thought of that. And really, you know, perhaps that wouldn't be quite fair. You cannot use Cissy as some sort of…test.'

'What did you expect when you suggested having visitors, then, Robert?' Lydia fumed. 'Did you think I would keep her hidden away?'

'Well, no. But she spends most of her time in the nursery, anyway.'

'If anyone,' said Rose, 'says one unkind word to Cissy, I will send them packing.'

'It might be a little too late for Cissy by then, though…' said Robert pensively.

'She is not as fragile as all that,' said Lydia. 'Provided we are there to love her, she will not care what anyone else may say to her, or think of her.'

'Are you quite sure?'

'Oh, yes.' Well, probably. 'And as Rose has so astutely pointed out, what better way to find out what a person is really made of, than to force him to confront a girl with all of Cissy's disadvantages?'

It had certainly proved that she had made the right choice in accepting Colonel Morgan's offer. He might have blustered and barked orders, and lost his temper when things were not done to his exacting standards, but he had not been, at bottom, a cruel man. When he'd first seen Cissy, he had lost his temper—oh dear me, yes. But he had done so to good effect, reducing those who had been maltreating her to quivering wrecks.

There was a great deal of difference between a man's manner and his true self. She only had to think how she'd been taken in by Rothersthorpe's charm when she'd been a naïve girl. Looking back now, she could see that though he had it in him to be kind, those random acts that had so impressed her were all of a rather showy variety. And none of them had cost him anything.

Even when he'd caught her up in his arms and carried her indoors, it had been the kind of act that would have caught the eyes of all the other ladies in the party. When he returned to them, she would wager they had mobbed him, treating him as though he was some kind of hero.

But she couldn't help reflecting that he'd managed to leave her side before she'd emptied the contents of her stomach all over the drawing-room floor. Nor had he meant a single word he'd spoken to her in such tender tones.

'Men,' she said with just a touch of bitterness, 'can appear to be all that one would wish for in a husband, but turn out to be far from what you first thought them to be, only when it is too late. Invite who you will to Westdene, Rose. So long as I am there to support her, nobody will be able to do Cissy any harm.'

'Anyone who tries will have to answer to me, too,' said Robert gruffly, taking her hand.

'And we will send them packing,' said Rose with a militant lift to her chin and the light of battle in her eyes. 'For I wouldn't dream of marrying a man who could not accept Cissy exactly as she is.'

Chapter Four

Rose was all for getting into their carriage and leaving town at once, then writing to the people they would invite to stay with them for a week.

Robert said it was the worst thing they could do.

'People will become intrigued if we all just up and leave in a hurry. And they will ask questions. If we prevaricate, their curiosity will be roused to fever pitch. Do you really want Cissy to become the topic of gossip?'

'Mama Lyddy,' said Rose, turning to her imploringly. 'What do you think we should do?'

While the two siblings had been squabbling, Lydia had been sitting quietly, thinking. There was only one event she still really wanted Rose to attend and it was only a few days away. She would be willing to put off their departure from town until after the soirée at Lord Danbury's house, so important for Rose's future did she believe it could be.

'On this occasion,' she therefore said, 'I concede that Robert has raised a good point. I do think it would be for the best if people thought we were leaving town because we'd decided to throw a house party, rather than having been called home for an emergency. And if I were to write to Marigold and tell her the exact date on which we will return, she and Michael could help Cissy to count down the days. It might help her to calm down, a little.' Perhaps.

Once they'd agreed this was the course to take, she had written to Marigold, outlining their plans. She had left it to Rose to write out the invitations to her favourites, merely requesting a copy of her list so she could warn their housekeeper, Mrs Broome, how many people to expect.

She could not stop worrying about Cissy, but she thought she managed to hide the depth of her concern from Rose. The last thing she needed was to hear that she did not believe anything would calm Cissy down but her own return to Westdene.

At last it was the eve of their departure and there they all were in Lord Danbury's house, courtesy of his daughter, Lady Susan.

She had her suspicions that the lady in question had her eye on Robert, though her invitation had included them all. Robert had wealth and reasonable looks, and, from what she could see of the other guests, Lady Susan had a kind of fascination for the unusual. And from the way she had questioned Rose, upon their arrival, at such length about her mother and her life in India, she had appeared truly interested, if a bit patronising in her manner.

Perhaps, after this, when they returned to town, other society hostesses would begin to admit Rose to their ranks. If only Rose managed to make a good impression while she was here. The trouble was, even though Lady Susan had told Robert this was to be 'a gloriously informal evening', she wasn't too sure what that meant. She had a horrid suspicion that the daughter of an earl could get away with much, under the banner of being 'informal', but that if the dark-skinned daughter of a colonel in the East India Company army behaved in exactly the same way, she would be condemned as 'fast'.

Not that Rose was doing anything more outrageous than attracting a group of her admirers and holding court in her usual, impartial manner.

But ought Lydia to be part of the group? Was it acceptable to stay on the far side of the room, observing? Or should she, as chaperon, stick much closer to her charge?

She did not really want to intrude and put a damper on Rose's enjoyment. It was just that several rather haughty-looking people had looked down their noses at the jolly group of youngsters as they had stalked past. Was it the fact of finding a nabob's daughter, and a couple of junior naval officers in Lord Danbury's house at all, or their free and easy manner of interacting, which was drawing down such disapproving stares?

She had almost decided that she ought to go and stand a little nearer, just to give them more of an appearance of respectability, when she was startled by an all-too-familiar, dark-brown voice drawling into her ear.

'Champagne?'

She did not need to look round to know that it was Lord Rothersthorpe standing behind her, offering her a drink. She knew his voice only too well.

Though for the life of her, she could not think why he had approached her tonight. They had seen nothing of him since his visit to their house on the day they had decided to leave town. And on that occasion he had made it quite plain that he despised her for having *die-away airs* which made her so vulnerable she could only ever have been an *encumbrance* to him.

Though it made no difference to her, not now. How could it?

'It does not have poison in it,' he said, moving to stand in front of her, which gave her no choice but to acknowledge him. 'I just thought you looked as though you could do with some fortification.' He glanced across the room to where Rose was holding court.

'I don't know what you mean,' she said, though she took the glass from his outstretched hand. It was the only way to make his arms go back to hanging by his sides. It was ridiculous of her, but having his hand stretched towards her like that made her remember things better left forgotten. Like how it had felt to be held in his arms. And taking a drink would give her something to blame for the peculiar fizz that was rushing down her spine. For it was not, it *could* not have been, created merely by the sound of his voice.

'You were debating whether you ought to go over there and lend an air of respectability to the proceedings,' he said.

Since it was ridiculous not to look at him while he was talking to her, she lifted her head, and did exactly that. The initial fizz turned into a sort of slow burn.

'And I would guess, from the look of trepidation on your face, that you were also imagining the beauty's reaction should you attempt anything so heavy-handed.'

She hated the way he'd read her so accurately. But what she hated even more was the way her body leapt to attention, just because he was standing so close and giving her his undivided attention. Bother her heart for fluttering and her lungs for needing to drag in extra amounts of air, and her knees for behaving exactly as they always did in his vicinity. Could they not pay attention to her head? It had been a *mistake* to been so taken in by him when she'd been a girl. She'd known it then and he'd confirmed it by the way he'd spoken to her since. He was not, and had never been, the man for her.

'I fail to see why it should concern you,' she retorted waspishly.

'Nor do I, to be perfectly honest.' He rubbed the back of his neck with the hand that had just held her champagne glass, his eyes growing uncharacteristically perplexed.

'I have come to town to look for a wife, but ever since discovering that you are here, I keep looking out for you instead. And now that we happen to be at the same event, I have not been able to stay away from you. Have you any idea how annoying that is?'

He couldn't stay away from her? He had been looking for her? Didn't he mean, for Rose? She instinctively looked across the room and saw Rose looking back at her with open curiosity.

Oh dear. She hoped he would not linger talking to her for long, or Rose was bound to want to know what they had been discussing. And Rose was far too perceptive and inquisitive to be fobbed off for very long. Though her own thoughts in regard to Lord Rothersthorpe were far too muddled for her to comprehend, let alone attempt to explain to anyone else.

'Perhaps,' Lord Rothersthorpe continued, having raised his glass to Rose in salute, 'it is just that something about the expression on your face reminded me of the girl you used to be. Which, in turn, made me behave like the green boy I used to be, too. An attack of nostalgia.' His expression cleared. 'Yes, that must have been it.'

'You must certainly have changed since those days,'

she said, with a touch of asperity, 'if you have to examine your motives for wanting to speak to an old friend.'

'And thank God for it,' he replied, his face turning cynical. 'In those days I was completely taken in by that air of fragility you used to cultivate. Though fortunately, you have lost it, now.' He frowned. 'At least I thought you had.' He gave a short, harsh laugh. 'And yet you only have to look the slightest bit troubled to have me galloping to your rescue all over again.'

'You never once galloped to my rescue,' she retorted.

'Oh? That is not what you used to say. Whenever I asked you to dance, you used to hang on my arm, looking up into my face as though I was a knight on a white charger.' He bit the words out between clenched teeth. 'You used to plead with me to take you out for air on the terrace, or a walk in the park...'

'I did no such thing!'

'Perhaps not in so many words, I will concede that point. But you used to plead with your eyes. They used to have such a speaking expression in them. Like a spaniel,' he finished on a sneer.

'Well I...that is, m...' She finally managed to untangle her tongue. 'I wonder that you b-bothered with me, then, if I reminded you of a d-dog. And exactly how did taking me for a walk equate with rescuing me?'

'I took you out from under the shadow of that chaperon of yours, that's how. The minute I pried you away from her you blossomed. You lost your stutter, you laughed and smiled. Sometimes, you looked so pretty I wondered that other fellows did not notice it. Though I gather that was the whole point, wasn't it?'

'Pretty?' The shock of having a compliment flung at her in a way that made it sound as though he would rather have been insulting her filled her with a strange mix of emotions. 'You thought I was pretty?' The past swirled round her, like a gossamer cloud. She'd adored him and he'd secretly thought she was pretty. He'd never said so, but then he'd done all he could to keep things between them light. Paying compliments would have led her to hope for things he wasn't prepared to offer.

Still, she had dared to believe he genuinely liked her, because nobody had forced him to take her for walks in the park. He had not needed to dance with her every time they attended the same balls, either. There were plenty of other damsels in need of a hero to brighten up their evening, were he really indifferent to her. But he had not been indifferent to her. Which was why, when he'd started to talk about marriage, she'd very nearly believed he'd meant it.

'No,' he said in a tone she'd never heard him use before, harshly scattering the shreds of memory to the four winds. 'I thought you could *become* pretty, if someone were to take care of you properly. Well,' he said with another harsh laugh, 'time has proved me correct in that respect.'

He ran his eyes over her body with an insufferably insolent intensity. It made her blush all over.

'You have become just as beautiful,' he grated, 'as I always suspected you could be.'

'B-beautiful?' That surpassed pretty. Prettiness was something that was easy to dismiss. Beauty implied a kind of power over the beholder.

'Oh, come,' he sneered. 'You know very well exactly how alluring you are. I despise you and everything about you, and yet you only have to hang your head, or look the slightest bit anxious, to have me running to your side.'

Her heart was beating very fast. He thought she was

beautiful? Alluring? She could scarcely believe it. And yet here he was, pressing champagne on her and telling her he despised her, yet being completely powerless to stay away from her.

For the first time in her life, she felt as though she could almost be dangerous. It was a heady sensation. But the feeling only flared for a moment before fizzling out and plummeting her back down to earth.

'You despise me,' she repeated, looking up into his face in pained bewilderment.

'Are you surprised? You made me believe you needed gentle handling, someone to cosset and care for you. What an idiot I was. All you needed was a man with an open purse. Any man, to judge by the indecent haste with which you dragged Colonel Morgan to the altar.'

Anguish coiled inside her like a snake. And like a snake, it reared up and struck out.

'At least he was prepared to go to the altar. Which you,' she reminded him, 'were not.'

He clenched his jaw against the words that clamoured for release. He could not tell her what he thought of her inconstancy, not here in this crowded drawing room. And as for claiming that he wasn't prepared to go to the altar… He raised his glass to his mouth and drained it of its contents. Better than calling her a liar to her face.

How could she say he hadn't been prepared to go to the altar when he'd asked her, outright, to marry him?

At least, his conscience nudged him, he'd asked her to *think* about it. And she'd given him her answer by marrying someone else.

'I don't know how many times you warned me you were never going to marry,' she said, sending a cold sensation swooping through him.

Had he been as adamant as that? If he had, he'd conveniently stuffed that fact to the back of his mental wardrobe. But now that she'd dragged it into the daylight, he supposed he could see exactly how he might have given her that impression. At first it was because he'd begun to suspect *she* might have been falling in love with *him*. He'd wrestled with his conscience, wondering if it would be better for her not to have any more to do with him. He hadn't wanted to hurt her.

But he hadn't been able to stay away from her either. She'd exerted a fascination which he'd been increasingly powerless to resist.

Until he'd decided to stop fighting it and simply surrender to marriage.

Only she hadn't trusted in him, had she? While he'd been raising the funds to pay for a wedding licence, she'd gone and married her nabob.

Though that hadn't been the only reason she'd spurned him.

'You certainly did not want to marry a fribble like me anyway, did you?'

She'd told him she loved being with him because he made her laugh. At the time, he'd taken it as a compliment, fooling himself into believing she actually liked him. It was only later that he'd realised it was the exact opposite. All he'd been to her was a bit of light relief during intervals between the serious business of husband-hunting. She'd actually admitted that she used him to make her look attractive to other men. In short, he'd been the equivalent of the clown during the intermission.

'You never took me seriously. You even went so far,' he said resentfully, 'as to say you did not have to bother trying to impress me.'

'I never said any such thing! I valued the time I spent with you. You made me feel as though I could just be myself. It was such a relief to think I had one friend in town who liked me just as I was.'

She looked up at the cold, hard stranger who had once spent hours coaxing her out of her shell.

'What happened to you? It is as if all the laughter has gone out of your life.'

'You could say the scales fell from my eyes.' Which they had done, the moment he heard she'd married that dried-up old stick of a man. Because he'd been rich.

The money he'd had in his pockets, of which he'd held such high hopes, had suddenly seemed pathetic. He'd felt ridiculous when he'd heard about the opulence of her wedding, compared to the one he would have been able to pay for. He'd congratulated himself on having enough of the ready to obtain a licence and a ring. But she'd got lace and jewels from her nabob. A generous allowance, no doubt, and a life of utter luxury which he'd had no chance of matching.

He'd slunk back to Hemingford Priory after the encounter with Robert, rather than return to his rooms in town. He couldn't face the prospect of having to give explanations to the crowd he ran with in those days. How could a man admit to feeling incapable of resuming his life of drinking, gaming and kicking up larks, simply because a woman had jilted him? He would have been a laughing stock.

Hemingford Priory, of course, had been purgatory in the state he was in. He'd never been much of a one for country pursuits. Fishing was dull work and shooting entailed tramping through muddy fields ruining his boots.

And to crown it all, his father had been in residence,

throwing one of his infamous house parties. He'd taken to riding out during the day, in order to avoid the roistering. And before very long, he started to put up in whatever wayside inn he happened to be closest to when he felt exhausted enough to sleep as soon as his head hit the pillow. It beat the alternative—tossing and turning all night in his own bed, lurid visions of what Lydia would be getting up to with her husband stoked by the noise of what amounted to an orgy going on all around him.

It hadn't been long before he'd begun to notice that all was not right with others, besides himself. Wherever he went, he found surly faces turned upon him. At first, he'd thought he was imagining the way conversations between the labourers would cease whenever he strolled into the taproom. But he could not mistake the open hostility of the man who'd spat on the floor one day, as he'd been leaving, after muttering, 'Like father, like son.'

And he'd started to look, really look, at the state of the villages over which his father held sway.

And what he saw was that although his father entertained his cronies in lavish style up at the house, his father's tenants lived in hovels. His own gardens might be well groomed, but the fields that should have been productive were left unploughed. A lot of the villagers looked ragged and hungry. In fact, everywhere he looked, he had found evidence of neglect and mismanagement.

For the first time in his life, he'd actually had a good, hard look at himself, too. And what he'd seen was that the lifestyle that he had taken so much for granted had beggared these simple, labouring folk. He'd been ashamed of the way he'd been idling his life away, drinking and gaming, following blindly in his father's footsteps, letting himself be carried along with the crowd of bucks who were also frittering away their inheritances in a veritable orgy of waste.

He'd even conceded that Lydia might have had a point, when she'd looked down her nose at him the day he'd admitted losing all the money he'd won on the mouse by backing the wrong horse.

And a wave of something hot and bitter had swelled up inside him. He was damned if he was going to end up like his father. He'd show these locals how wrong they were to write him off without giving him a chance to prove himself.

And he'd show Lydia, too.

'You say you think I have changed,' he said coldly. 'And I am glad to say I think I have, too.'

In a strange way, he supposed he owed it all to her. She'd certainly started it, by making him wish he could be a better, more stable man. And even though she'd flung his good intentions back in his face, that desire to prove himself had only grown stronger.

'Clowns,' he drawled, 'are all very well, in their place, but a man of my rank has an obligation to behave responsibly.'

'A clown? I never thought of you as a clown,' she said. 'I don't understand why you have become so…'

'So what?'

She lowered her head. She had been going to say cold, or hard, or bitter. It appalled her to think that, for a moment, she had been so upset she had forgotten her manners.

'I beg your pardon, Lord Rothersthorpe,' she said, pulling herself together with an almighty effort. 'I almost forgot that you have, as you pointed out, come into

a very noble title. Naturally, you would not behave as
you did when you were a young man, without the cares
and responsibilities that go with the role. And I apolo-
gise if I spoke out of turn. It is just that we were used
to talk to one another so freely, that—'

She broke off.

'Yes, we did, didn't we?' He stroked his chin as he
looked at her downbent head. Perhaps it had not all been
an act on her part. Perhaps she had begun to develop
a little bit of genuine affection for him. As much as a
woman so shallow was capable of feeling.

And perhaps, given that her stammer had put in a re-
appearance, she really had been as timid as he'd thought
her, too. He could not discount the amount of pressure
that Westerly woman had been putting on her to marry.
If she really hadn't believed he was in earnest when
he'd asked her to marry him, maybe she just hadn't had
the strength to hold out against such a glittering offer.

Perhaps he had to take some responsibility for her refusal. He had, after all, deliberately hidden his true feelings from her, even once he'd admitted them to himself.

It had certainly been easier to assume he'd been
taken in by her, than admit he'd made a total mull of
proposing. Easier, too, to make himself believe he hated
her, whenever he imagined her willingly opening her
legs to…

He slammed the door on that train of thought. But
even so, he did not feel the terrible roiling jealousy
that permitting himself to veer in that direction normally produced.

It was as though confronting her like this, and finally
hearing her point of view, had released a great deal of
the poison that had been festering inside him.

He tried to recall, without the veil of resentment,

what she had really been like, back then. And what he had been like. It was not easy to regard the past with impartiality.

Though one thought did manage to swim clear of the maelstrom of clouded memories. And it was the knowledge that they had both been very young and not very wise.

But what did it all matter? He was no longer looking for someone who would make him feel as though his life had some purpose. He had a purpose in life. He had responsibilities, as she'd just said. He had a duty to his tenants to find a wife who would work alongside him, in the areas particularly reserved for that sex.

He did not want a frail, delicate blossom who needed constant care. He was looking for a partner in his life's work. He wanted to marry the kind of woman who would visit the sick and do something about the education of the village girls so that they wouldn't leave in droves for work in the mills.

And from what he'd seen of the mills he would one day inherit, he wanted a woman of compassion, and vision, who would stand shoulder to shoulder with him as he did something for the lot of the miserable wretches who currently slaved for a pittance there, too.

Lydia would have been of no help whatsoever. In fact, her constant demands for attention might well have hampered him in his quest to turn his estates around. He threw his shoulders back. He'd achieved everything he'd set out to do without her.

He hadn't needed her.

And he didn't need her now.

So why was it, dammit, that he was still standing here, letting the awkward silence between them lengthen, when all round the room were women who *were* eminently suitable?

'I wish…' she eventually said, very softly.

He'd been impatiently scanning the room, but at her words, he looked down into her upturned face. And his heart thudded.

God, not only was she more beautiful than any woman had a right to be, but no other had ever managed to have such an instant, visceral effect upon him.

Even though he knew that she was nothing but a worthless piece of fluff, he still wanted her.

And by the look in her eyes, the faint flush that was spreading across her cheeks, the pulse that fluttered in her throat, she wanted him too.

An intense surge of lust coursed through his veins. So intense it sickened him. All she had to do was flutter her eyelashes at him and murmur something that might be taken for an invitation, and he was ready to take up where they'd left off. Even though she hadn't been prepared to stand by him when it would have mattered. Even though she was the very last woman he should ever wish to get entangled with again.

'Don't look at me like that, dammit,' he snarled.

'Like what?'

'It is no use opening your eyes wide and feigning innocence.' He leaned forwards, so that he could hiss his resentment into her ear.

'You want me. You are practically licking your lips and imagining what you will do with me if you ever succeed in getting me into your bed.'

And the worst of it was that he wanted it as much as she did. By God, she was like a kind of sickness. He'd thought he was cured of her, but after only one exposure to her, he'd gone down with the fever all over again. Even down to making excuses for the inexcusable.

For had not even her stepson said there could only be one reason for a girl of age to marry a man like his father? And he should know. If Robert said that Lydia was mercenary to the core, it must be true.

Lydia reared back in indignation and had actually opened her mouth to refute his allegation when she realised she couldn't. For it would be a lie.

She did want him. She'd always wanted him.

She couldn't help it.

And even though she was rather shocked at the way he'd spoken so bluntly about sexual desire, her traitorous body was responding with an enormous great wave of it. It totally eclipsed the pattering of her heart and the weakness of the knees she'd previously experienced in his vicinity. If he led her out of the room right now and they could find a secluded, horizontal surface on which to lie, he would find her completely ready for him.

She had never, ever, responded in this way to talking about the marital act. When Colonel Morgan had asked her if it would be convenient for him to visit her room, though she had never refused, the knowledge that he would be availing himself of his conjugal rights had never had *this* effect upon her.

'Perhaps,' he suddenly said, 'that would be the answer.'

'W-what is the answer? Answer to what?'

'The answer to what we should do about this inconvenient attraction I feel for you.'

'What? I…I don't understand you.'

'Oh, yes, you do.' He closed the distance she'd put between them and murmured into her ear again. The heat of his breath slid all the way down her spine. 'We should become lovers, Lydia. And lay the past to rest in your bed.'

He straightened up, and gave her a slow, sultry perusal. 'Just send me word, Lydia. Whenever you are ready, I will be more than happy to oblige.'

'N-no...' she tried to say. But somehow the word barely managed to make it past the huge lump in her throat. When she'd started to try to tell him what she wished might happen between them, it hadn't been *that*. She'd just hoped they might be able to recapture something of the friendship they'd used to feel for each other, that was all. She wouldn't have asked anything more of him, if only he could try to set aside the animosity that kept flaring in his eyes, that kept spilling from his lips.

Instead of which he'd grossly insulted her by assuming she was the kind of woman who could indulge in an extra-marital affair. She should have slapped his face.

And then he wouldn't have given her that knowing look. And he wouldn't be stalking away with that self-satisfied smirk on his face.

At least, she couldn't see it, but she could tell from the set of his shoulders. She'd never seen such a smug back. It was no use saying it was entirely her own fault for gasping and melting when he'd suggested they should go to bed together. He was the one who'd made her gasp and melt, with his wicked suggestion.

Ooh, if only she had a heavy object to hand, she would throw it at him. Never mind who was watching.

Though people were watching. People who mattered to her.

People she'd forgotten entirely, for the entire time Lord Rothersthorpe had been talking to her.

Though the moment she looked at Rose, she knew that *she* had not taken leave of her senses. Her eyes were flicking from Lord Rothersthorpe, who was stalking from the room, to her.

And they were brim full of speculation.

Chapter Five

Lord Rothersthorpe reined to a halt, pulled a kerchief from his pocket and mopped his brow, muttering a string of oaths under his breath. Lydia had driven him to take to his horse yet again.

The moment he'd received her note, delivered to his door at dead of night by one of her footmen, he'd realised it had been a mistake to issue her a challenge. He should have known she wouldn't let him escape her clutches now she'd reeled him in again.

He'd thought that telling her the truth—that nowadays he found her only fit for bedding, not for wedding—would have put her in her place.

Instead, he'd discovered just how different Mrs Lydia Morgan was from the girl he'd believed Lydia Franklin had been. *That* Lydia would never have taken a lover.

But then *that* Lydia wouldn't have taken a shrivelled-up old man for a husband, either. Had he learned nothing? How could he have been so taken in by that little show of outrage she'd put on when he'd made his proposition? She'd been so convincing he'd wondered if he owed her an apology for insulting her, even though he'd cloaked it under an air of nonchalance as he'd taken his leave.

Just as well he hadn't turned round and made that apology. Or he would have felt a great fool when he held that note in his hand.

It had all been an act. Put on lest someone had overheard him, he supposed. She must really want people to believe she was a respectable widow.

He grudgingly conceded that she did at least draw the line at flaunting her affairs to the detriment of her stepdaughter's chances at making a good match.

Then he shut his eyes and shook his head, unable to credit the fact that he was sliding into an attitude of looking for some good in her. When was he going stop letting his youthful folly affect his judgement as an adult?

She was the kind of woman who used the cover of a batch of eager suitors for an innocent girl's hand to embark on a clandestine affair.

So what did that make him for taking her up on it?

What kind of man dragged on his clothes at first light, dashed straight round to the mews and saddled his horse as though getting to Westdene was a matter of life or death?

The horse in question snorted, and gave its head a little shake. He stopped wool-gathering, stuffed his handkerchief back in his pocket and urged his mount into motion.

To think he would actually have been glad if she'd accepted his proposal back then. Though, he grudgingly conceded, she might have made him happy, to begin with. But the truth was he'd had a lucky escape.

Lydia was too avaricious to have understood, let alone supported him in his quest to improve life for his tenants. When he'd started sacrificing so much of his own personal wealth to redress the imbalance that had so appalled him, she would soon have ceased looking up at him with those puppy-dog eyes. She would have pouted and rebelled by running up enormous bills at the dressmaker's.

The way he saw it, his life would then have gone in one of two directions. Either he would have stayed enamoured of her and ended up living to please her. Or he would have grown disgusted at having tied himself, in his youth, to such an ambitious schemer. In either case, it would have spelled disaster for his self-respect and his tenants in about equal measure. He shuddered as he imagined his estates still lying waste, his tenants driven to rioting through hunger, while all their rents went on buying her silken gowns.

He trotted along, his face grim. Whichever version of married life he envisioned, she was very far from being the helpmeet he yearned for now.

So what was he doing, riding his horse through this insufferable heat, just because she'd summoned him to her bed?

He rested his horse when he came to the brow of the next hill, scowling along the road that descended through a narrow, steep-sided valley. If he had any sense he would turn round and send a note expressing regrets, saying he had pressing engagements which would keep him in town for the entirety of the next week. And she would have her answer. She could damn well find some other man to slake her carnal appetites!

No sooner had he pictured some other man in her bed than his stomach clenched in revolt.

Anyway, why the hell should he deny himself the satisfaction of possessing her, just for a few nights, simply because he had a few qualms about her character? Did a man look for virtue in a mistress? No.

So what was the matter with him?

It could not be that he was afraid she could inveigle her way into his heart again. This time round, he was not some green boy, blinded to her faults by infatuation. He was older and wiser, and could see exactly how worthless she really was. This time round, her attraction for him was merely physical.

He was keen to bed her, yes, but that did not put him in a position of weakness. There was no point in taking a lover unless his level of interest was such that she could make all the sneaking around involved worth his while. And if he felt that it would kill him to let her slip through his fingers, then it was only because she had been his secret, sexual fantasy for such a long time.

She might still be disturbing his peace of mind, but she no longer had the power to touch his heart. She could not deflect him from the future he'd mapped out for himself. This was just a short interlude before he commenced on the serious business of finding a suitable wife.

A hard smile curved his lips at the notion of treating her as nothing more than a passing sexual adventure, after the way she'd used him as light relief during her own Season of spouse hunting. There was a pleasing symmetry to it.

He urged his horse onwards. Hadn't he recently likened her to a kind of pernicious disease? Well, this week would be the equivalent of taking the cure. He would immerse himself in her for the duration of this house party, or however long it took for this inconvenient obsession with her to burn out.

And once he'd slaked his lust for her, he wouldn't

have that gilded image of her, ethereal and fragile, shimmering in the background of his mind whenever he looked at any other woman.

This week, he would take that image and shatter it beyond any hope of repair.

He was amazed that it still existed in any form, given the years he'd spent hating her for marrying for money. Yet he'd only had to look at her across that ballroom, to feel a jolt of yearning so strong it had almost stopped his breath.

Very well, she was still the most beautiful, the most desirable woman he'd ever seen. But her beauty went no deeper than her porcelain-fine skin. Apart from being mercenary, she was also damned insensitive. She must be, to have given him directions to the jetty where the barge carrying all her other guests was moored. Had she really forgotten the only other time he'd gone by water to Westdene? Had that day meant so little to her?

He could still recall every single minute of it.

Ironically enough, when he'd gone to collect her, she'd wanted to cry off. She'd said she wasn't well enough to go out anywhere. Her chaperon had been deaf to her entreaties, practically thrusting her into the hack he'd hired to take them down to the jetty. When she'd winced at the brightness of the light reflecting off the water he'd been livid with her chaperon. Though rouge had given Lydia's cheeks some semblance of normality, her lips had been completely white. And while the others had bounced, laughing, out of the barge once they'd reached their destination, her legs had almost given way. She'd stood on the jetty swaying, her hand pressed to her forehead. And all her chaperon had done was rather impatiently tell her to go and sit in the shade, and stop making such a fuss.

Over the years since then, he'd often wondered if the Westerly woman had known her charge better than anyone. Perhaps her impatience with her die-away airs stemmed from a knowledge that Lydia had been acting all along and disapproved of her methods. But at the time, as a young man rather given to fits of chivalry, he'd sworn that someone had to rescue Lydia from that woman. And that, in spite of his youth, and the assumption that went with it that he wouldn't have to consider marriage for years yet, he was going to be the one to do it. That decision reached, conventions and propriety seemed irrelevant. He'd scooped her into his arms and carried her up to the house. For she'd told him once that only complete darkness and absence of sound would bring any relief from the devastating pain she suffered when she got one of her headaches.

Robert had been too busy with his other guests to pay him much attention. He'd taken the opportunity to put his proposition to Lydia, but there had not been time for her to give him any kind of answer before the Westerly woman had come panting into the house behind them, vociferously objecting to his actions. He'd only managed to appease her by promising to go and fetch the housekeeper, the moment he'd laid Lydia gently down on the nearest sofa.

And that had been the last time he'd seen her, as a single woman.

Dear God, did she really think he could take part in a parody of that day by getting into a barge with a load of young people intent on their party of pleasure? When they both knew that at some stage over the next few days, they would become lovers? It would have been like rubbing salt into all the wounds she'd ever inflicted on him.

His mouth flattened into a grim line. Even after all these years, he was still angry with her. *He'd* got her into that house. She'd *used* him to effect an introduction to Colonel Morgan, then turned all her charm upon *him.* She'd seduced the old man into making a proposal within the space of a few days.

As effectively as she was seducing him now, he supposed, darting him those heated looks with those luminous great eyes of hers. While still managing to project an air of fragility—no, make that utter femininity.

Oh, what the hell did it matter how he chose to describe what it was about her that called to everything that was masculine in him? The fact was that he wasn't going to be fit to court another woman until he'd dealt with this obsession with her. If he did not take this chance to finally get to know her, in the biblical sense, he would forever wonder what it would have been like. He might even, God forbid, still find himself hankering for a version of her whilst selecting his own wife. Which would be disastrous.

He *needed* to take these few days, or even weeks, or however long was necessary. Only then could he start looking for a virtuous young woman who would become a life partner. A woman he would be proud to have for the mother of his children. A woman who would care for his tenants compassionately and run his household with intelligence and tact. A woman he wouldn't want to alternately strangle, or kiss, or shield from the slightest breeze.

And speaking of breezes, he wished there was one now. Heat poured down the hillside and pooled in the valley floor, making the atmosphere insufferable. There was not a scrap of shade to be had anywhere. The only way to escape was to press on, climb the next hill and hope for a village with an inn, or at least a stand of trees so he could give his mount some respite.

For the first time that day, he could see the point of travelling to Westdene by water at this season of the year. His lips curled in self-derision. He'd been in such a rush to set out that he'd only paused to give his valet instructions about packing and transporting clothes. It had never occurred to him that he ought really to have consulted a map. He knew, roughly, the location of Westdene in relation to the river. Knew where the nearest large town was, too. And assumed he could get there just as well on horseback, without having to have anything to do with the arrangements she'd made.

This was the effect Lydia had on him, even now.

Eventually the road, as all roads do, brought him to an inn where he got not only water for his poor beleaguered horse, but also an excellent pint of ale for himself. The landlord had not heard of Westdene, but he did introduce him to a wagon driver who often went up past Chertsey and that excellent fellow gave him detailed directions, liberally peppered with landmarks, culminating in the information that he wanted to look out for a dirty great big set of stone gateposts topped with pineapples.

Since Westdene was set on the brow of a hill, he caught glimpses of it through the trees long before he found the gateposts in question. And he was glad of it, for otherwise he might have been confused by the fact that the gateposts were actually surmounted by a pair of delicately carved marble lotus blossoms.

He paused in the gateway, his jaw working as he gazed at the still far-off slender towers and domed turrets of the house, just visible above the tree tops. The eccentricity of its architecture had been a talking point when Colonel Morgan had the place built. It looked for all the world as though he'd transported a miniature Indian palace from the heat of the tropics and dropped it whole into the rolling Surrey countryside. But to him, those turrets and domes did not represent interesting architectural features. They were images that recurred in his most lurid nightmares, even after all this time.

It was a while before he could tear his eyes from the outlandish structure and make himself enter the grounds that had belonged to Lydia's husband.

But after a few minutes, though he hated to admit it, he had to acknowledge that he'd never seen such spectacular gardens. Last time he'd been here, he had not taken much note of them, but now he could see exactly why people had vied for those invitations of Robert's. Whoever had designed the place had taken advantage of the gradient to create a succession of weirs and cascades, and sweeping expanses of water, round which the drive wound so that at every turn he encountered a new, but equally enchanting, view. He did not know the names of most of the plants he saw, which told him they must be specimens imported from far-off lands. All of which added to the impression of having strayed into a realm where everything was out of the ordinary.

Every now and then he caught glimpses of another horseman, cantering up the drive ahead of him, and, further on still, an unwieldy travelling coach, lumbering up to the house itself. Evidently, he was not the only one who had chosen not to travel to Westdene by water.

He was crossing the last of the stone bridges before the final sweep up to the house at exactly the same time that the coach lurched to a halt beside the shallow front steps.

So he had a ringside view of everything that happened next.

First of all, just like a creature from one of his heated nightmares, a wild-haired woman came rushing out of the house. Screaming.

The horseman dug in his spurs, urging his mount to intercept the screaming woman before she could reach the carriage.

As the woman tried to dodge round him, Robert—for Lord Rothersthorpe now perceived that it was he—kicked his feet free from the stirrups, dropped to the ground and caught the creature in his arms. She struggled frantically with him, screaming incoherently at the top of her lungs. Robert's horse shied away, but after shaking its mane as though thoroughly disgusted by the behaviour of the nearby humans, trotted off round the corner of the house with its ears pricked up. Only once the horse was well on its way to what Rothersthorpe assumed was its comfy stable did Robert slacken his hold, allowing the she-demon to rain down blows upon his head and chest with clenched fists. She knocked off his hat and even caused him to stagger back a pace or two under the force of her attack.

And yet Robert made no move to either defend himself or restrain her now that the horse had taken itself off out of range. He just stood there, absorbing the blows, whilst very deliberately blocking her access to the coach.

It was such a bizarre sight that Rothersthorpe brought his own horse to a standstill. Robert's horse had a place of safety, well known to it. But his own mount was far from its home and he wasn't at all sure what its reaction would be. If the wild woman darted out of Robert's range, it might rear and lash out with its hooves and injure her. He reached down and patted its neck, murmuring soft words of reassurance just in case.

Eventually the woman slumped in exhaustion against Robert, though her shoulders still heaved through the force of her sobbing. Only then did he allow her to approach the coach. He pulled the door open and Lydia stepped out. The sobbing woman tottered over to her, they flung their arms round each other, and then, because the wild woman was much larger than Lydia, the pair of them collapsed in a froth of petticoats on the gravel beside the coach steps.

The woman's weeping grew less noisy as Lydia stroked her tangled hair, so that when Lord Rothersthorpe's horse pawed at the gravel, impatient at being obliged to stand so long in the heat when it could smell a stable close by, Robert's head flew up.

He scowled, then stalked back down the drive towards him.

'Best come straight round to the stables,' he growled. 'This way.'

He turned and strode away. Rothersthorpe followed, though it wasn't easy to tear his eyes from Lydia, who was crooning something softly to the wild woman, whilst somehow managing to rock her rhythmically. As he passed the stationary coach, he glimpsed another girl, a little boy and a dog clustered together just inside the front door of the house, as though undecided whether it was yet safe to approach the heap of tangled skirts and splayed limbs that was Lydia and the sobbing female.

The boy had a look of Lydia, somehow. Rothersthorpe supposed it was something about the shape of his face, and his flaxen hair.

For a moment, it felt as though the sun had gone behind a dark cloud. He shook his head, impatient with himself. He'd known she had a child by the Colonel. Somebody had told him, not long after the event. So the sight of the boy should not have come as a shock.

He didn't care that Lydia had a child by another man. Why should he? She was nothing to him now.

'I hope,' said Robert as they entered the stable yard, 'that I may rely on your discretion about the incident you just witnessed.'

Rothersthorpe dismounted and saw his horse led into the shady stable by a capable-looking groom while he puzzled over Robert's peculiar choice of words. But curiosity got the better of him. Raising one eyebrow, he turned to Robert, and said, 'My discretion?'

Unabashed, Robert looked him straight in the eye, and said, 'Fact is, this is a bit of a tricky situation. Cissy will calm down soon enough now Mama Lyddy is home to care for her, but if Rose were ever to find out about the state she was in just now, she might take it into her head never to leave again. And I won't have her tied here. It wouldn't be fair.'

'You don't wish Rose to become distressed,' he echoed. What the hell was going on here? And who was that screaming, violent woman that Robert had left Lydia alone with?

'I don't want Cissy distressed either,' said Robert with a scowl. 'Dammit, I should have paid more attention to what Lydia tried to tell me. She has not travelled so far from Westdene for years, so I didn't realise...' He struck at his boot with his riding crop a couple of times, his frown deepening. 'Her problems, you see, were nowhere near so obvious when she was younger.'

'Your sister Cissy is—'

'Careful what you say,' snapped Robert. 'I won't

have her described as a lunatic, whatever appearances to the contrary might indicate. And if you cannot deal with that, perhaps you had better leave right now!'

Rothersthorpe raised both eyebrows. 'No need to take that tone with me, Morgan. I merely wished to understand the situation.'

'Beg pardon,' said Robert, though his scowl did not abate one whit. 'Fact is, having Cissy throw a tantrum like that has rattled me. This whole house party I wanted to throw for Rose is going to be a damned sight more difficult than I'd thought if she doesn't take to the guests. We've always sheltered her from strangers, do you see, so this is going to be a monumental challenge for her.'

Something flickered in the back of his memory. Robert telling his guests on that long-ago picnic that they could have the run of the grounds, but that the house was out of bounds. He'd made some jest about his father having a nasty temper and warning his guests to avoid him if they didn't want to feel the lash of his tongue. He'd taken that statement at face value, but if Cissy had been so easily disturbed, perhaps there was another reason why strangers were not welcomed within doors.

And perhaps that was why all Robert's parties had ceased. He'd known that Robert had fallen out with his father over his marriage to such a young woman and had avoided Westdene for some time. But he'd assumed, when he did not resume throwing parties, and inviting people for picnics in the grounds, after the Colonel's death, that Lydia had somehow been the cause. Now it looked as though it might have had more to do with the strange woman—Cissy—who was, apparently, not quite right in the head.

Not right in the head, and very, very dependant upon Lydia.

His vision of her lifestyle wavered and shifted. He'd always wondered why she had not returned to town sooner after her husband's demise. With the amount of money she must have at her disposal as the widow of a nabob, anyone would have thought she would make frequent trips to town, for shopping sprees.

But she hadn't.

Robert sighed. 'I wanted Rose to have the freedom to choose a husband, without having to worry about how it would all affect Cissy. But I *should* have thought how the disruption to her routine would affect her.'

Rothersthorpe's eyes narrowed. Robert had expressed concern for Rose's freedom, and Cissy's welfare, but none at all for Lydia. He seemed to assume it was Lydia's place to look after them both.

It was damned peculiar for the old man to have kept a child like that within his household at all, let alone have his young wife become the creature's nurse. If ever anyone in his own circle had a child that was abnormal in some way, they paid someone to take them off their hands. Someone trained to deal with that kind of infirmity. And they would keep them at a safe distance from the whole members of the family, in order to prevent disturbances of the kind he'd just witnessed.

Instead of which, he seethed, Colonel Morgan had married a girl with no family to protect her and given her the job of looking after his unbalanced daughter. For some mysterious reason, she had not balked at the task. And she'd somehow slipped in to the role of being the poor creature's security. Well, perhaps he could see how that might have happened. Lydia might have many faults, but he'd seen with his own eyes that she had a way with the poor demented creature.

Maybe he could understand why Lydia felt entitled to take a lover. It sounded as though she'd been virtually incarcerated down here, caring for Colonel Morgan's children by all his previous wives, and the unbalanced one in particular.

It struck him as supremely ironical that as he'd been making his way along the driveway, he'd imagined her reigning over it all like a queen. Colonel Morgan, he could see, was something of a collector and he'd assumed the man had installed his pretty young bride in this lush setting like the jewel in his crown.

Instead, it looked very much as though she'd earned every penny the old man had spent on her. Ah, poor Lydia, he thought, with a cynical smile.

And it hadn't ended with the Colonel's death. It sounded as though Robert permitted her no personal freedom at all. No wonder she'd snatched at the chance of getting him down here, while she could.

He eyed Robert with curiosity. His words indicated an attitude of putting everyone's needs before Lydia's. In public, in London, he had presented a façade of friendliness with his very young stepmama. But how deep did it really go?

He remembered the hostility he'd displayed on the announcement of his father's latest marriage and the names he'd called Lydia. And the way he'd stood guard over both women in his charge, at that ball, his hand clenched on the back of his sister's chair. He had not deferred to Lydia in the matter of his sister's possible dance partners. Why had he not picked up on that marked lack of respect before?

Because he'd been too busy dwelling on his own resentments, that was why.

'Look, I'd better show you up to your room,' said Robert, 'where you can freshen up. I shall have to go and reassess the situation before I risk introducing Cissy to any of our guests.' Shoulders squared, he began to march towards the rear of the property.

'Do you plan,' asked Rothersthorpe, setting off behind him, 'to keep the girl hidden away then?'

'Plan?' Robert snorted. 'No, that was not the plan. Damned if I know what will happen now. Rose swore she'd send everyone packing if Cissy got upset, so the whole party might have to be abandoned, for neither she nor Lydia would countenance shutting Cissy out of sight.'

Robert shot him a level look as they reached the back door. 'You must do as you please. You have seen her at her very worst. If you've a mind to stay, and you have it in you to be kind to her, we need say no more about it.'

'Thank you,' he replied, without making the slightest attempt to disguise the sarcasm.

'If you decide to grace us with your presence,' Robert replied, with an equal measure of sarcasm, 'send me word and I will have you collected from your room in about an hour. The others will have arrived by boat by then and will be picnicking down by the Persian Pools. We will walk down and join them.'

Lord Rothersthorpe remained silent while Robert led him through the house and up some backstairs to a corridor that led to a guest wing.

But there was no question of him leaving. For good or ill, he'd made the decision to come down here and lay his first love to rest. Even though now it appeared there was more to Lydia's subsequent lifestyle than met

the eye, it made little difference. He was going to be
her lover. Purge her out of his system so he could get
on with his life, mad stepdaughters and vengeful step-
sons notwithstanding.

So, as Robert flung open the door to a small, rather
Spartan room, he said, 'There is no need to send word.
Just come and get me in an hour.'

Robert's expression eased into something approaching a smile. He made no comment, but the way he
clapped Rothersthorpe on the back expressed his approval clearly enough.

Rothersthorpe shucked off his riding jacket and
tossed it on to a chest that sat at the foot of a rather
narrow bed, feeling as though he'd just passed some
kind of test.

Not that it mattered. He neither needed nor wanted
Robert's approval.

He wanted to wash off the dust of travel and change
out of his sweat-dampened shirt. He went across to the
marble-topped washstand, which stood next to the window. There was a pitcher full of water ready for his use,
though since his valet had not yet arrived, there was
no chance of changing his shirt. He poured water from
the pitcher into the basin, knowing he would have to
make do with just washing his face and hands. Then he
ran his wet fingers through his hair, in lieu of a comb,
which he devoutly hoped his man would remember to
pack, and inspected himself in the mirror.

He saw an idiot looking back at him. An idiot who'd
come haring down to Surrey the minute Lydia had
crooked her finger at him. An idiot without so much
as a change of clothes, so eager had he been to get here.
An idiot who'd spent the entire journey reminding himself of all Lydia's numerous faults. Who had not been

on the premises five minutes before he'd started to see her as a victim of circumstances, rather than a woman getting her just deserts.

An idiot, who had listened with mounting anger as Robert revealed what her life here must be like, and who had actually started to sympathise with her.

What difference, he admonished his reflection, did it make if Robert was holding Lydia prisoner down here? This was a luxurious prison. She'd walked into her marriage with her eyes wide open, and if she'd subsequently found that caring for Robert, Cissy and Rose was no sinecure, it was none of his business.

And if he could see why she might want to conduct a secret affair, right under the nose of her tyrannical stepson, that made no difference either.

Whatever her reasons for inviting him down here, his had not changed.

He simply had to get over her.

Chapter Six

'How is she?'

The moment Lydia entered what had once been his father's study, Robert strode across the room and took her hands. It was all she could do not to snatch them away.

Except, for once, he really did look contrite.

'I had no idea she would have become so upset whilst parted from you, Mama Lyddy. I would not have acted as I had…'

'You mean,' she replied coldly, 'in keeping all news about her *tantrums* from me whilst I was chaperoning Rose to balls and parties?' Since arriving home she'd found that not only Marigold, but also Mrs Broome, had written to Robert expressing concern.

'Yes. Unforgivable of me, I can see that now, but you must believe me…'

'No, Robert, *you* should have believed *me*. Did you really think anyone could know her better than I?'

'No.' He had the grace to look a bit shamefaced. 'It was just that I thought you were being over-protective. You…well, you and the girls…you all fuss over her in a way that seems totally unnecessary.'

'Unnecessary.' Lydia blinked, once, then nodded her head. It was pointless staying angry with him when his repentance was so genuine. He loved Cissy and she knew he would never do anything to hurt her, not deliberately. It was just he had this irritating tendency to think he knew best. About everything.

'You can only say that,' she pondered aloud, 'because you were not here when she first came to live at Westdene. By the time you forgave your father for marrying me and came to visit, she had settled down.'

Now that she was not so angry with him, it became possible to withdraw her hands from his, go across to the window and hitch her hip on to the broad sill.

'But Marigold or Rose could have told you about her,' she said.

A tide of guilty colour swept across his cheeks. She sighed.

'You are so like your father.'

His brows drew down into a sharp frown.

'You never actually ask what those who depend upon you want. You assume you know best and just expect to have your orders obeyed without question.'

He flung himself into his father's chair and scowled at her, silenced, for once, by the accuracy of her observation.

'But no matter. I understand that, like him, you are trying to do your best for us all.'

'I…' He looked down at a pile of papers, stacked neatly on the desk, and moved them fractionally to one side. 'We are getting away from the point,' he growled. 'Which is Cissy and why she went so completely to pieces, just because you were not here.'

'Ah, yes. Perhaps I should begin with the nightmares she used to have when she first came to live here. Nightmares from which she used to wake up screaming, night after night. Or perhaps we should talk about the way she would not let either me, or your father, out of her sight for one moment during the daytime.'

'What?'

'It was her fear that broke through both Rose and Marigold's tendency to resent having another mother foisted on them.' She smiled wryly. 'They are, at bottom, good girls. And so it wasn't long before they threw their hearts into coaxing Cissy out of her tendency to cling to me all day.'

'I have to admit,' said Robert gruffly, 'that I was surprised that they had finally started to think about someone other than themselves. Surprised and impressed. For when they were very little, they both seemed rather spoiled. Father's little hothouse flowers,' he said with a bitter twist to his lips. 'I suppose,' he said thoughtfully, 'Cissy is the sort of girl who brings out the best in people.'

'In this family, that has been true,' she corrected him. 'But I have discovered that she can also bring out the worst in people. My guardian, for example. When my parents died and I met the new holder of my father's title for the first time, he seemed like a decent sort of man. He said he was willing to be quite generous to me, in respect of franking me for a Season. But he flatly refused to give Cissy house room. He said he had no intention of being saddled with what he termed a halfwit. He would not listen to my explanations of her condition, but packed her straight off to an asylum.'

'Yes. I know that…'

'What you do not know is what she suffered there.' Lydia paused, steeling herself to speak of a time that had been so horrific she didn't even like to think about it.

'When we went to collect her, we found her locked in a room no bigger than a cupboard, manacled to her bed. When your father remonstrated with the governor of the place, he said it was for her own good. That he did not want her to accidentally hurt herself, when she was in a wild state. That he found patients learned to behave with more docility if he had them strapped down when they rebelled against his regime. And then he began to expound the scientific basis for the methods he employed to effect a cure for what he termed the feeble minded.' Lydia screwed up her face in revulsion. 'It involved strapping his patients to a chair and repeatedly plunging them into baths of freezing water to stimulate blood flow to the brain. Or turning them upside down, and suspending them thus, for hours at a time.'

'Good God…'

'And all the time he was boasting about his scientific methods,' Lydia went on as though she had not heard his shocked utterance, 'she was lying there, in her own filth, crying and straining towards us. And then your father…well, you know how terrifying he could be when he got into one of his rages. That first time I saw him lose his temper it was just like how I would imagine it would feel to witness a volcano erupting.

'But I felt like cheering him as he reduced Cissy's tormentors to quivering, apologetic jellies. And from that moment on, your father was her hero. When I told her he was to be her new father, she flung her arms round him and kissed his cheek. In all her filth.'

At that point, Lydia had to rub at her eyes with the cuff of her long-sleeved gown. A lesser man would have repulsed her. But he had not. He had not even wrinkled his nose as he'd hugged her back.

'And it was Cissy's total adoration of him that made

all the difference to the way your sisters behaved towards me after that,' she said. 'Her face lit up whenever he walked into the room. Because I'd told her he was her father now, she treated him exactly as she had done our own father. When he sat down, she would just climb into his lap and cuddle him.'

She had to take a deep breath and screw her eyes shut for a moment to hold back the tears. It was when she'd seen how he thawed whenever Cissy demonstrated her affection openly that she'd begun to see him in a new light, too. Under all that bluster, he was, really, quite a sentimental sort of man.

'So,' said Robert, 'by the time I'd cooled off and come home for my first visit, there you all were hugging and kissing the old martinet, and him revelling in all the affection you showered on him…'

'Oh, your face when you walked in that day,' said Lydia, with a watery smile.

'Did my jaw actually drop as far as I thought? I thought you had wrought nothing short of a miracle,' he said, regarding her with fondness.

Lydia sobered at once. 'It was nothing to do with me.'

Robert shrugged. 'It was a miracle, though. The girls looked pleased to see me. My father was pleased to see me. There were no recriminations for having stayed away so long. No lecture about my lifestyle. For the first time, instead of all snapping and snarling at each other, it felt as though we could become a real family.'

His voice had turned very soft and reflective, but all of a sudden his face flushed and he started fiddling with a letter knife.

'Well,' she said briskly, recognising the symptoms of embarrassment in a male tricked into speaking about his emotions. 'We really do have more pressing business to consider than what happened years ago and that is the question of Rose's suitors.'

'Yes, indeed.' Never had a man looked so relieved to have the subject changed.

'I came in here primarily to tell you that I think we should continue with the house party.'

'What? Are you quite sure?'

'Oh, yes. I looked over the guest list carefully after Rose sent the invitations out. And I believe each person on it has the potential to cope with Cissy.'

In fact, she thought Rose had shown remarkable perspicacity for a girl of her age. For one thing, she had invited two of the gentlemen to bring their sisters, which was bound to have the effect of broadening her social circle, as well as leavening the mix. It would have been rather awkward if the house party had consisted solely of single gentlemen.

'As she *usually* is, yes, but—'

'She will be fine now. The reason she became so upset was because somebody—' she gave him a loaded look '—told her, just as we were leaving, that Rose was going to London to look for a husband. Which reminded her that, once upon a time, *I* had gone to London to look for a husband.'

'But she can't have thought…'

'Cissy never did understand why she had been sent to that asylum. I never spoke of it once we'd rescued her, since it upset her so much. Except to assure her it was over, that she was safe here. Only…' she pursed her lips '…the longer we stayed away, the more the memories of what it had been like last time I was absent for any length of time must have preyed on her mind. I do not think she really believed any of us would ever send her back to a place like that. But…'

'Oh, God,' Robert groaned. 'To think I was trying to offer her reassurance. I could see she was unhappy at the thought of you going away, so I reminded her of how good it had been for you to find a husband in my father. And I said it would be good for Rose to find someone, too. I was trying to pave the way for some new person to come into her life.'

'Yes, I do realise that,' she said. 'But please, in future, do not attempt to think you know what is best for Cissy. Or try to keep anything about her condition from me. I am best qualified to judge what she needs. She is *my* sister, Robert. Not yours, no matter if your father did adopt her.'

He gave her a jerky nod, grudgingly acknowledging her point.

'And another thing.' She was sick of him undermining her, just because he was now head of the family. 'It is about the addition to the guest list, which you did not run by me. I refer, of course, to Lord Rothersthorpe.'

She had not been able to believe her eyes when she'd looked up from the ground, where she sprawled with Cissy cradled in her arms, and he'd been there, gazing down at them in appalled fascination. She'd felt as though the bottom had just dropped out of her world. He was the last person she had expected to see. What on earth had prompted him to ride up to Westdene, today of all days?

'D-did you invite him here? I suppose,' she ventured hopefully, 'you thought it would be pleasant for you to have someone nearer your own age to bear you company while the place is taken over by all the youngsters that Rose has asked down here.'

It would be just like Robert to invite a guest of his own, without bothering to check how his decision might impact on anyone else.

'He is not here at my invitation at all,' said Robert. 'It was all Rose's idea.'

So that was that. There was no point in hoping Robert was using the occasion to mend fences with a man who had once been his friend. The lure of Lord Rothersthorpe's handsome face, and his title, had overcome Rose's scruples about certain aspects of his character. She was giving him another chance to prove himself.

And he had taken it.

'She did discuss it with me,' said Robert, 'since she needed my permission to send Peters out at dead of night.' He gave her one of his piercing looks. 'And when she explained her reasons, I decided there would be no harm in letting her have her way. Amidst the crowd already approaching, what difference does one more make? Can you really object to a last-minute addition on the strength of place settings, or vacant bedrooms, or any such rot?'

'No.' But then that was not the reason she objected to having him here. She had been so relieved that he had not made it on to the original guest list. Now it appeared she was going to have to deal with the painful emotions caused by having him numbered amongst Rose's suitors after all.

'Then let us not quarrel over such a one as Rothersthorpe. For heaven's sake, Lyddy, let us concentrate on what really matters here.'

'By all means,' she said dejectedly. And what mattered was most definitely not her. This week was about Rose's future. Cissy's welfare naturally came a very close second. And she…well, as usual she was of no importance in the scheme of things at all.

She got to her feet, smoothed her skirts and went to the door. She was used to putting the needs of others before her own. It was just that the strength of her feelings for Lord Rothersthorpe would keep rearing up and demanding she listen to them.

'I shall go and see if Cissy is ready. I made her understand that Rose and her friends are coming by water, and that if she wanted to see her today, she would have to wash her face and tidy herself up. I left Betsy helping her choose one of the new gowns we bought her in town.' Seeing the trunk full of presents, which Lydia had brought with her in the carriage, had done much to improve Cissy's frame of mind. Michael's reaction had helped, too. On seeing all the mysteriously wrapped parcels, he had dived in, gleefully searching for labels that bore his name, and Cissy had caught his highly infectious enthusiasm.

'I think it would help her if we all walked down to the Persian Pools to join the others, together, if you do not mind waiting? I know you wanted to be there to greet everyone the moment they stepped ashore, but…'

'There are two naval officers on board to deal with all that,' he said, making a gesture of impatience. 'Mrs Broome has the picnic well in hand and Rose is there to act as hostess. It is more important to support Cissy. Besides,' he added with a hard smile, 'I wish to observe their reactions to her. Then we shall see what they are all made of.'

Lydia wondered if the grim look on his face had anything to do with Lord Rothersthorpe's reaction.

'And Lord Rothersthorpe?' She paused in the doorway, her hand clenching convulsively on the doorknob.

'What did he make of the scene he witnessed?' If he was really as repulsed by Cissy's behaviour as he'd looked, and Robert had sent him away, then good riddance to him! He was not worthy of Rose.

'And what,' she added with a frown, 'was he doing coming here on his horse anyway, instead of upriver with the others?' Did he have such bad memories of the last time he'd come here that he could not bear to replicate even one aspect of it? She could well imagine him having nightmares over the time he'd very nearly stumbled into parson's mousetrap. So he must be very, very keen on Rose, to force himself to visit Westdene at all.

Robert shrugged. 'A couple of the other male guests have arranged to have their horses or curricles transported here. They won't want to be confined to the house and grounds all the time. There are some very good rides in the vicinity. But in answer to your first question,' he said, 'Lord Rothersthorpe asked one or two searching questions, but he did not seem unduly perturbed by my answers. And when I made it quite plain that if her behaviour offended him, he was at liberty to leave, he chose to stay.'

That was not as comforting as Robert had probably intended it to be. It just meant she had to relinquish the last shred of hope that she might be spared the sight of Lord Rothersthorpe dazzling her beautiful stepdaughter.

Mustering a wan smile, Lydia left Robert's study and went back upstairs to the nursery, where she'd left the children unwrapping their presents.

She paused for a moment just outside the door to blow her nose and straighten her shoulders. There were happy sounds emanating from the room and she had no intention of lowering anyone's spirits by revealing the state of her own.

Pinning a bright smile to her face, she flung open the door and strode in. The sight which met her eyes wiped the smile from her face at a stroke.

Shredded wrapping paper littered the floor like so much bark mulch. It originated from Cissy and her dog, Slipper, who were sitting on the floor playing tug-of-war with any large pieces they could find. There were not many left. Dog slobber, she observed with horror, had a rapid and highly deleterious effect upon brown paper.

She turned an indignant face to Marigold, who lifted her chin mutinously.

'It is the first time she's been happy for weeks,' she said by way of excuse.

Michael came running over to her, his little face creased with anxiety.

'I kept telling Cissy you were coming back any day now, but it didn't make any difference,' he said. 'I know you wouldn't leave us, Mama. Not for ever and ever!'

'Of course I wouldn't,' she said, pulling him into a hug. Oh, it felt so good to hold his warm little body in her arms again. How she had missed him.

'You aren't cross with me?'

'Of course not!' She looked down into his upturned face and smoothed back the fringe that would keep flopping into his eyes. 'You did your very, very best to try to make Cissy understand. But, sometimes, nobody can get through to her.'

'You can,' he said.

'Not always.' She sighed. 'It is just that she is happier when I am near. And so she is less inclined to be… naughty.'

Slipper had just destroyed the last substantial piece of wrapping paper and flopped down on the floor with his nose in Cissy's lap. She ruffled his soft velvety ears with one hand and put the thumb of her other hand in her mouth, only the occasional shudder hinting at the emotional storm she'd just weathered.

'Are we all ready?' Lydia asked Michael and Marigold. 'Because Robert is waiting to take us all down to the Persian Pools to meet Rose's new friends.'

Marigold leapt to her feet, her face alight with excitement. 'Oh, she has written all about the two naval officers who are vying for her favours. I am so looking forward to seeing them. Are they really as handsome as she says?'

'They are both very handsome,' Lydia confirmed. Well, she supposed young girls would find them so. It was just that she found it so hard to tell them apart. It had even occurred to her, when she'd seen their names side by side on the guest list, that Rose might be having the same trouble. Why else would she have listed them in the same way she'd done with the sets of brothers and sisters, unless she thought of them as a matched pair?

Marigold ran to the mirror to check her appearance, patting her bright auburn curls swiftly into place. With her huge green eyes, and her tendency to freckle, it was sometimes hard to believe she and Rose were sisters— until she recalled they'd had different mothers.

Michael ran to Cissy and put his thin little arms round her shoulders. 'Picnic, Cissy,' he said, slowly and clearly. 'You will like it. And if you don't we'll steal some cake and come back here.'

It looked very much as though, in her absence, Michael had become her closest friend. She supposed this was inevitable. Marigold, who had been her playmate for the last few years, was growing up. But Cissy would never start primping in front of a mirror, or wondering whether men found her pretty. Though her body was of a similar age to Rose's, her mind had not progressed at all since she had been about Michael's age. For the next few years, he would be closest to her in temperament.

As though to prove her point, he went across to the toy chest and got out a ball for Slipper to play with while they were out. The moment the dog saw what Michael was about, he got up, barked once and nosed at his mistress to get up, too.

Cissy clambered to her feet. Her face was clean, though her eyes were still red-rimmed. She had allowed somebody to tidy her hair and put her in one of her new dresses—though it was now crumpled, and liberally sprinkled with bits of soggy brown paper and dog hairs. In short, she looked as respectable as she was ever likely to look.

Michael took her hand and tugged her towards the door. Marigold twitched the folds of her shawl one last time before setting out, by which time Lydia could hear Cissy and Michael thundering along the corridor. She and Marigold followed at a much more decorous pace. When they reached the back hallway, the rest of the schoolroom party had checked and were staring up at Lord Rothersthorpe who, beside Robert, was leaning against the door jamb, his arms folded across his chest.

Cissy broke away from the power of his scrutiny first.

'I'm sorry, Robber,' she said plaintively, 'for being so naugh-y. I shoul-n't 'ave hi' you. Or knot off your ha'.'

'That's all right, little love,' he said, opening his arms wide. Cissy ran into them and gave him one of her hardest hugs.

'Now,' he said, putting her from him, and making sure she was looking at his face. 'Make your curtsy to Lord Rothersthorpe.'

Cissy did as she was bid. Lord Rothersthorpe, in turn, bowed to her with great formality, which had the effect of making her crow with laughter. She had never, Lydia realised, been formally introduced to anyone before. No wonder she was a little startled.

Cissy clapped her hands and curtsied again.

'For the lord's sake, don't bow to her again, Rothersthorpe,' said Robert out of the corner of his mouth. 'Or we shall be here all day. Michael,' he said, much louder, 'make your bow to his lordship.'

Michael bowed very correctly, and Lord Rothersthorpe returned the compliment, causing Cissy to laugh again.

Lord Rothersthorpe did not even attempt a polite smile, Lydia seethed. He clearly found the whole situation most uncomfortable. Though he did at least have the grace not to make his disapproval of Cissy obvious. Instead, he was gazing with narrowed eyes at her six-year-old son, Michael.

'Come now, Cissy,' said Robert, taking her very firmly by the arm. 'It is time we went down to the Pools.'

'There will be cay'.' She beamed. 'Miker said so.'

'Indeed there will…'

Robert led her inexorably away, and although Marigold fidgeted about in front of Lord Rothersthorpe he did not take the hint and offer her his arm.

'Come on,' said Michael, when nobody else seemed inclined to make a move. 'Or there won't be any cake left!'

When he charged out of the door, Slipper frisking at

his heels, Marigold heaved a sigh, rolled her eyes and set off after him.

Which left her alone in the doorway with Lord Rothersthorpe.

'Alone at last,' he said, once the others had moved out of earshot. 'I was beginning to wonder how I was ever going to get a chance to speak to you in private.'

'With…with me?'

He crooked his arm and she laid her hand upon his sleeve.

'Of course with you,' he said with a touch of impatience. 'How else are we to arrange things?'

'What things?'

'Mrs Morgan,' he said, 'will you cease this stupid pretence that you do not know what I am talking about? It is all very well acting the innocent when your family is within earshot, but they are not.'

Indeed they weren't. What with Robert's long strides and the way Slipper was dashing about madly, they had all drawn quite some distance away. Even Marigold—in spite of her initial attempts to behave like a young lady. Michael kept throwing the ball for Slipper to fetch back and she hadn't been able to resist getting drawn into the game.

'So,' said Lord Rothersthorpe, setting a leisurely pace which ensured they would never catch up with the rest of the party, 'let us make the most of this chance to make arrangements.'

Arrangements? Whatever could he mean?

'Normally,' he went on, when she'd remained in baffled silence for several paces, 'in this kind of affair, the gentleman in question would make his way to the lady's bedchamber at the appropriate time. But since I am not at all familiar with the layout of this house and there seem to be an amazing assortment of corridors leading to various wings, you will have to come to me. Or,' he said sarcastically, 'was it your intention to furnish me with a map?'

'A map? Whatever for?'

'Perhaps you are right. I confess, I had qualms about visiting you in the same bed you once shared with your husband. What, then, was your plan?'

'My plan?'

'Yes.' He shot her an impatient look. 'I take it this is not going to turn into the kind of house party where the ladies wander through the corridors at dead of night. Think, woman. Think of a place where it will be safe for us to be quite alone. A place where we will not be disturbed.'

Only then did his odd choice of words finally make sense.

'You are speaking of conducting an affair with me!'

He hadn't come here because he wanted to marry Rose, at all! Oh, how marvellous!

Oh, poor Rose. She was going to be so disappointed.

But then she did have five other single gentlemen down here dangling after her to make up for it.

She glanced up at Rothersthorpe's handsome profile, her spirit soaring again. He wanted *her,* not Rose. Not young, fresh, vibrant Rose with all her money and beauty.

'Why else,' he growled, 'did you send me that note, begging me to join you down here for the duration of this house party, if not so that we could become lovers?'

He thought *she* had invited him? Why would he think…? Oh! That was right. The last time they had talked, he had briefly mentioned having an affair with her. And said that she would only have to send him word and he would oblige.

Well, she hadn't thought he'd meant it! He never meant the half of what he said. In fact, most of what he said was designed to amuse or charm. So she had just thought he was trying to insult her when he'd implied she was the kind of woman who would indulge in that kind of behaviour.

But he *had* meant it.

And to prove it, the moment he got Rose's last-minute, no doubt hastily scrawled invitation, he'd come straight down here. In pursuit of her.

For a moment, she had the feeling that the whole world had turned upside down. And she wasn't sure whether to be grossly insulted, or immensely flattered. In fact, she was so flustered she couldn't say a word.

'Not in the room you once shared with your husband,' he said, mistaking the confused shake of her head. 'No, I suppose that would not be in very good taste. Though if that was not your intention, I wonder that you should have put me in a room with such a very narrow bed.' He chuckled. 'You obviously have no experience at conducting this kind of intrigue, do you? Am I the first since your husband died? If so, I have to tell you that I appreciate the compliment—'

'Oh, stop it, stop it!'

He took her words literally, bringing their progress along the path to a halt and turning to face her.

She took a faltering step back, pressing her hands to her burning cheeks. The moment he had put the notion of how one would manage…congress…in a single bed, her mind had supplied a series of quite shocking images.

'I…' she gulped. 'I…'

'I know,' he breathed.

Their eyes met. And she knew he was thinking more or less the same thing she was.

Something like a bolt of lightning flashed between them. He seized her upper arms and manoeuvred her behind a stand of saplings, even though the rest of the party were disappearing round a bend in the path that would have hidden them from view.

'Just the thought of us together, at last, has the same effect upon me,' he said gruffly.

And before she quite knew what he was doing, he'd pulled her roughly into his arms and was kissing her.

Whenever, in the past, she'd dreamed about kissing him, he had been gentle and respectful. Now he was neither.

For a moment, she stood quite stiff in his arms, resenting him for treating her so roughly. For thinking she was the kind of woman who...

Oooh, but he *wanted* her. He was making no attempt to disguise his rampant ardour. And she was so tired of always holding back. Of watching what she said and how she behaved, and even what she thought.

She could not rein back her natural impulses one second longer.

With a small cry of desperation, she flung her arms round his neck and gave herself up to the kiss. He gave a low growl of approval, and, although she had not thought it possible, took the encounter to another level, thrusting his tongue into her mouth and clutching her bottom in his hands to hold her in place while he ground his pelvis against hers.

She gave as good as she got.

By the time they broke apart, they were both panting, and rather red in the face.

'My God,' he grated, 'I don't know how I'm going to wait until night time, not now you've let me see... what you are really like.'

What she was really like...?

'Dammit,' he said, looking around the grounds as though searching for something. 'Is there not a summerhouse or something where we could go, and just... quickly...well, slake this thirst?'

He might as well have spat in her face.

Her response had not just been physical. She had once cared for this man, even though she'd known he was not at all dependable. And lingering echoes of that affection had driven her to do what she had dreamed of doing, all those years ago.

How could she have been so stupid?

Chapter Seven

⁓⧉⁓

She wrenched herself out of his arms and set off along the path, wiping her mouth with the back of her hand.

She could not have an affair with him! Nor any man. What kind of woman did he take her for?

Oh, he might have acknowledged that this would be her *first* affair, but he still thought her capable of jumping into bed with a man to whom she was not married. Which was unthinkable. Outrageous.

He caught up with her, grabbed her arm and yanked on it.

'Slow down,' he murmured in an urgent undertone. 'And for goodness' sake, let me straighten your dress before we catch up with the others.'

She forced herself to stand completely still while he tugged her bodice back into place, then walked round her, brushing off all signs of their recent encounter against the trunk of a tree. But she had to screw her eyes shut while he did it. It would probably be quite some time before she could look him straight in the eye again. Because if he did think her the kind of woman who was keen to have affairs, then she had only herself to blame for plastering herself up against him, clinging to him, writhing against him, and kissing him as though her very life depended on it.

Although—her eyes popped open to glare at him—he had assumed it *before* the kiss. He'd assumed it in London.

'And now tell me,' he added, clamping her hand firmly into the crook of his arm and urging her into forwards motion, 'when we can carry this thing to its completion.'

She shook her head. 'I am not...' *the kind of woman you think I am.* But saying it would sound hypocritical after the way she'd kissed him.

'I cannot...' *just have an affair with you.* But if she said that, he would be furious. He'd got his poor horse all of a lather galloping down here because he was so keen to get started.

'In a moment, I am going to have to play hostess to Rose's guests,' she ended up saying. Decent, respectful young men who would offer marriage, she reflected bitterly, and only beg for a kiss once a betrothal had been announced. She was still trembling from the effect of his kiss. Now a wave of resentment and hurt added to her physical reaction. He still had the power to raise her hopes, then dash them all down. He'd kissed her first, then assumed, because she was so susceptible to him, she would be flattered at the invitation to become his lover.

When he'd told her he was actively seeking a *wife*.

'Please do not press me now,' she begged him. If he carried on urging her to accept his proposition, when he didn't consider her fit to become his wife, she might do something even more stupid than kissing him. Like... shout at him. Or burst into tears.

And she didn't want Rose's house party ruined before it started by creating either kind of scene.

He just had time to give her a searingly impatient look before they rounded the last bend in the path. He swore softly under his breath as he caught his first glimpse of the area they called the Persian Pools, which comprised a series of velvety lawns surrounding a staircase of rectangular pools, each one overflowing into the next. Rose's guests were mainly assembled near the pavilion, a building designed to give either shade from the sun, or shelter from the rain, and in which Mrs Broome had set out a veritable feast. And they were all looking in their direction.

It was nothing to do with them, of course, although that did not stop Lydia from feeling extremely self-conscious. It was Robert who was drawing their attention, having not long since emerged from the same path himself.

'Ladies, gentlemen,' Robert was saying in a parade-ground voice that bore a marked resemblance to his father's. 'Permit me to introduce the remainder of Rose's family to you.' He waved a hand towards Michael and Marigold as she and Lord Rothersthorpe began the descent to the lower lawn.

'This is her sister and mine, Miss Marigold Morgan,' he said as Marigold dropped a curtsy, 'and this our young brother, Michael.' Michael bowed.

'And this lovely young lady, on my arm, is Cecilia. We usually call her Cissy.' He cleared his throat. 'She cannot hear very well, so if you wish to speak to her, please call out *Cissy* in a clear voice and Slipper here will alert her to your intent.'

Lord Abergele's sister wrinkled her nose in distaste and tried to catch Miss Lutterworth's eye. Only the girl was leaning over the lower pool in an attempt to spot one of the ornamental fish, which were sheltering from the heat of the sun under the lily pads; and missed it.

But Lydia had not missed it. All her own concerns were promptly swamped by her need to protect Cissy from that kind of look. She was old enough, and tough enough, to look after herself, even against such a one as Lord Rothersthorpe. But Cissy was so vulnerable.

She was just wondering how she might diffuse the slightly tense atmosphere when Mr Bentley strode forwards, his hand outstretched. 'Cissy,' he said in a firm voice.

Slipper nosed at Cissy's free hand, then looked at Mr Bentley, in the manner of a pointer, though she'd always thought there was more spaniel in him than any other breed.

'I say, dashed clever dog,' said Mr Bentley, bending down to ruffle Slipper's ears. Then he looked up, grinned and said, 'Pleasure to meet you, Cissy.'

Lydia could have hugged him for ignoring Cissy's impairment altogether and focusing on her dog.

'That was kind of the boy,' murmured Lord Rothersthorpe, drawing her a little distance apart from the rest of the family group. 'I had wondered if Morgan's introduction was not a little challenging for some of the present company.'

Well, that was typical of Robert—disguising any anxiety he might feel behind a mask of belligerence.

'Mr Bentley is a good sort,' said Lydia. 'I have always thought so.' Even if she had also thought him a bit lacking in personality. But now she could completely understand why Rose had invited him.

'Rose did not invite anyone she feared might be unkind to Cissy.'

'You are all very protective of her,' he mused.

'Of course!'

'My father,' Robert was explaining to Mr Bentley, and anyone else within earshot, 'wanted Cissy to be able to enjoy as much independence as she can and so he trained Slipper to be her ears.'

'Have you never,' said Lord Rothersthorpe to Lydia, with a frown, 'considered employing a nurse for her, rather than allowing her condition to dominate the entire family?'

'Never,' she snapped, withdrawing her arm from his.

It was as well Lord Rothersthorpe had not come down here with the intention of paying his addresses to Rose. Neither she, nor Robert, would countenance her marriage to anyone who could suggest they relegated Cissy to some darkened backroom of their lives. Especially not now Robert knew what Cissy had suffered when given into the keeping of strangers.

'Please do help yourself to the refreshments,' she said coldly, indicating the pavilion which her husband had modelled on a shrine he had once seen on his travels.

He bowed briefly, a mocking smile lurking about his mouth, before he turned and sauntered through the milling throng of Rose's friends.

What had she ever seen in Lord Rothersthorpe? He wasn't a very pleasant man *at all*. She eyed him with disfavour as he climbed the steps of the open-sided structure. When he had been younger, she'd refused to admit that his devil-may-care attitude towards life was a symptom of selfishness. But in the intervening years, it had hardened into a carapace which could not be mistaken for anything else. She could quite see, now, the trace of that original pirate ancestor in him. The

man who'd taken what he wanted to enrich himself.
Mrs Westerly had warned her that the taint had never
been eradicated, not through any amount of generations. The Hemingfords had only survived by plun-
dering the wealth of more sober, industrious families.
Admittedly by marriage, rather than actual violence,
but still…

So why was she still admiring the elegance of his
movements as he made his way through the throng?
How could she still want to glimpse the line of his leg
as he mounted the steps into the pavilion? And why was
it that when he reached for a slice of bread and butter,
and folded it into his mouth, she could not help salivat-
ing at the memory of what it had felt like to have those
lips pressing down on hers?

'Cissy is enjoying this, isn't she, Mama Lyddy?'

Lydia jumped. Rose had somehow managed to reach
her side without her noticing quite where she'd come
from.

'Yes,' she said, pulling herself together and her eyes
away from Lord Rothersthorpe's lazy inspection of the
tea table.

To judge by the new configurations, Robert had introduced most of the guests to Cissy already.

'Mr Bentley's manner with Slipper was good, was it
not? After the easy way he spoke to them both she has
not been the least bit shy with any of the others either.
And most of them took Robert's announcement about
her deafness in their stride. With only one exception.'
Rose shot a scathing look at Mr Lutterworth. 'Did you
see the way he rolled his eyes when she betrayed how
much she was enjoying having the ladies curtsy, and
the men bow to her? I overheard him saying something
not very kind about his own sister, Cynthia, too,' she

added darkly. 'About how he wished he could train a dog to wake her up whenever she starts daydreaming.'

Lydia clucked her tongue, annoyed with herself for not paying closer attention to what had been going on. Damn Lord Rothersthorpe! She shot him a resentful look.

Rose glanced towards the pavilion herself, then smiled at Lydia.

'He is the one, isn't he?'

'The one?'

'Now confess…'

Lydia's heart bumped in alarm. Surely nobody could have perceived they had been kissing?

'Confess it. He is the one who sent you those violets. And from the way your eyes dwell on him, with the same faraway look you had when you first showed me your scrapbook, I know I was right. He *was* your first love. For even in the aftermath of one of your quarrels, you cannot keep your eyes off him. I am not surprised.' She pretended to fan herself. 'He is a very handsome man.'

'Rose, such talk is not at all seemly,' she snapped, her cheeks glowing with guilty heat.

As usual, Rose dismissed her attempt at remonstrance with a giggle. 'Mama Lyddy,' she said, shaking her head. 'There is nothing wrong with saying that a man is handsome.'

'Yes, but you are implying—' She broke off in confusion. Rose could have no notion of the kind of relationship Lord Rothersthorpe wanted to have with her. Surely?

'Why should you not have a beau, as well as I?'

'A…a beau.' She heaved a sigh of relief. For Rose, sheltered from the harsher realities of life, interest from a man would only have an honourable outcome. She probably had no idea what men could be like.

'You are correct, Rose,' she admitted wistfully. 'He is very handsome. But…'

'And he obviously has feelings for you,' put in Rose cheerfully.

Lydia made a sound that was not quite a snort, but was expressive of her opinion of that statement.

'No, truly,' Rose protested. 'Otherwise, why would he have been so cross with you? At that ball? You had not seen each other for getting on for ten years, and the very first time he spoke he could barely bring himself to be polite. If he had not cared about you, he would have forgotten whatever it was you did to annoy him ten years ago.'

'You think he cares about me, because he was rude?' Lydia shook her head. 'Rose, really…'

But even as she gave voice to her doubts, she wondered if there might be a grain of truth in what Rose said. She'd wondered why he'd seemed so antagonistic towards her, when he was the one who'd let her down. But perhaps he resented her for having so very nearly lured him into marriage, well before he'd been completely ready for such a commitment.

'And you like Lord Rothersthorpe, too. So you just need to spend some time together and it will all work out,' said Rose confidently.

Not the way Rose thought, it wouldn't. But she did not say so. She had no intention of spoiling her day by explaining the grim realities of her life. Let her keep her youthful belief in happy endings, for now.

Although Rose was the kind of girl who would get a happy ending. She was so sure of her own worth she would not settle for anything less.

But in her own case, Lord Rothersthorpe had already made it quite clear that he only wanted an affair. Today he had even been quite crude about it—talking of going somewhere and slaking his lust for her *in the open air*. He'd implied it would only take a few minutes.

But then, the night of Lord Danbury's informal soirée, had she not been so aroused by standing close to him, talking about intimate topics, that she'd known that if they had gone somewhere secluded, all he would have to do was hitch up her skirts, and he would have found her ready to receive him?

Her eyes strayed to where Lord Rothersthorpe was talking to one of the naval officers as he piled a plate with food. And something inside her wound up tight, then shot sparks through her bloodstream, rather like some kind of firework going off inside her. For a moment, she wondered what it would be like to have the freedom, and the courage, to strip him of all his clothing, so that she could feast her eyes on that utterly delectable body of his, then run her hands all over it while he was running his hands all over her.

And just like that, she was ready for him once again. In fact, if they really did go somewhere secluded where he could take advantage of her readiness, she thought the whole episode might very well reach its natural conclusion within a very few moments.

Gracious heavens. When he'd suggested they do exactly that, she had been shocked. Outraged. Insulted.

Yet she could not stop thinking about it.

At this point her legs became so weak that she only just managed to totter to one of the benches dotted about the edges of the lawn before they gave way under her, depositing her upon the cool stone surface.

However was she going to be able to concentrate on

entertaining Rose's guests, and maintaining some semblance of dignity, when the mere sight of him leaning against the door jamb of the pavilion made her want to slam herself up against him and wind her legs round his waist?

She leaned forwards, shading her eyes with a groan.

What was she to do?

'Are you ill, Mama?'

She lifted her head quickly to see her little son, Michael, standing beside her with a troubled air. Robert, too, was watching her, a frown on his face.

She opened her arms and drew Michael into a hug.

'A little tired, love, that is all. And I was thinking so hard that I quite forgot people might be worried by my frowns and sighs.'

Michael reached up and rubbed at the crease between her brows.

'Don't think any more, Mama,' he said. 'Just come and have some pie. And a drink of lemonade.'

Just like a male, she thought with a smile. Thinking that food would cure everything.

But she took his hand and allowed him to lead her to the shady pavilion, even though it would mean walking right past Lord Rothersthorpe.

She tried not to look at him. But when she passed within an arm's length of him, she was very aware that all she would have to do was stretch out her hand and she could touch him.

She blushed, darted a glance his way and found him looking back at her with such blatant hunger that she was amazed none of the other guests appeared to have noticed. She glanced round, to see if anyone had.

The two naval officers were bearing down on

Rose—each with a rather incongruous-looking glass of lemonade clutched in their large, work-worn hands.

Mr Lutterworth and Lord Abergele were making steady inroads upon the buffet table. Their respective sisters were strolling around the pools, arm in arm, still hunting glimpses of the exotic fish. And Mr Bentley had taken a plate of food outside and was sitting on the grass, alternately ruffling Slipper's ears and offering slices of cake to Cissy.

Just as Michael had assumed all would be well with her, if only she had a plate of food. Men, she reflected, were always ruled by their appetites. In that, they were the more straightforward of the sexes. Only the females of the party required something more.

Lord Rothersthorpe, she saw in a flash, saw nothing wrong in slaking his appetite for her, just as he would slake his thirst with a glass of ale, or his hunger with a plate of sirloin. See a woman who rouses desire? Take her to bed. Problem solved. There was nothing of emotion about it, any of it. It was all about appetite.

Although perhaps that was not only because he was a man, but also because of the class of man he came from. He'd spoken to her about the habits prevailing in the kind of house parties he was used to attending, where the men wandered the corridors at night to spare the ladies' blushes, as though it was perfectly normal.

But it wasn't! Why, the Colonel would never have dreamed of dealing with his sexual needs by taking a mistress. Or embarking on an affair with a willing widow—and she was sure there would have been plenty of those, given his wealth. Colonel Morgan had firmly believed that sexual incontinence was a weakness.

That was one of the reasons why he'd never been long without a wife. No matter what Robert had thought of his multiple marriages, she had applauded his moral values, which, she supposed, Lord Rothersthorpe would condemn for being irredeemably middle class.

Rather mutinously, she piled her plate high with a selection of cold cuts, pie, and bread and butter.

'You won't wan' your dinner if you eat all tha',' said Cissy, bouncing up with Slipper frisking at her heels. Then she frowned and carried on, a little uncertainly, 'That's wha' you always say to me when I ea' too much cay at tea time.'

'Cissy!' Slipper nudged her hand and they both turned to see Robert, who had also followed Lydia into the pavilion. 'Mama Lyddy only says that because you always do eat too much cake.' He said it with a smile, so she knew he was not reproving, but teasing her.

Then he leaned forwards and asked Lydia quietly, 'Are you well? You look a little strained. It has been a rather difficult day for you, has it not?'

More than he knew.

'I think perhaps it might be a good idea if I went for a rest before dinner,' she admitted. 'If you do not mind?'

'Not at all,' he said. 'All our guests are quite happy milling about down here for now. When it is time for them to go in, Rose and Marigold and I are quite capable of showing them to their rooms and settling them in. You really have nothing to do except dress for dinner.'

He had meant it kindly, but to her, it was yet another reminder of her position in this household. She had very little importance in her own right. Westdene was Robert's house. For now, he wanted her to carry on living here, because she was a familiar female influence for Rose and Marigold. But once they had husbands and homes of their own, or even if he married himself, what then?

Head bowed, she left the pavilion and made her way back to the house that she'd never quite come to think of as her home. It was not that she needed to worry about her ability to look after Cissy and Michael, once her usefulness to Robert came to an end. Colonel Morgan had left them financially secure. It was just…

She shook her head impatiently at herself. There were enough problems to worry about for now without imagining possible new ones cropping up in the future. Chief among them being Lord Rothersthorpe, and the unsettling effect he was having on her.

She'd always thought of herself as quite a moral person. And yet he only had to talk about…well, sex…and she became a woman she hardly recognised. Surely she could not seriously be contemplating doing all those things with a man to whom she was not married? But she was, she admitted. She *wanted* him. With a ferocity which puzzled and disturbed her.

For she had never thought of herself as having any kind of sexual needs. The marriage act was not unpleasant, but never, until Lord Rothersthorpe had come back into her life, had she ever really thought much about it during the hours of daylight. It was a duty that she was willing to perform for the man to whom she owed so much. How many men would have taken Cissy into their household, in the state he found her in at that dreadful asylum? Or taken such pains to calm her, reassure her, and then to help her reach her full potential?

No, she had never once thought of denying Colonel Morgan, when he asked if it was convenient to visit her bedroom. But it had not been an activity that she actually anticipated, never mind yearned for.

She rubbed at the frown which was slicing its way into her forehead. Ever since Lord Rothersthorpe had come back into her life, the firm foundations on which she'd thought she'd been standing had become shaky. They were not married. The days when she had almost dared hope that love might have blossomed between them had long since passed. So how could she be filled with such…lustful longings? She did not like him any more than he appeared to like her, yet the desire that flared between them was frighteningly intense.

And yet, because there could be no happy ending, in the way Rose meant, it was very tempting to see his point of view. Indulging in a brief, passionate, intense affair would harm nobody else, as long as nobody found out.

She came to a standstill, her fists clenched at her sides.

Dear Lord, she was actually contemplating it. Actually wondering if she dared go down the road Lord Rothersthorpe was tempting her to take. Questioning the moral code with which she'd grown up. Abandoning her principles.

And just letting herself go, for once. Letting herself do something that was just for her. That was not about anyone else's needs or expectations.

That was, in a word, selfish.

Chapter Eight

As Lydia climbed slowly up the stairs that led to the family wing, she tried to recall when she had last done anything that anyone could have accused her of doing out of selfishness.

When she got to the landing, she paused, her hand on the banister. She shook her head. The opposite was true. Ever since her mother's death, she had been hedged about by obligations of one form or another. Not that caring for her family was an obligation, exactly…only she had felt responsible for both her father and Cissy. She had failed with her father. There had been nothing she could do to prevent his downward spiral into despair. But at least she had been able to find a husband who had rescued Cissy from the fate to which her legal guardian had condemned her.

She went to her bedroom and pushed open the door, wrinkling her nose with distaste. Her husband had designed this room and installed her in it as soon after their marriage as he could. Her eyes roved over the bed with its opulent silk hangings, made to look like a tent, or something out of a harem. She supposed she could have got rid of it and insisted on something plainer, once he no longer came to visit her in this shrine to the pleasures of the flesh, but it would have seemed… ungrateful. And how could she have explained to a grieving Rose and Marigold, not to mention Cissy and Michael, that all the silk, cushions and cords, and vials of oils and perfumes, did not equate with love at all— that she would feel better about herself if she could sweep them all away and sleep in a room that was plain and…wholesome?

Even here, she had to consider how her own actions affected others.

Her lips thinning, she entered the room and shut the door firmly behind her.

She had told everyone she needed a rest, but in the mood she was in, she simply could not lie on that bed.

Instead, she went to the window and flung it wide open.

If truth were known, she was absolutely sick of being a slave to duty. She'd had no freedom since she'd been scarcely more than a child herself. She had never experienced the feeling that she could choose to do whatever she wished. Not like Rose. Although the house was full of her suitors, she did not have to marry any of them, not if she did not want to.

Not that she was jealous of Rose. Exactly. It wasn't as if she wanted to marry again. Not even if it were possible, which it wasn't. Cissy had been so upset by her prolonged absence that she'd promised she would never leave her alone again.

Which raised the problem of what that would mean for Rose's Season.

What she would like to do was to take Rose back to London after this house party and take Cissy with them. She thought she could manage it, too, if only she could hire someone to help take care of her. She took a deep breath of air that smelled of good earth and growing green things as she admitted to herself that, in that one respect, Lord Rothersthorpe had made perfect sense. She had only objected because he had described the person they needed to hire as a 'nurse'. They had called the female warders in Cissy's asylum, 'nurses'.

But if they all went up to London, there would be a perfect excuse for making all sorts of changes to staff. If she were to hire a lady's maid for Marigold, then casually say that all young ladies needed someone of the sort, if they went to London, maybe Cissy would accept that. After all, they had engaged extra help for Rose at the start of the Season. And it was true that a young lady could not walk about unaccompanied in town. It just was not done. She had to have a maid to go with her. Then one always had to look one's best, to receive callers and such like. London life involved several changes of garments each day.

A great weight rolled off her shoulders. She could see Cissy accepting a personal maid on that basis. And then, when they returned to Westdene, they would just keep the woman on. It would mean keeping Marigold and Rose's ladies' maids on, too, but it wasn't as if they could not afford the extra staff.

Now all she had to do was find a sensible, motherly sort of woman, who would be able to look on Cissy as a child inhabiting an adult's body and would therefore be able to deal with her occasional tantrums accordingly.

And she would have a measure of freedom.

A bumble-bee buzzing past the window made her start back. Freedom? What would she do with it, if she had it? Shutting the window, she went across the room to her dressing table, sat down and asked her reflection what it was she wanted, if she could indeed have *anything*.

Her reflection shook her head at her, reprovingly. She already knew the answer. It was Lord Rothersthorpe. As he'd been when she'd first met him. Laughing and carefree. And, she thought, perhaps teetering on the brink of falling in love with her.

Her lips twisted in scorn. She was hankering after a dream. For one thing, Lord Rothersthorpe had always been too shallow to ever fall in love with anyone, let alone her.

She sighed and fiddled with the stopper of one of the bottles littering the table, absentmindedly dabbing a little attar of roses on to her wrists as she considered the second obstacle that stood in the way of having her dream.

Which was the fact that any fondness he might have felt for her had been superseded by a resentment she didn't really understand. When he looked at her now, there was nothing that she wanted to see in his eyes.

Except passion.

Such passion.

Though it shocked her, confused her, even scared her a little, at least it made her feel…something.

Ever since the Colonel's death, she had been sort of drifting along, putting off making any decisions about her future.

She could have moved straight out of Westdene and set up house with Cissy and Michael. Only she hadn't liked to leave Rose and Marigold, shattered as they were by their father's sudden and unexpected death. They had been a touch nervous about Robert coming back and taking over, too, and had wanted her to stay and shield them.

Even when it had become clear there was no need for her to do anything of the sort, she had still not made any preparations for her removal from this house.

But in a way, this house party marked the end of one era and heralded the dawning of another. It wouldn't be long before Rose married and then Marigold. Did she really want to stay on here, keeping house for a stepson who would one day wish to install his own wife as mistress of Westdene? No. Not when she could guarantee that any such woman would not want such a youthful mother-in-law, not to mention a 'backward' female cluttering up the place.

If she did not start making choices soon, somebody else would be making them for her, yet again. And she'd had just about enough of staying in the background, dutifully catering for everyone else's needs while her own life drifted along, getting nowhere.

She always seemed to come last in a whole long list of people who were more important. Why, even now, when she'd started out wondering whether she could really succumb to the temptation of what Lord Rothersthorpe was offering, she'd veered off into making plans for Cissy and Rose and Robert and Michael.

With an expression of impatience, she got to her feet, went to the bell-pull and rang for a maid. She was not going to waste this afternoon drifting about her room, getting nothing done. She could at least take a bath and start preparing for dinner.

One thing she did know, she reflected as she went to her armoire to select an evening gown, and that was that she was not going to get married again. She did not want to be so dependent on a man that she felt like a chattel. Not that it was very likely that any man would want to take her on, with both Cissy and Michael in tow.

Especially not a man like Lord Rothersthorpe. Her mouth twisted in wry self-mockery. Why, even when she'd been young, and a virgin, she hadn't managed to rouse sufficient interest for him to go through the ordeal of marriage.

Now that she was a widow he'd assumed she would be willing to indulge in a little sexual adventure. But that was all. That was all he thought she was good for.

But then, wasn't that more or less how she felt about him?

Her hand stilled between her blue-silk and the silver-satin gowns.

He only had to look at her in a certain way, and she started melting. Oh, who was she trying to fool? He only had to walk into the room and she began to burn. And after that kiss, she knew that their bodies would match perfectly. That if they once got into bed they would both go up in flames. In spectacular fashion.

A shudder of longing went through her, so fierce she had to bite down on her lower lip. No wonder widows got a reputation for being wanton.

At that moment her maid arrived.

'Could you bring hot water and fresh towels?' she said, grateful for the timely interruption to such disturbing thoughts. 'I find that I cannot sleep after all, so I may as well relax in a warm bath, then dress for dinner so that I am ahead of Rose's guests. Oh, and, Betsy,' she added as though it was an afterthought, 'I quite forgot to enquire when I arrived, but I do hope Mrs Broome was not too put out,' she said, plucking a gown at random from the selection hanging in her cupboard, 'by the last-minute announcement we were to have an additional guest? Lord Rothersthorpe.'

'Oh, no, ma'am. Not at all. She said as how it was about time this house was opened up for visitors again.'

'I am pleased to hear it.' She frowned at the damask rose which was far too heavy for the time of year and hung it back up. 'There was no trouble about preparing a room, then?'

'No, ma'am. She aired them all as soon as she heard you was throwing a party, just in case. So it was only a question of making up just the one extra bed.'

Betsy bustled up to her and caught hold of the blue silk. 'This one, I think, Mrs Morgan,' she said. And before Lydia even had to prompt her, Betsy volunteered the information that Mrs Broome had put him in the single gentleman's guest room number three. Which was a huge relief, since she hadn't dared ask bluntly if he had a room to himself. Even though it was just one along the corridor set aside for single male guests, at least the housekeeper had not put him in with one of the other bachelors. It had been a real concern, because in the Colonel's time, he had often put the welfare of his own staff before the comfort of guests.

'Guests come and go,' he'd snapped the first time she'd entertained his visitors. 'If they don't like it here, they needn't come again. But it's devilish hard to get, and keep, decent staff.'

But since Betsy might think it odd if she only enquired about his accommodation, she continued with the topic while they selected the accessories to complete her outfit.

'So all the guests have a room of their own?' She hid her blushes by delving into a drawer for her stockings. It was just so wicked to hide enquiries about how safe it might be to conduct an *affaire* with one of the male guests, amongst spurious concerns about the others.

'Mrs Broome did think about putting both the naval officers in together,' Betsy confessed, 'but in the end she thought it would not do to treat them any different than any of the others. Why, only think how dreadful it would be if Miss Rose was to show a preference for one of them! We would not want him thinking we hadn't treated him right, the very first time he stayed here, now would we? And we have plenty of rooms. And nobody begrudges Miss Rose the extra work, not for an occasion like this.'

She tried to smile, though it was hard when she felt such a fraud.

'Thank you for telling me all this, Betsy. I know that I really should have come and spoken to Mrs Broome about the arrangements as soon as I got here.'

'Never you mind about that, ma'am,' said Betsy. 'You was busy with Miss Cissy, wasn't you? We can see to the guests, and their baggage, and valets and whatnot. But Cissy needed you.'

'Why, thank you.' Lydia blushed even harder. For Betsy would not be looking at her with such trust, and admiration, and sympathy if she only knew what she was planning.

'Once you have helped me out of my clothes, you may go,' she said, unable to look Betsy in the face one moment longer. Embarking on an affair, she could see, was going to involve employing one stratagem after another. She had already duped Betsy into thinking she was being a dutiful hostess, when all she wanted to know was where Lord Rothersthorpe would be sleeping, and whether it would be feasible to visit him in that particular room.

'I am sure you have plenty to occupy you elsewhere.'

'Thank you, ma'am. The others will all be coming

back in soon and no doubt they'll all be ringing for hot water.' Betsy dropped a curtsy and bustled out.

Once she'd gone, Lydia paced to the window and looked out blindly, her arms wrapped round her waist.

Why should she feel guilty? Didn't she deserve some reward for all she'd endured, this last ten years? All her adult life had been one of unremitting sacrifice and duty. Why, even Colonel Morgan had acknowledged that she'd sacrificed her virginity on the altar of duty, in order to provide for Cissy.

Didn't she deserve to have a man in her bed whom she'd *chosen,* just for the sheer pleasure of it? Just once? No, more than once. They would be lovers for the duration of this house party. He wouldn't want her any longer than that, she shouldn't think. He'd made it quite plain that he found his desire for her rather irksome.

Though that hadn't stopped him from jumping on his horse and galloping straight down here when he thought she'd indicated she was ripe for an affair.

And what was so wrong with having an affair anyway? All they intended was to share mutual pleasure for a short while. In many ways it would be perfect, since she did not want yet another male thinking he had the right to take over her life, which was what marriage would entail.

And Nicholas had never wanted anything permanent from her. Hadn't she already learned, the hard way, that it was pointless trying to hold out for love? She was not the type of woman to inspire it.

And in her own case, all that was left of her youthful, romantic attachment was the physical attraction.

All? She laughed at herself. It was an attraction so strong that it bordered on desperation. It had not diminished with the years, but developed into something so visceral that it was too…necessary to even attempt to fight.

Four nights.

That was not much, in the scheme of things, was it? Four nights of untrammelled pleasure. Four nights of giving rein to impulses of which she was already quite ashamed…but which were growing stronger by the minute.

Footmen arrived then, bearing the hipbath and cans of hot water, obliging her to act as though she was still the dutiful, blameless widow they all believed her to be.

While inside, she was turning into someone she wasn't sure she recognised.

When they'd left and she sank into the rose-scented water, it was all she could do not to moan as she half-closed her eyes, dreaming of the night to come. She would tiptoe along the corridor to his room, barefoot. She wouldn't need to carry a candle. The moon would light her way.

The warm water was like silk sliding over her skin, rousing rather than relaxing her.

Though he would have cotton sheets, in the bachelor bedroom of his, not silk.

They would feel cool and crisp against her back.

And he would feel hot and hard as he pressed her into them.

With a swoosh, Lydia abruptly stood up and got out of her bath. Lying luxuriating in the warm water was far too sensual. She would never make it to midnight if she did not, somehow, get her mind off her body and what it was anticipating.

Besides, as hostess, it was positively her duty to be the first down to the music room, where everyone would gather before dinner.

And hopefully he would be just as impatient to see her, too. For she had to find a moment to tell him what she'd decided.

She would be going to his room. Tonight.

Lord Rothersthorpe faltered on the threshold of the room to which a smart young footman had directed him.

It was a testament to the Colonel's career in India. And the wealth accumulated there. Many-armed marble goddesses flanked the fireplace, ivory elephants supported glossy ebony tables scattered throughout the room and the carpet was such a work of art, it seemed a crime to walk on it.

He took perverse pleasure in doing just that, stalking across to the piano, leaning up against it and folding his arms across his chest.

This was what Lydia was used to now. This…rather tacky opulence. His mouth twisted in disdain as he wondered what she would make of Hemingford Priory. Most of the carpets there were threadbare, the tables were scratched and the walls sported rectangular stains where paintings had once hung.

Not that they'd added anything to the décor. He'd been glad to see the back of the rather gloomy Rembrandt in particular, and all those writhing bodies on the Tintoretto which had given him nightmares as a child. Besides, it had been obscene to have such things hanging on his walls when his tenants did not have decent roofs over their heads.

Suddenly, she was there. Like him, she hesitated in the doorway, though it could not have been on account of the décor, since she was used to it.

No, it was the sight of him that had made her eyes

widen. She just stood there, looking at him, a pulse visibly beating in her throat. And she was trembling.

'G-good evening,' she said, then blushed.

For a few moments all he could do was gaze at her. Just drink her in. She was so damned beautiful. No woman had a right to be so beautiful. In fact, she did not look like a woman at all, with that blue silk shimmering round her body, but rather like some kind of naiad. Even her hair was swept up and contained with something that resembled hundreds of tiny water droplets, but was in all probability just crystals.

Or, knowing how wealthy her late husband had been, perhaps even diamonds.

His mood darkening, he pushed himself off the piano and bowed.

'Good evening Mrs Morgan,' he just about managed to say without betraying his disgust at this fresh evidence of her mercenary nature. He hoped.

'P-please, won't you take a seat? I do not know how long it may take the others to arrive.' She darted an anxious look over her shoulder.

'Why, thank you, Mrs Morgan,' he said, walking to one of the sofas and folding himself down on to it. He patted the cushion at his side. 'Let us not waste these few moments alone on opposite sides of the room.'

She'd only taken one hesitant pace towards him when they both heard the sound of footsteps in the hallway. It was some comfort to see she looked as vexed as he felt when Marigold and Cissy came tumbling into the room, all breathless blushes, the dog not far behind.

Though he was annoyed the moment was lost, he got to his feet and made his bow.

Cissy beamed at him as she rose from making her own curtsy.

'I ly' parties,' she said. 'This is my firs' party. And Marigold's.'

Marigold looked a bit put out. He supposed she was at that age where she wanted, very much, to be thought grown-up, and she clearly did not like Cissy blurting out the fact that this was to be her first attendance at an adult party, too.

'You both look charming,' he replied gravely, wondering why Cissy was downstairs at all. Surely she should be taking her meals somewhere else? With Lydia's son, for example. Although perhaps it was better not to leave her alone with the boy, not if she might be a danger to him.

'Pretty.' Cissy nodded, stroking the silk of her gown.

'I kept on telling her,' Marigold complained to Lydia, as Cissy skipped towards him to show off her finery, 'that we were making her a pretty dress for a party. There was no need for her to go getting so upset. Why she would imagine we would make her such a dress if I was only making up tales about lots of guests coming here…'

It was the kind of remark that revealed her immaturity. Lydia ought to tell her that if she wanted to be treated as a grown-up, then she ought to behave like one.

Instead, she very calmly explained, 'Nobody could have prevented Cissy from surrendering to her fears.'

She'd half-turned away, while Cissy prattled on to him, so that, he guessed, she would not know they were talking about her.

'You did,' replied Marigold, moodily. 'Look at her now. For weeks all she's done is cry or suck her thumb and now she's bouncing around as merry as a grig. Just because you have come home.'

'Robert, too, don't forget,' said a determined voice behind them. Rose had managed to float into the room in a cloud of pale-gold muslin and lace without either of them hearing her approach. 'Mama Lyddy might be able to comfort her, but when she's being naughty, it takes Robert to make her behave.'

Naughty? Was that what they called it? She'd attacked Robert with a ferocity that might have resulted in injury, had she turned all that wildness upon someone smaller or weaker.

'Yes,' Lydia confessed. 'I am afraid I do tend to be rather too soft with her.'

Although that softness had produced the desired effect. Cissy had crumpled to the ground, completely transformed by Lydia's soothing presence.

'As you are with us all.' Rose smiled, linking arms with both her and her sister, and drawing them deeper into the room.

Cissy, who had taken the place on the sofa that he'd intended for Lydia, leapt to her feet.

'Left on a Mullet,' she cried, as though pleased with herself for remembering a mangled version of his name.

'Lieutenant Smollet,' the stern-faced naval officer, who had just come in, corrected her.

'Left on a Mullet,' said Cissy again, bouncing across the room to him and sweeping him a deep curtsy. He answered it with a very correct bow, while Marigold placed her free hand over her mouth and creased up with mirth.

Cissy, fortunately, had not noticed. She had eyes only for the handsome lieutenant. 'Do you ly' my dress, Left on a Mullet? I have never had such a pretty one.' She whirled round to show him the entire creation.

A minute ago she'd been showing it off to him. Were all the Morgan girls such incorrigible flirts?

'Marigold,' hissed Lydia out of the corner of her mouth. 'Behave.'

Lieutenant Smollet, meanwhile, completely unruffled by the girl's boisterous and inappropriate behaviour, took command of the situation by crooking his arm, and, the minute she laid her hand upon his sleeve, leading her firmly across the room towards another sofa.

'I ly' you, Left on a Mullet,' she confided, plucking at his sleeve as he sat her down. 'I ly' your shiny buttons.'

Lieutenant Tancred, who had just come in himself, paused only for a second before remarking, 'Cutting me out, Smollet?'

To his surprise, the lieutenant did not take advantage of Smollet's preoccupation with Cissy to monopolise Rose. Instead, he sat down on the sofa on the other side of Cissy and got her attention by tapping her on the arm.

'I think I might just point out,' he said with a smile that displayed nearly all his teeth, 'that since I wear the same uniform, my buttons are just as shiny.'

'He got here first though, Left Unanchored, because I spec' you spend more time polishing 'em up.'

The look on Tancred's face surprised him into a bark of laughter.

'I think this young lady has just accused you of vanity,' he said.

Lieutenant Tancred was still smiling, but there weren't so many teeth in it.

'What can I say? A man likes to look his best for such an important occasion as this.' He shot Rose a very meaningful look.

Rose smiled at him, but not with the warmth she had shown Lieutenant Smollet when he'd steered Cissy across the room, sat her down and calmed her down.

Suddenly, he saw why the two officers were giving the sister so much attention. They were vying with each other to win Rose's favour. These were two professional men who were clever enough to spot when they were being given a test. *This* was why Cissy was on display all the time. Rose meant to judge her suitors by the way they reacted to her unfortunate sister.

There was no further opportunity for private conversation with Lydia. The other guests came down in ones and twos, and she was busy circulating, until it was time to go in for dinner.

Robert took the head of the table, and she the foot, with the others ranged according to rank. Which meant that he was beside her.

It was an exquisite form of torture, sitting so close to her that he could smell her perfume, yet not being able to yield to the temptation to touch her. Or speak to her of the burning issue of where and how they were going to become lovers.

His only consolation was that she appeared as tense as he. She ate scarcely anything, merely pushing the food around on her plate.

But she took frequent sips of her wine.

And then licked her lips, making it almost impossible not to groan out loud. He wanted to taste those lips again. Soon. The kiss they'd shared that afternoon had been so heated he was amazed they had not burst into flames on the spot.

He tore his eyes away and took a deep draught of his own wine. When he next turned to look at her, she was staring fixedly at his mouth. Her own lips were slightly parted. Her pupils were dilated, making her look somewhat dazed.

'You had better not,' he said softly.

'What?' She started, almost dropping her fork.

'Look at me like that,' he said. 'As though you would rather be eating me than what is on your plate.'

She blushed and looked away.

'But I would,' she murmured, so softly he might almost have imagined it.

The witch! He was instantly so hard he was glad he was sitting down with the tablecloth concealing the entire lower half of his body.

'Mrs Morgan?'

They both looked up to see Mr Bentley giving them a very odd look.

Ye gods, he hoped the boy had not overheard.

'Mama Lyddy has a lot on her mind, Mr Bentley,' said Robert smoothly. 'I am sure she did not mean to ignore your request. But as for myself, I think it would be a very good idea.'

Lord Rothersthorpe let out a slow sigh of relief as the conversation flowed on, without requiring any input from either of them.

He spent the rest of the meal struggling to get his body under control. It would never do to rise from table with his erection straining against his breeches. He could take his napkin from table with him, he supposed, to conceal it, but...

He shook his head ruefully. He had not been so excitable since his voice had started to break. If then.

Fortunately, the ladies left the table before the gentlemen. And once she was not within touching distance, it became a bit easier.

None of the men wanted to linger over their port for very long. Robert led them all back to the music room, where Lord Abergele's sister was tinkling out a tune on the piano. Lydia had taken up a seat in a far corner, well away from the younger ladies. Which suited him perfectly. While the other men jostled for ways to impress Rose, he made straight for her side.

'When are you going to put me out of my misery?'

She glanced away as he sat down next to her, but he'd caught a tormented expression in her own eyes.

For a moment, panic seized him.

'Don't, for pity's sake, tell me you have changed your mind.'

She shook her head.

'This is not easy for me,' she said in a voice so low he had to bend closer to catch the words. 'I did not intend…and I have never…' She blushed, and reached for her fan.

Relief and elation surged through him in about equal measure.

'You are telling me that I will be your first lover since your husband died.'

She nodded. Then looked up at him, over her fan, with such open longing he could not mistake the message.

It was more than an admission of the fact. It was a promise, too.

She cleared her throat and folded her fan, running the struts nervously between her fingers.

'I shall have to take Marigold and Cissy up to their rooms quite soon, Lord Rothersthorpe,' she said in a tone that anyone could overhear, should they be curious about what they were discussing. 'And it is unlikely that I shall return to the party after that. There has been a lot of excitement, one way and another, today. Cissy might take some time to settle.'

She got to her feet.

He naturally did likewise.

'I hope you enjoy the rest of your evening,' she said. 'Once the other ladies retire, Robert is likely to try to inveigle you into a game of billiards. Though I hope you won't let him keep you up all night.'

She stared at him, as though willing him to under-stand.

'I am touched that you show such concern over my health. Do I look tired?'

'I think your journey down here on horseback must have been very tiring, given how hot it has been today,' she said, looking a little cross.

He smiled at her. 'And you think that having an early night would do me good, is that it?'

'Yes,' she said vehemently.

'I think you are correct, Mrs Morgan. I think an early night is just what I need.'

She looked relieved.

He chuckled as she walked away and began shep-herding the younger girls out of the room. Did she really think he could not take a hint? He had known straight away that she wanted him to go to his own room, as soon as he could, so that she could join him there. But she had not picked up on his own subtle acknowledge-ment of her hidden message.

It just went to show how new all this was to her. How naïve she was, in her own way, in spite of having been married and bearing a child.

Chapter Nine

It was not as difficult to settle Cissy as she'd feared. She had not slept well for the entire time Lydia had been in London. Relief that she was home, coupled with exhaustion, meant that she was actually quite content to get into bed, with Slipper curled up in his basket on the floor beside her.

It was Marigold who proved fractious. Lydia had to be quite firm in pointing out that very few young ladies of her age were permitted to so much as eat dinner with adult guests, never mind mingling with them for half an hour afterwards. It was only when she threatened to restrict her to the nursery altogether that she ceased arguing and went rather grumpily to bed.

By the time she got to visit Michael's room, he was already fast asleep. She sat on the edge of his bed, just gazing at him. How she wished she'd come here first, so that she could have kissed him goodnight. She only just managed to prevent herself from brushing his fringe from his forehead. He'd wake up and sit up, and twine his arms round her neck and beg her for a story, and probably a kiss while there was nobody to see. Which she would love. But it would be selfish of her to disturb him now. Tomorrow, though…tomorrow she would arrange her evening better. She would be the one to tuck him in and say his prayers, not his nanny.

He was one reason why she could never regret her marriage. The Colonel had always been kind to her, in his way, but after Michael came…

His delight, both in his son, and in her for presenting him with the boy, had been overwhelming. He'd doubled her allowance. Showered her with gifts. She'd even begun to wonder if he'd started to feel some genuine affection for her. She had never measured up to his first wife, Robert's mother, of course. No woman on earth could ever compare with her.

But then Maggie had been his first love. And nothing could quite match the strength of feelings experienced in youth, before adversity and experience made people more cynical about the opposite sex. So he'd told her.

'You should marry again, when I'm gone,' he'd said, during his last winter, after suffering a debilitating inflammation of the lungs. 'You are still young and quite lovely, and I have not placed any restrictions on your jointure. No matter what you do, I have made sure you will always be comfortably off, both you and Cissy.'

'I don't want to think about it,' she'd replied, a little uncomfortable about the way he seemed to be trying to plan her future even when he'd gone.

'Marriage to me put you off for life, is that it?'

'Not a bit of it,' she chided him, tucking the rug more firmly round his knees. 'But I have Cissy to think of. There are not many men with a heart big enough to take her into their home.'

He'd grasped her hand then, and kissed it, his hard face working as though suppressing some strong emotion.

He had never asked her if she loved him. He had neither expected, nor seemed to want it when they'd struck their very practical bargain. Yet she could not doubt that hearing that she thought so well of him had touched him deeply.

He had known, though, that someone else would come along one day. Someone she would want with every fibre of her being. If ever there was a man who knew what it was to be driven by desire, it was Colonel Morgan. It was just that he'd always held such rigid views that he'd assumed she, too, would marry rather than forgo the pleasures of the flesh.

She got to her feet and trod softly to the door, so as not to disturb Michael as she left him. She had only one more duty to see to, before she would be free to go to Lord Rothersthorpe.

She tapped on Rose's bedroom door. Given the amount of time it had taken to settle Marigold, and what with all the woolgathering in Michael's room, Rose was just about ready for bed.

They spent a fruitful few minutes talking about how the guests were shaping up and discussing tentative plans for the next day. By the time she left, she was fairly sure that nearly everyone would be settling down for the night by now.

At last she could return to her own room and prepare herself for the night ahead. She'd already asked Betsy to lay out the sheerest of her silk nightgowns, which she covered with a rather more functional wrapper for the walk along the moonlit corridors. She dabbed her favourite perfume on all her pulse points, then went and sat on the window seat for a few minutes, with her knees drawn up, listening to the sound of the house quieting down.

She was trembling with anticipation and nerves by the time she thought it safe to set out. And even then she drew her hand back from the door latch several times before muttering, 'This is ridiculous!'

She had every right to walk about her own house, at any hour of the day, or night. If she met anyone else, *she* would be the one to demand what they thought *they* were doing, prowling about in the dark.

Yes, that was the attitude to take. With a firm nod of the head, she flung open her door and, barefoot, walked boldly through the dark and silent house to the single gentlemen's quarters.

The Colonel would have been thunderstruck if he could see her now, striding down the corridor to the guest wing, with the full intention of getting into bed with one of her male guests. It was one of the things that had made her decision so hard to make. She'd spent so many years living up to his exacting standards that the habit of wondering what he would think of every action she took was hard to break.

But she was free now and more than capable of making her own decisions. And deciding on her own moral standards.

Given her circumstances, taking a lover was a logical, practical solution.

Though she felt neither logical nor practical by the time she reached Lord Rothersthorpe's room. She felt excited. Scared.

Driven.

If she did not go in, now she'd got herself here, she would never, ever forgive her cowardice.

Taking a deep breath, she seized the door latch, went in and shut the door.

The room was not as dark as it had been in the corridor. Although there were no candles burning, he'd left the shutters open, so that moonlight streamed in across the bed where he was sitting propped up against the pillows. Waiting for her. Naked to the waist, at least.

For a moment, she stood quite still, just looking at him.

'Oh, my…' she breathed. She had never seen such a perfect specimen of masculinity. She drank in the firmly sculpted arms, the broad shoulders, the wide expanse of chest which was just made for a woman to lay her head against. And as for that stomach, with the line of dark hair drawing the eye downward to all the possibilities still concealed beneath the blankets…

A smile crooked one corner of his mouth. He flipped the covers aside. Her eyes widened.

He was ready for her. Magnificently ready for her.

'Oh, my…' she breathed again.

He made as though to swing his legs out of the bed.

'No,' she said. 'Stay where you are.'

It had been such a struggle, getting to this moment. She was casting aside a lifetime of good behaviour and breaching all her own self-imposed boundaries. She couldn't allow him to take over, not at this point. He'd never been reliable. And she wouldn't be able to bear it if all he did was take his own pleasure without seeing to hers. No, if she was going to do this, then she couldn't allow it to be anything less than perfect.

She untied the belt of her dressing gown with trembling fingers and shrugged out of it.

'Lie back against the pillows,' she said. She had worked herself up to such a pitch that her voice sounded quite harsh. Stern, even.

His eyes widened, just a fraction, but then one corner of his mouth kicked up in a wicked smile and he did as she'd bid him, lacing his fingers behind his head as he settled back against the pillows.

Her stomach swooped at the sight of him, lying there, roused and ready for her to do with as she willed.

She needed to get her hands on him so badly she couldn't waste time with all the ties that held the front of her nightgown closed. She just reached down and seized two fists full of material at her hips, pulled the whole gown up and over her head and tossed it aside.

A sleepy, satisfied smile curved his lips as she stalked across the room to the bed.

'What have you in mind for me?'

'No talking,' she commanded, placing her hand lightly over his mouth when she reached him. She wasn't going to let anything spoil this. And whenever they talked, all the bitterness and disappointment that lay between them swam to the surface.

Leaning forwards like that left her breasts level with his mouth. His eyes fixed on them. His lips parted under her hand, his head straining towards her.

She shook her head. She wasn't interested in ceding to his wishes. This was her time.

'Later,' she said. 'If you are good.'

His eyelids lowered. His lips spread into a smile under her fingers—though they opened in shock when she got on to the bed, and straddled him.

He drew his hands out from under his head, and reached for her hips.

'No!' She grabbed his wrists and pushed his arms back up above her head.

He was very much stronger than her. So the fact that he'd let her do so demonstrated that he was willing to let her take charge. Which was crucial.

She rewarded his submission by leaning forwards

and brushing a kiss on his forehead. Then on his cheek. His chin. His throat. She licked round his Adam's apple as he swallowed convulsively, then she sat back, releasing her hold on his wrists so she could run her hands along his arms, tracing the contours of his biceps, then his wonderfully powerful shoulders. She smoothed her fingers over his hair-roughened chest. Stroked his flanks. His stomach.

Oh, but he was gorgeous. So well formed. So masculine.

And all hers.

He sucked in a sharp breath as she shifted back, to look at what she could feel nudging her soft warmth. She drew one finger tentatively along its length, then slipped her whole hand between his legs to cup him.

He gasped and surged up beneath her. She glanced up. At some point during her exploration of his body, he'd grabbed hold of the iron railings of the bedstead and was hanging on to them for dear life, if the tortured expression on his face was anything to go by.

She lifted off him, kneeling up and leaning forwards so that she could nuzzle the tendons straining in his neck. Her breasts just brushed his chest.

With a muted groan, he writhed from side to side, straining upwards towards them. But he didn't grab her. Or try to wrest control from her.

He could have no idea how much that meant to her, but her heart swelled with gratitude just the same.

And something darker. The unaccustomed feeling of power was heady. She could do whatever she wanted. Whenever she wanted.

And what she wanted was to explore and taste every single inch of this glorious body. So she started to kiss her way along the same trail her hands had taken. Licking at his nipples, nibbling at his flanks. Raining light kisses on his stomach.

Running her tongue the entire length of his erection and swirling it round the tip.

By the time she stopped playing with him and shifted over him so that his thick shaft brushed against her slick folds, he was trembling. And panting. His hips undulated as though he couldn't quite help just that tiny amount of movement, but still, he waited until she was ready. Until the moment was perfect for her.

She leaned forwards, rubbing her breasts the entire length of his quivering body, delighting in its strength, its hardness against her softer, womanly flesh. Her whole bloodstream was fizzing. She had never felt so alive, so bold…or so aroused. She had to have him inside her. Now. She reached down and took the most masculine part of him in her hand.

He was panting hoarsely now, a sheen of sweat standing out on his brow as she positioned him at her entrance, then sank slowly, deliciously slowly, down upon him. Feeling him filling her, meeting her need… oh, completing her.

As though she'd let him off the leash, he thrust up hard, once, twice.

She leaned forwards, bracing herself on his shoulders to increase friction at the spot where she ached and yearned.

He thrust once more and sensation exploded inside her. Her entire body shook with the force of the most intense orgasm she'd ever experienced.

And he was coming, too.

He throbbed and pulsed inside her. So deep inside her.

And then he caught her as she collapsed down on top

of him, wrapping his arms round her as she lay shaking and spent, listening to the thunderous heartbeat pounding beneath her cheek.

She couldn't believe it was all over so quickly.

Although…perhaps it hadn't been as quick as all that. She'd been simmering with arousal ever since that kiss. Each word they'd spoken, each look they'd darted each other had been a form of extended foreplay.

'Lydia,' he murmured, placing a kiss on the crown of her head. 'Lydia.'

The tenderness, the awe in his voice, matched how she felt, exactly.

When he rolled her to her side, kicking his legs free of the sheets, she made no protest. Apart from the fact she was as limp as a rag doll, she was curious to know what he would reveal about himself now.

She'd just discovered he was nowhere near as selfish as she'd thought. A selfish man would not have let her play with his body, surely? Or let her take her pleasure exactly as she'd wanted it?

He kissed her. Stroked her hair. Told her she was the most beautiful woman he'd ever seen.

She kissed him back, grateful that he was ending their session this way, with caresses and words of praise.

He could have just closed his eyes and started snoring while she peeled herself off him, grabbed her clothes and slunk back to her room.

Instead, he was making the whole time together absolutely perfect.

'Please don't tell me I may not touch your breasts now,' he murmured, wriggling further down the bed so he could nuzzle them.

It was surprising and flattering, too, that he should still want to, now that he'd got his release.

'You may,' she whispered, running her fingers through his hair, holding him to her breasts.

It was prolonging her pleasure. A glorious, warm extension of what they'd just shared.

Until he ran his free hand down her back, cupped one buttock and began to squeeze it rhythmically.

'N-no…'

He lifted his head, a frown creasing his brow.

'Why not?'

'Because I'm getting…you are making me…'

He grinned that wicked grin again.

'That is the whole point.'

'But…'

To answer her confusion, he let go of her bottom, took her hand and drew it down to his groin.

She gasped. He was…

'Again?'

He nodded.

'And this time,' he growled, 'we can take it slowly.'

And they did. Side by side they lay in that narrow bed, legs entwined, kissing and touching languorously. Until mounting desperation had her clawing at him for closer contact, harder touches, deeper kisses.

'Now…please,' she breathed into his mouth, willing to let him flip her on to her back, this time, if he wanted, just so long as he would stop the slow, aching torment and give her the release she craved.

Instead, he rolled on to his own back, pulling her on top again.

Only this time he didn't let her have it all her own way. He caressed her hips, ran his hands up her waist and tilted to one side so he could cup one breast. Then

half-sat, pulling her forwards so that he could flick his
tongue over her nipples.

In this position she could rock herself to orgasm
in seconds. But then it would be over. And she didn't
want this to end.

So she tried to calm down. Relax the inner muscles
that were straining and clenching.

But her heart was pounding so hard, and his hands
and mouth were working her so relentlessly that she
couldn't seem to stop. Her hips ground against him.
She arched back, increasing the pressure.

And a second orgasm took hold of her and flung
her to the stars.

He seized her by the back of her neck, dragging her
down and smothering the strangled cry that tore from
her throat, with a wild and masterful kiss.

And she collapsed on to him again, trembling like
a leaf.

He stroked her back, soothed her with gentle kisses.
And only when she'd stopped shaking did he deftly flip
them both over, reversing their positions.

Mentally she braced herself for him to pound to a
swift release while she still floated in the warm aftermath.

Instead, he entered her slowly, and began to rotate
his hips gently, insistently rocking against her most
sensitive spot. Deliberately attempting to stimulate her
again.

'I can't,' she protested. She could not believe she'd
just had two orgasms in such rapid succession. It was
surely impossible to reach such heights a third time.

He just smiled against her throat and kept right on
doing what he was doing.

And in spite of thinking it was impossible, her inner

muscles twitched, and came back to life. Her hips instinctively undulated to match the rhythm of his own.

He shuddered, and when she looked into his face she could see he was gritting his teeth. He was deliberately holding back, waiting for her.

Time after time he almost came to the brink and had to slow down. She could only marvel at his self-control. He clearly intended to hold back until he made her come again. No matter how long it took.

By the time she was teetering on the brink of yet another orgasm, every muscle in her body was straining to bring her to release, while he was quivering with the effort it was taking him not to. Her inner thighs ached, her buttocks ached. She was becoming exhausted. She didn't think she was going to be able to keep going long enough to get there.

But then he reached down between their two sweat-slicked bodies and found that sweet spot. With a few deft strokes he pushed her straight over the edge and she was falling, falling, and yet climbing, oh, she was flying into white-hot oblivion.

And he was flying there with her. Shuddering and pulsing and burying his face into the pillow to stifle his groan of bliss.

When she came to herself, it felt as though all her bones had melted in that last conflagration. He didn't seem to have fared any better. For a while, they both lay fused together in mutual satiation. Panting for breath, while their heartbeats thundered through their lax limbs.

And a great swell of emotion brought tears to her eyes. It was no longer possible to block out what she felt for this man, not after what they'd just shared. No wonder she'd exploded with rapture the moment she'd taken his body into hers. She had not just been waiting for the moment for one afternoon, but for eight long, lonely years.

She'd wanted him with every fibre of her being when she'd been a shy and insecure young débutante. Every bit as much as she'd wanted him when she saw him again as a mature and sexually experienced woman. The intervening years might as well have not happened for all the difference they made to how she felt about him.

How she would probably always feel about him.

One large fat tear ran down her cheek and into her ear.

For eight long years she'd been telling herself she didn't love him. That her heart had not been broken when his disappearance had given her no choice but to marry another man. But now she knew better. The sex could not have been so spectacular if she did not love him.

She, more than anyone, knew the difference between a mechanical coupling, designed to sate a physical appetite, and an act of love. And she had just given herself to Lord Rothersthorpe heart and soul.

As for him…

He'd made no secret of the fact that he wanted her. But it was only in a physical sense. He could not have exerted such self-control if she, if this, had meant anything very much to him.

While she had made love, for the very first time in her life, he had just enjoyed a satisfying sexual encounter.

It no longer felt like glorious closeness, to have him lying on top of her like that, now she'd faced up to the fact that they were both in such very different frames of mind.

'Will you please get off me now?' She had to get out of here, swiftly. She couldn't bear it if he initiated the kind of sophisticated, post-coital conversation she imagined men conducted with their paramours.

He did not respond. His face was buried in her neck, his arms holding her tight, even though he appeared to be only semi-conscious.

She pushed at his shoulders.

'You are crushing me.'

He sucked in a sharp breath. Every muscle in his body tensed.

'How appallingly ill mannered of me,' he drawled, sliding to one side. He kept one arm draped over her waist, leaned up on one elbow, and looked down at her, his expression sardonic.

Just as she'd feared.

With a determined grimace, she pushed his arm aside and swung her legs over the edge of the bed.

For a moment, she went a bit light-headed, and had to sit still until the feeling passed.

He took advantage of her momentary weakness to trail one finger lightly down her spine.

'I wonder at you putting me in a single bed. It would have been more pleasant to lie for a while in comfort after—'

'That was nothing to do with me,' she snapped, getting to her feet. She felt so naked and not just physically, but emotionally, somehow. If she wasn't careful, he would guess how much this had meant to her. And he…

She shook her head. She didn't know how he would react, exactly. Except that it would mean humiliation for her, in one form or another.

But at least she could set him straight about one thing. She had not been as desperate to take him as a lover as he'd assumed, with his typical, monumental, masculine arrogance.

'In fact,' she blurted over her shoulder as she went to retrieve her nightgown, 'it was not I who invited you down here at all.'

'What do you mean? You sent me that note…'

'*Rose* sent you that note,' she retorted, shaking her gown out and slipping it over her head. She felt better for having the barrier between them. Flimsy silk it might be, but at least it shielded her to some extent.

'And before you ask, I am quite sure,' she said, bending to pick up her dressing gown, 'that it was not so that we could embark on an affair.'

He was still propped up on one elbow, his face set in a scowl.

'When I arrived,' he said slowly, 'you…'

'You assumed I was a wanton widow, ripe for an affair,' she said bitterly.

'Well, if that performance was anything to go by,' he said mockingly, 'I was correct.'

He might as well have slapped her.

Thanking heaven that she'd got dressed so quickly, she marched to the door and went straight out.

'Lydia! Wait!'

He hadn't shouted. It had been more of an urgent hiss. She noticed him frantically attempting to fight free of the tangled sheets as she turned and shut the door on him, but she did not even think about waiting to hear what else he had to say.

She just went striding down the corridor. Away from him.

Tears streaming down her face.

Chapter Ten

There was no fathoming the riddle that was Lydia Morgan. And there was no point in trying. This was, after all, just a brief affair, on which he'd embarked to purge himself of her, once and for all.

And if last night had left him longing for more, well, that was no bad thing. On the contrary, it would have made staying here deuced awkward if he'd felt reluctant to have her back in his bed again.

Nicholas took one last look at himself in the mirror to check that his face revealed nothing of the turbulence coursing through his mind. He was going to have to greet Lydia in a few moments, over the breakfast cups, without raising suspicions about what they'd become to each other, to any of the other guests.

So the last thing he should be doing was dwelling on the way she'd discarded her clothing so impatiently, before fulfilling every fantasy he'd ever had. Or how she'd looked like a goddess, her limbs bathed in moonlight as she'd stalked imperiously to his bed. How it had all seemed more like a dream than anything he'd ever experienced.

Until the end. When they'd descended into bickering over…well, he still wasn't sure quite what.

He tugged his waistcoat down, strode to the door and snatched it open. That was what he should be remembering when he next looked at her. The disappointment—nay, the rancour of their parting. That would give him a demeanour totally suitable for a public breakfast table.

It had been so typical of Lydia. If anyone had the right to feel annoyed, surely it was he? For the way she'd pushed him aside when she'd had enough of him, for one thing. Just as she had all those years ago. She'd used him to keep her spirits up while she'd been husband-hunting, but actually *marry* him? Oh, no. And he might be good for a romp, but actually *feel* anything? Not she.

He grimaced. That very prosaic little voice, complaining he was crushing her, had brought him back down to earth with a bump, and just as well, too, or heaven alone knew what he might have said, or done. For it hadn't been tenderness he'd thought he'd detected under all those passionate kisses at all. He'd seen, and only just in time, that she had not been making frantic love to him at all. That she was nothing more than a sex-starved widow, revelling in finally getting her hands on a firm, young male body.

A bitter smile curved his lips as he descended the stairs to the main part of the house. He'd exceeded all her expectations, to judge by the shocked look on her face when he'd started taking her for the second time. Oh, yes, he'd given her a night to remember, all right. And the irony was that if only she hadn't dismissed his proposal out of hand they could have had eight years of nights like that one.

So what had she meant by her parting shot about not

having invited him down here? Why was she claiming Rose had been the one to send that invitation at dead of night? And why had she seemed so upset when she left? If he didn't know her better, if he hadn't already worked out that she was using him, he might have gone back to wondering if he held a special place in her heart. He'd already considered that might account for her apparent shyness when he arrived and her spectacular about-face after he'd kissed her.

And the expression on her face when they'd been making love.

Ah, damn! He was right back where he'd started. Trying to understand her. Wanting her to *feel* something for him. When what he should be doing was just thanking his lucky stars that she was so spectacularly uninhibited in bed.

He scowled impartially round all the people already assembled at the breakfast table. Though he didn't suppose they noticed. Most of them were clustered at the far end, near Rose, chattering away like a flock of starlings.

He pulled out a chair next to Lydia, who was staring fixedly at her plate, a blush mounting to her cheeks.

It was a wonder she could blush—a woman who could behave like *that* even if it was in the privacy of a darkened bedroom.

'Coffee, tea or ale, sir?' The deferential tones of one of her footmen jolted him from his torrid memories of the apparently demure woman sitting by his side and forced him to speak.

'Ale,' he grunted.

Lydia was breathing hard. And trembling just a little. Dammit, now he felt all...protective towards her. He could see she had no idea how to conduct herself with him in front of others, after being intimate with him. She'd never taken a lover before. She didn't know how the game was played.

It was up to him to lead the way.

'You should bid me good morning,' he said softly. 'And enquire how I slept, just as though you had no idea I was not alone.'

'Anything else I have done wrong?' she replied, going from demure and bashful to waspish in the blink of an eye. 'From the look on your face as you came in, it is quite obvious you are nursing some kind of grievance.'

'If I have a complaint,' he replied, stung by her ingratitude, when he was only trying to make things easier for her, 'it is…that my bed is too narrow. I found it rather…restricting.'

Her face turned scarlet.

'However,' he continued, nodding his thanks to the footman who'd just deposited a tankard of ale by his plate, 'I have decided to look upon it as a challenge. I intend to spend the day,' he said in a deliberately provocative tone, 'thinking up ways to compensate for its limitations.'

She gasped and hastily set her cup down in its saucer before she slopped it all down the front of her dress.

'In fact, I am really looking forward to the night and exploring new possibilities.'

For a moment she looked as though she couldn't decide whether to run out of the room, throw her coffee in his face, or crawl into his lap and start exploring possibilities right now.

In short, he'd succeeded in reducing her to the state she always got him into, whenever they got within five feet of each other.

His mood much improved, he took a long, satisfying pull from his tankard.

She picked up her knife, sliced off a hefty chunk of butter and slapped it onto her toast.

He sighed. It was all very well scoring points off her, but it would not make conducting this affair any easier. It would be wiser to smooth her ruffled feathers by finding out what had provoked her ill humour with him the night before and putting it right. If he could.

'One possibility,' he began tentatively, 'would be to avoid turning our time together into another battle.'

White knuckled, she tore her toast in the attempt to spread her butter evenly.

'Please believe me when I tell you that I regret the way we parted,' he said. 'I do not know what it was I said, or did, to anger you, but whatever it was, can you not forgive me for it?'

She glanced at him, suspiciously, out of the corner of her eye, and seemed to come to a decision as she reached for a pot of jam.

'Of course I forgive you, my lord.'

Which was not good enough. Nowhere near good enough. Not when she bit the words out between clenched teeth.

'Yes, but what for? Why were you so upset?'

'Because I had attached far too much importance to the event,' she snapped, then bowed her head, as though regretting her outburst.

'It is entirely my own fault…' she sighed '…that you spoke as you did. I had no right to feel that you were insulting me.'

'Insulting you? How? I assure you, I never meant…'

'I…I know. Afterwards, I realised that you acted and spoke as you did because you came here looking for an uncomplicated affair with a woman you thought was experienced and…sophisticated. I should have told you, the moment you told me you thought I had sent you that invitation, and for what purpose, that I am not that kind of woman.' She dropped a dollop of jam on to her mangled slice of toast. 'But you are never going to believe that now, not after the way I…'

'Do you regret…what we did?' His heart thumped painfully fast. 'Do you wish to discontinue our…?'

She'd been about to replace the spoon in the jam pot. His question appeared to startle her so much she dropped it on to the tablecloth.

'No,' she hissed, frantically scooping up the worst of the spill and tapping it from the spoon on to a side plate. 'I suppose I should,' she added almost mournfully. 'But it seems that when it comes to you, I just cannot help myself.'

The sense of relief made him quite light-headed for a moment.

'But something about…us…distresses you. Won't you tell me what it is?'

She shook her head. 'This is hardly a fit topic for the breakfast table. Anyone might overhear.'

So there was something. And heaven help him, but he wanted to know what it was. His heart had leapt when she said she'd attached too much importance to the event. Which might mean she did feel *something* for him.

Or perhaps it was only that she was irritated about losing control. There had been more than a touch of exasperation about the way she'd said she couldn't help herself…

'Come for a walk with me. A ride with me.'

'No. I have my duties.'

He seized her hand when she waved it towards the young people at the other end of the table.

'Stop this, Lydia. We need to talk to each other. I need to understand you.' If only he could get to the heart of her mystery, perhaps her hold over him would slacken. She would no longer tantalise him, drive him to distraction, once he could see her as just a woman, like any other. Not that he would tell her that. So instead he added, 'So that we won't ruin this short time together by quarrelling so often.'

He was shocked to see something very much like torment in her eyes.

'What have I said now?'

But before she could answer him, Robert came in. He glanced round the table, taking in Rose sitting in state amidst her courtiers, and then, with a narrowing of the eyes, Lord Rothersthorpe's hand on Lydia's wrist.

With a rueful grimace, he let go, wondering how on earth he would explain *that* to her stepson, should he choose to take issue with him.

But then, fortunately for all concerned, Michael came skipping in, ran straight up to Lydia and flung his arms round her neck.

She rested her cheek on his hair, closed her eyes and appeared to breathe him in.

It was such an entirely instinctive reaction that he had the sense that for the very first time he was seeing a side to Lydia that she did not have to fabricate. She was, without doubt, a mother who loved her son.

But what else was she, that was the question? Every time he thought he caught a glimpse of the real woman, she turned into something else, right before his eyes. It was like being led across marshland by a will-o'-the-wisp. She shimmered, she tantalised, she beckoned to him, but remained always just out of reach.

Was that the secret of her fascination? If so, then getting to know her well would definitely ensure her power over him would cease.

But then Robert drew up a chair beside him, putting an end to any chance of talking freely.

Or of arranging a private meeting during the day, so that they could just talk and break the spell she invariably cast over him.

But she was in no hurry to set him free. As was the way with house parties, everyone dispersed after breakfast to amuse themselves according to their tastes. Lydia let him catch glimpses of her, flitting from one group to another, or disappearing through a plain door that led to the kitchens and staff quarters. But not once could he catch her alone.

Not even at lunch, where she monopolised the earnest young son of the local vicar, who came in daily to tutor Michael, and, if his ears did not deceive him, Cissy too. She used the excuse of her prolonged absence to demand a progress report.

Eventually, though, the tutor made his excuses and left. Lord Rothersthorpe was just about to take the vacant place at her side when Robert got to his feet and tapped a spoon on his glass to attract everyone's attention.

'It looks as though it is going to be a lovely afternoon,' Robert said. 'So I thought we could make the most of the gardens.'

There was a general murmur of assent.

Michael went to his side and tugged at his sleeve.

Robert bent down and Michael whispered something in his ear.

'That is a grand idea. Ladies, gentlemen, Michael would very much like to invite you to a game of crickers on the orangery lawn.'

'Crickers? What is that?' Mr Bentley strolled over and ruffled Michael's hair.

Michael ducked away from the over-friendly hand of Mr Bentley, a scowl which made him look very much like his older brother darkening his countenance.

'It is a game we have adapted to suit the shape and size of the lawn hard by the orangery,' said Robert. 'Not quite cricket, though we do use stumps, and not quite rounders, though the players of each team guard their bases.'

'Oh, yes, that would be such fun,' cried Rose, going to his side and swiftly flicking Michael's disordered hair back into place. 'And Michael, of course, must be captain of one of the teams.'

Rose's suitors fell into line at once, declaring that it did indeed sound like capital fun. After a surreptitious dig in the side from her brother's elbow, even Lord Abergele's sister adopted a patronising smile and declared she didn't mind humouring the children.

'Marigold, I think you had better be the captain of the other team,' Rose declared.

Lord Rothersthorpe bit back a smile as the sixteen-year-old struggled between worry that the haughty baronet's sister would regard her as childish and delight at being about to play what was clearly a favourite game. And being captain of a team to boot.

Delight took precedence as Robert tossed a coin and the two captains began to pick their teams.

Michael, having won the toss, got first choice. He

chose Cissy, which was very noble of him since the girl
was not likely to be much of an asset. Marigold showed
no such sentiment. She chose her own brother Robert,
then himself, Lieutenant Smollet, the Prince of Pickles—who'd been known as George Lutterworth when
he'd entered this rather eccentric household—and finally had to accept Lutterworth's bespectacled sister
Cynthia, since she was the last person left.

It shouldn't have mattered, but Lord Rothersthorpe
was rather pleased that he was on the team that was
the most likely to win. Michael had ended up with not
only Cissy, but also Lord Abergele's sister, who was not
likely to put in any effort at all. It was hard to tell how
Lord Abergele himself would fare at any kind of sport.
So far he had not observed him doing anything with any
enthusiasm apart from eating. He'd started to think of
him as the Hungry Baronet, somehow succumbing to
the prevailing atmosphere of this house party, where
everyone was rapidly acquiring nicknames. Mr Bentley might, possibly, make up for the deficiencies of
the other members of his team. But he rather thought
Lieutenant Tancred was the only one who posed any
real competition. He had the determined jaw of a man
who would do whatever it took to win. In any situation.

'What about Miss Morgan?' enquired the Hungry
Baronet's haughty sister archly. 'On which team will
she be playing?'

'Well,' said Rose, with a rather mischievous smile,
'since Mama Lyddy always acts as umpire, I cannot
possibly play. Or the teams would be unequal. Which
would not be at all fair.'

'You could exchange places with me,' the girl suggested. 'If you wish to play.'

'Oh, no, I could not deprive you of that pleasure,' Rose insisted. 'You are my guest,' she said sweetly.

Poor Lord Abergele. His title was nowhere near grand enough to outweigh the hostility steadily mounting between the two girls. In fact, of Rose's five suitors, he would hazard a guess that only three were still in the running, Lutterworth having dished his chances the very first day by speaking ill of his own sister, a crime the family-oriented Rose would never forgive.

Marigold ended the potential spat by shepherding the entire party to the orangery, a strange building that was joined to the house, yet not quite a part of it. It was, he supposed, a kind of conservatory, since the walls were almost entirely comprised of glass and the floor of terracotta tiles. Yet the structure did not cling to the rear wall in the accepted fashion. Rather, it curved out like a glittering arm embracing a large, lush lawn. But it did house a stunning collection of exotic plants growing in immense containers, which gave out the typically damp, green scent he would have expected. Dozens of intricately wrought brass lamps were suspended from the ceiling, adding to the oriental feel of the place. These, and the selection of comfortably upholstered chairs which were scattered amidst the towering plants, suggested a room that was frequently used, by day and by night, for anyone wishing to enjoy the magnificent view that could be obtained from this spot.

By some means he hadn't observed, his own team got to bat first, which meant most of them could sit and watch the game from the chairs set out round a refreshment table, over which Rose presided.

Only Robert strode to the open doorway, possibly so that he could shout encouragement to his fellow batsmen. Or perhaps so that he could maintain some kind of guard over Lydia, for she had taken a seat just inside that doorway, from where she could get an unimpeded view of the entire lawn.

There was an empty chair beside her. In spite of Robert's proximity, Lord Rothersthorpe decided this was as good an opportunity as he was ever going to get, and made straight for Lydia's side.

'May I join you?' He indicated the vacant chair. He saw Robert stiffen, though he did not turn round. There was nothing wrong with them sitting side by side, talking after all. How could the man possibly voice an objection?

It was only Lydia's response that mattered.

She lowered her eyes to the slate lying in her lap, which looked as though it had come from the schoolroom.

'Of course,' she said crisply, using a stick of chalk to write 'Marigold's Team' to one side of the line she'd already drawn down the centre of the slate.

Robert made a sound like a low growl as Lord Rothersthorpe sat down, before gathering himself up and taking a step forwards on to the flagged area between the orangery and the lawn.

'Do you think he suspects?' He kept his voice low. The glass partition, and the open door, provided scant privacy.

'I doubt it,' said Lydia, eyeing her stepson's rigid back. 'I think his reaction just now is more to do with the fact that since his father's death, nobody has actually sat in that chair. It was a favourite spot of his, you see. He would sit here, come rain or shine, admiring what he'd achieved...' She gazed out over the gardens, her eyes misty. 'I suppose somebody should have removed it. It is not as if he's ever coming back.'

He gave her a sharp glance. His ears might be deceiving him, but it sounded as though she'd actually been fond of the old man.

Out on the lawn Marigold was marking out a kind of clock face with squares of what looked like old matting. He could hear Michael, in his little-boy treble, attempting to explain the principles of the game to the uniformly bewildered adults gathered round him. And the low hum of conversation taking place at the far end of the orangery round Rose's tea table.

Nobody was paying him or Lydia the slightest bit of attention.

'I had no intention of upsetting anyone,' he said softly. 'But you have made it so difficult for me to get close to you today.'

'Yes.' She nodded, though she did not look at him. Instead she kept her eyes fixed on the team fanning out across the lawn into what he assumed must be strategic positions.

'I shall go into bat first, to give you an idea what you should be doing,' he heard Marigold shout, bringing a smile to Lydia's lips. Something inside him clenched hard when her smile grew fonder, loving. Once upon a time he'd dreamed of having her smile at him like that.

Annoyed with himself for harking back to the days when he'd hoped for so much from her, he tore his eyes from her luscious mouth and turned to see what she was looking at, to make her smile so.

It was her son, solemnly bowling the first ball of the match to his sister, with a great deal more enthusiasm than accuracy.

Nothing daunted, Marigold went to meet the ball and just managed to get her bat to connect with it. Slipper, who had followed Cissy on to the lawn, and taken up a station at her heels, tore off after the ball before any of the others in the fielding team could make a move.

He couldn't help smiling himself when Slipper took the ball straight back to Michael, who patted his head and told him he was a good dog. Who would have thought an animal could have picked up the principles of the game before his human teammates?

Robert groaned. 'Those children seem determined to undo all the training that my father put that dog through. Slipper is not a pet!' He shouted the last to Michael, who grinned, waved, then turned away to concentrate on his next throw.

He looked at Lydia again, who was still smiling in a way that made her look like a total stranger. Not just a warm, loving mother, but a woman totally at ease with herself and her surroundings.

'The more I see of you,' he mused, 'the less I feel as though I know you. Who are you, really, Lydia?'

'I don't think I know what you mean,' she said, with a perplexed frown. 'I am just…me.'

He gave her a long, steady look.

'Since I have come here, I have seen quite a new side to you. One which I never would have guessed existed.'

She stiffened and blushed.

'I did not mean that,' he continued swiftly, guessing she was still thinking about the night before. 'Delightful though it was. No, I am speaking now of your relationship to the members of this family.'

At that moment, there was a cry of 'out!' from the lawn, swiftly followed by Marigold's anguished protest that she couldn't be.

From the corner of his eye he'd seen Marigold hit the ball straight towards Cissy and Slipper leap up to catch the ball in his mouth.

Now the whole fielding team was looking to Lydia to pronounce judgement.

'I cannot be out,' Marigold said again. 'Slipper is not on the fielding team. Or if he is, then we should have another person on our side to make numbers even.'

Lydia got to her feet and went to the doorway to stand beside her stepson, who was looking at her with a mixture of amusement and enquiry.

'Slipper is not on anyone's team,' Lydia said firmly. 'He is just a dog who cannot resist chasing after a ball. We all know he will be as much danger to whichever side goes into bat.'

'Then I am not out?'

'On the contrary, Marigold, you are out.'

Marigold threw down her bat in disgust. 'That is so unfair!'

'Mama Lyddy is the umpire,' said Robert reprovingly. 'Her word is final.'

'Pick up your bat, Marigold,' said Lydia firmly. 'You need to pass it on to whoever is in next.'

Marigold scowled, but did as she was told, stomping into the orangery and up to the refreshment table, where she thrust the bat at Lieutenant Smollet.

He took it from her as though he had no idea what to do with it.

But then Rose smiled at him and said, 'I am sure you will pick up the rules in no time.'

Giving her one last smouldering look, he got to his feet, squared his shoulders and marched to the door as though he was about to go into battle.

'Your stepson appears very fond of you,' Nicholas said as Robert clapped the hapless lieutenant on the shoulder.

'Why should he not be?'

Lord Rothersthorpe studied his boots in silence for a few seconds, before continuing. 'At the time of your marriage to his father, he led me to believe that he was very much against it.'

'Oh, I see,' she said, looking at the stiff set of her stepson's shoulders. 'Yes, he was. But that was before he even met me.'

'Before he...' Rothersthorpe frowned. 'But he told me you were a greedy, grasping, conniving...'

'Pray do not stop now,' she said sweetly when his voice faltered. 'I am a greedy, grasping, conniving what?'

He shook his head. 'Never mind. Besides, I am no longer sure you are any of those things.'

'Then why say it?'

His gaze strayed out of the bank of windows. Michael was handing the ball to Cissy, while Lieutenant Smollet was adopting a protective stance in front of his wicket.

'I suppose I am trying to explain...well, it is just that, for years, I've had this image of you as somebody entirely different from...what you appear to be now, amidst your family, and in your home.'

'Is that an apology?'

It had been more in the nature of an observation, but if an apology was what she wanted, he didn't see why he shouldn't let her think so.

'What else could it be? If you were the woman I thought you, those girls would not all adore you the way they do. You would not be able to pass messages to your stepchildren with just a look and tease each other the way you do unless you all trusted and respected each other. Nor would you have the close, affectionate bond I can see you have with your son, either. I imagined you making their lives a misery all these years. Instead of which…' he made a sound that was halfway between a laugh and a click of his tongue '…I can't help thinking that the whole lot of them walk all over you. You have earned every penny your colonel bequeathed you, have you not?'

She sucked in a sharp breath.

'What do you mean?'

His mouth flattened into a grim line.

'Robert acts more like a gaoler than stepson. Rose is so headstrong I would describe her as being well on the way to being a minx. Marigold is set fair to becoming just the same once she leaves the stage of being a sulky schoolgirl behind her. And as for that Cissy…' He paused to watch her make an ungainly attempt to bowl for the man who'd finally, stoically, accepted his name was now 'Left on a Mullet'. 'She is doomed to perpetual childhood, though her body is that of a woman, is she not?'

'Yes, she is,' said Lydia, coldly. 'What of it?'

'Your late husband may have had his reasons for wanting to keep her in his own household, but he should not have laid all the burden of her care upon you. He should have hired a professional person to manage her.'

'I do not regard Cissy as a burden,' she said vehemently. 'I love her.'

'Which only goes to prove you are not the woman I mistakenly thought you were all these years. Instead, I have discovered…' he half-turned in his chair and gazed at her beautiful face '…you are still the gentle, rather easily put-upon girl I met and I…liked so much when I was just plain Mr Hemingford. I only wish…' He reined himself in. Dear God, he couldn't *still* be wishing she'd chosen him, rather than Colonel Morgan, could he? Hadn't he reached the conclusion that he'd had a lucky escape?

Yes, but that had been when he'd been sure she was just a mercenary harpy. When he'd thought she'd made her choice coldly and deliberately. Before he'd recalled how little cause he'd given her to believe his proposal had been made in earnest. Before he recalled how much pressure her chaperon was putting on her to marry well. And God knew, back then he'd been *no* chaperon's idea of a good match.

And, to make no bones about it, before discovering how sensational she was between the sheets.

'Yes? What do you wish?'

'Nothing,' he grated. It was pathetic to beg for an explanation as to why she'd married Colonel Morgan and in such haste. Nothing could undo the past eight years.

Lydia allowed her eyes to follow the game in progress, as though it was taking all her attention. But in reality, she was struggling to keep her anger in check.

Who would have thought that *he* was one of those people, like her guardian, who thought that the simple-minded ought to be locked away, lest they contaminate the rest of society?

Perhaps he wouldn't have spoken so freely if he hadn't somehow got hold of the idea that Cissy was Robert's sister, rather than her own. But in a way, it was better to know the truth.

In spite of the heat of the sun, a little shiver ran down her spine. He had never done anything but disappoint her, and let her down. But to discover that he was the kind of man who thought it best to consign Cissy to the care of strangers…

And as for saying *he'd* never really known *her!* Well, clearly that cut both ways. They had never really been able to talk to each other, in private. Mrs Westerly might have been extremely keen to arrange a match, but she had never wished to do so at the expense of the proprieties. It had all been hands held across a cotillion, snatched moments on moonlit terraces, the occasional outing to the park, strictly chaperoned by a groom or a maid or both, when conversation had therefore of necessity stayed within very narrow confines.

No, she'd never known all that much about him. She'd been dazzled by his superficial charm. Blinded to his faults by her hunger for some respite from the gruelling task set her by her guardian. In short, she'd idolised him.

Actually, she frowned, she'd always known he had feet of clay. Handsome and charming as he was, she'd never liked the way he found it amusing to lose money on ridiculous wagers, or wriggle out of paying his bills. Well, now she could add uncaring to the list of his character defects.

So why had it felt so good to hear him explain why he had said such cutting things? And to hear his apology—grudging though it had been?

That was what made her shiver. The fact that in spite of all his faults, she still wanted him to think well of her. He exerted far too strong an influence over her.

Though she thought she knew why. The Colonel had told her that one never forgot one's first love. He had probably been trying to reassure her that it was not her fault that he could not feel anything warmer than fondness for her. But it also helped to account for her own reactions to Lord Rothersthorpe, who had been *her* first love. And now she'd discovered she'd never really stopped loving him, no matter how hard she'd tried to put him out of her mind, she could understand why she'd been on fire for him after that kiss in the garden, even though what he'd assumed about her had been so insulting. Why she wanted him to understand her, even though he did not really merit any kind of explanation.

She glanced at him. He was looking at her in a way he'd never done before—with open curiosity. The mockery, the flippancy of his youth, well, that had long gone. But now he'd lost that harsh, judgemental frown, too. He really did look as though he wanted to understand.

And he'd finally admitted that he *had* liked her very much when they'd known each other before. No prevarication. No making excuses and backing away from the statement the moment he'd made it, either.

She sighed. He'd told her, at breakfast, that he didn't want their short time together spoiled by quarrels. And even though it had hurt to hear his reminder that he only saw her as a temporary diversion, it would ease pain somewhat, if she could at least prevent him sniping at her.

'Firstly, I have to take issue with you referring to Robert as a gaoler. I know he can be rather autocratic, but he is his father's son, after all. And I learned, through the course of my marriage, how to deal with men of his stamp. He can make me do nothing I do not wish.'

'If you say so…'

'I do say so. And what is more, I do not feel *put upon* by his sisters, either.'

She paused, marshalling her thoughts into coherent, concise sentences which would not cause any trouble if anyone should overhear them. Although the din emanating from the enthusiastic spectators, as Lieutenant Smollet gamely swung at the next ball Cissy bowled for him, would have made it well nigh impossible anyway.

'Perhaps, since you do not have sisters, you do not appreciate how fortunate I consider myself to have been brought into this family. As their stepmother, and being so very near their age to boot, they could have taken against me and made my life a misery. But they did not. I don't say they welcomed me with open arms, not at first. It took time to earn their trust. But though I cannot dispute the fact they have rather forceful characters, they also have generous hearts.'

'Very well, I stand corrected,' he said. 'On that point. But I still…dammit, it sticks in my craw to think of you marrying Colonel Morgan at all. I suppose…I mean… did Mrs Westerly pressure you into it? Was that what happened?'

'Mrs Westerly was the one who first put the notion into Colonel Morgan's head, that I cannot deny,' she admitted sombrely. While she'd been lying there, trying to work out if she dare believe she could put her faith in a proposal that had clearly been made on a whim, Mrs Westerly had gone to work on the Colonel with a vengeance.

'While she stayed here with me, she wasted no opportunity of pointing out all the advantages of taking on a wife to manage his household. He could never manage to keep a housekeeper for long, because of his temper, you see. She convinced him that a wife would relieve him of the tedious chore of having to think about domestic issues at all.'

'He married you because he wanted you to keep house for him? And never have the freedom to escape his vile temper? Lydia, how could you have let the pair of them push you into such a distasteful union?'

'Nobody pushed me into anything,' she retorted. 'I made very certain, before I accepted Colonel Morgan's proposal, that he would give me exactly what I wanted out of the arrangement. And I drove a hard bargain, believe me.'

'So it was his money you wanted.' He sat back, crest-fallen.

If he hadn't looked so upset, she might have let him carry on believing the worst of her. But it was that hint that he wished to believe well of her that made her willing to allow him just a glimpse of the truth.

'You discussed my marriage with Robert, you said.'

When he nodded, she continued, 'He put ideas into your head which he could not possibly have verified, since we did not meet for months after I moved in here. So I forgive you for thinking it was money I wanted from marriage, when it was nothing of the kind.'

Lieutenant Smollet had finally managed to hit one of Cissy's rather wild attempts to bowl the ball in his direction. Lord Rothersthorpe watched it go sailing over the boundary hedge and into the region of the Per-sian Pools rather than look at her, as he grated, 'If not money, then what?'

With an excited bark, Slipper plunged straight through the hedge, while Lieutenant Tancred ran to an arched gap further along.

'Run, Left on a Mullet!' Robert darted forward, his attention wholly captured by the prospect of his team finally earning some points.

'Security,' she said simply, as the lieutenant set off round the pitch. It was as much as she was prepared to tell him, now she knew what he was really like.

'Security?' He turned to look searchingly at her. 'I don't understand…'

'No. I don't suppose you did. But did you never won-der why I suffered from so many headaches? It was the unbearable strain. The further into the Season I got, and the more impossible my situation grew, the less able I became to deal with it, physically. Even Mrs Westerly started to worry that my health would break down completely before she managed to get *someone* to give me a home.'

A home? That was all she'd wanted?

'I had no idea.' He shook his head, his face grim and pale. 'Though I feel now as though I should have done.'

It explained so much. The first time he'd seen her, she'd been a picture of health. He'd almost forgotten. He had not taken much note of her, beyond admiring her silvery-blonde hair, and those enormous blue eyes, and thinking what a catch she would be for some marriage-minded man. She'd only really started to pique his interest when she hadn't become the toast of the *ton*. When instead she'd started to fade away before his eyes.

'You were shy, painfully shy, weren't you?' He recalled now how she'd looked as though she'd wanted to bolt when men had, in those first weeks, begun to flock round her. All that blushing and stammering hadn't been an act at all. She really had hated putting herself forwards in order to snare a husband.

And yet she'd kept right on doing it.

Or at least…

'That dreadful woman kept on pushing you at men, didn't she? No wonder you grew desperate to escape her.'

There was an immense splash from beyond the hedge. It sounded as though the dog had dived into one of the pools to retrieve the ball.

She tapped the chalk on her slate, a frown pleating her brow as though she was choosing her words with the greatest of care.

'It was not quite like that. I suppose it must have looked as though Mrs Westerly was pushing me at men in far too forceful a manner, but in truth she was doing her very best to help me, in the limited time available to us. My guardian had told us both that he was only prepared to frank me for one Season. He had told her that if she could not get us...I mean, of course, me,' she amended swiftly, 'off his hands then he would no longer support me. I would have had to find some form of genteel occupation. You see, my father had not left his affairs in good order. The estate itself was entailed, but I was given to understand there was not much else left but debts.'

He recalled her saying she was going to be in trouble if she hadn't brought some man up to scratch before the end of her Season, but he hadn't thought she might actually have ended up with nowhere to live.

'You really needed a home,' he said, gazing down at his boots. After a moment or two he gave a harsh little laugh. 'I...I see.'

She was stronger now and more sure of herself, but back then, she had been a timid little thing. The prospect of being at the beck and call of some querulous old woman, if she'd taken work as a paid companion, must have seemed terrifying. And with that face, it would have been downright dangerous to go out as a governess to any household which had a son of anything above adolescence, or an employer with a roving eye. She might have fared reasonably well as a school-teacher, he supposed, given the boundless patience he'd seen she had with Morgan's wilful girls.

But what really stung was seeing that he could have been the man to give her the home and security she'd craved, if only he hadn't taken such pains to make her think he was not on the marriage mart. Because that was what he'd done. Alarmed by the strength of the feelings he'd begun to develop for her, he'd attempted to counteract them by declaring to both her, and himself, that he was offering nothing but a light, inconsequential friendship. She could have had no idea he'd been struggling with himself when he blew hot and cold upon her.

If it really had only been a home she wanted, then Hemingford Priory was as secure, in its own way, as Westdene. If he'd only not been so selfish, self-absorbed…such an utter idiot! If he'd spoken sooner, or even if he'd not made his views on marriage so plain, she might have waited for him. Or if he'd talked to her then, as they were talking now, instead of trying to amuse her with idiotic tales of his stupid pranks.

Or if he'd stood his ground when Mrs Westerly had shoo'd him out of the drawing room he'd brought Lydia to after stammering that feeble excuse for a proposal. Laid his heart bare. And explained where he was going, and what he planned to do. Oh, she might have turned him down anyway. But on the other hand, she might not.

He hadn't really done all he could to convince her that he was, for the first time in his useless, frivolous existence, in deadly earnest.

No. He'd been too busy protecting himself from the potential humiliation of a rejection.

A chorus of shouts and laughter erupted from the lawn as Slipper wriggled back through the hedge, the ball in his mouth, Lieutenant Tancred hard on his heels.

While guilt curdled his insides into a writhing mass of bitter regrets. He'd let her down by refusing to nail his colours to the mast. And made a monumental mess not only of his own life, but also of hers. He'd made her think she had no choice but to marry Colonel Morgan.

She had not betrayed him at all.

He had betrayed her.

Chapter Eleven

'Have you been happy? At least, tell me that becoming mistress of all this brought you some joy,' he grated in anguish.

'Happy?' She gave a light shrug as though she did not consider his question relevant. 'Happiness did not come into it. I have been secure. And…I have learned to be content with my lot.'

Content? She could have been *happy* with him. They could both have been happy—and not just *to begin with,* either. Because, since he'd been down here, he'd discovered that she was exactly the kind of woman he'd come to town looking for. She was nothing like the mercenary harpy Robert had painted her—*before* he'd even met her, as it turned out. She'd entered a family riven with resentment and melded them all into…his gaze swept across the lawn, at all the happy smiling faces…into *this.*

And if she could gentle such a strong-willed bunch of people, she could have helped him untangle the mess his father had bequeathed him, too.

If he hadn't been such a coward when it came to love, she could have been at his side all these years.

And that boy, Michael—a pang of complete wretchedness curled the writhing mass of regrets into a knot—could have been *their* son.

He got to his feet so abruptly his chair went skidding across the tiles.

At the far end of the orangery, Marigold's did the same. Though for an entirely different reason.

'Keep running, Left on a Mullet!' She need not have bothered screaming the encouragement. Lieutenant Smollet was running doggedly round and round the pitch, while Lieutenant Tancred struggled in vain to get Slipper to relinquish the ball. More and more members of the fielding team started chasing the dog, who appeared to think it was all part of the game to dodge them all, while Michael, who might have made the dog behave, was rolling on the ground with laughter.

Lord Rothersthorpe couldn't see how anyone could be laughing, nor even how the sun could still be shining, when he felt as though his whole world had come to a juddering halt.

Eventually he heard Lydia's chair scrape across the tiles as she, too, got to her feet. Would she come and lay a comforting arm on his back? Tell him she understood? And forgave him?

No. Of course not. She had no idea of the blow she'd just dealt him.

She was calling the dog and snapping her fingers in such a way that it knew the command was urgent.

Slipper dodged between Lieutenant Tancred and Lord Abergele, smearing their breeches with green pond slime as he did so, ran to Lydia, dropped the ball at her feet, then sat down, looking up at her expectantly.

It was Mr Bentley, who was supposed to be guarding third base, who grasped the fact that as umpire, she would not touch the ball herself. He ran over, snatched it up and threw it with deadly accuracy, knocking the bails from the wicket a split second before Lieutenant Smollet could touch the ground before it with his bat.

'Out!' the entire fielding team yelled in victory.

Lieutenant Smollet paused as he came in, to ask Lydia how many runs he'd just scored.

'Nine,' replied Lydia promptly.

She'd had the presence of mind to count. While he was standing there feeling as though someone had just hit him in the guts with a cricket bat, she'd been cool and detached enough to keep count of the score of that ridiculous, childish game.

'I think it may be your turn next,' said Lieutenant Smollet, holding out the bat, though his eyes were already darting past him, to see how Rose was reacting to his triumph on the playing field.

He took it with a low growl.

This might be only a childish game, but he had never felt more like hitting something a resounding blow with a wooden bat in his entire life.

He was glad Lieutenant Tancred was the one bowling for him. He would not have wanted to face any of the children, or ladies, in the mood he was in. One exchange of glances told him Lieutenant Tancred understood. There was not going to be anything the least bit gentlemanly about the way he bowled. This was war.

For a few minutes he let out his anger and frustration on the still-sodden tennis ball, slogging it as hard as he could.

If he'd only talked about her background, instead of himself, he might have learned about her desperate plight during her Season. But it had never occurred to him that girls who went to balls dressed to the nines could have any experience of hardship. There had been sufficient clues to have alerted a man with any brains. But he just hadn't wanted to look beneath the surface. No, he'd been content to drift along in a golden current, never stirring himself to imagine she might have lost parents, home and security at a *stroke*... He fumed as he set off at a run round the pitch. She'd told him she *needed* to get married. That she was only going to have one Season.

But he hadn't thought that if she couldn't find a husband, she would have ended up turned out into the world to earn her living in some menial role.

Apparently, each bowler only got three attempts to remove a batsman from his position. It was nowhere nearly long enough before Tancred handed the ball to the Hungry Baronet's sister.

She looked at the ball with distaste, looked at him with trepidation, lobbed the ball in his general direction, then shut her eyes and braced herself for impact.

Because she hadn't thrown with any great force, Lord Rothersthorpe had to step well away from his wicket to meet the ball. And his swing was therefore not as precise as it could have been. The ball sailed straight up into the air...

As he leaned his head back to watch it, he thought of how he'd pushed and probed, thinking that getting to know her better would free him from her. Instead, he'd learned that the hatred he'd nursed this last eight years had arisen from what amounted to a lie. Lydia was everything he'd ever wanted. He knew, at a deep, instinctive level, that she'd spoken the truth about what had happened at the end of her Season.

He knew, because he'd been unable to believe Robert's account of her. He'd been sickened to think she could be so different from how she'd appeared to him. That she could have ignored what he'd clumsily tried to offer, because a wealthier man had proposed.

But then she hadn't, had she? Not really.

All the pieces of the puzzle that was Lydia fell into place as neatly as the ball fell into Mr Bentley's out-stretched hand.

And changed everything.

She really was the girl he'd fallen in love with.

The girl whose loss he'd mourned for eight long years.

So unnecessarily.

A shout went up from the fielding team. He was out.

Out of *this* game, at least. But defending his wicket from the lieutenant's determined efforts to demolish it, and glorying in every run he notched up while the fielders scurried in various directions to retrieve his hits, had helped him work off much of his frustration. Now that he'd calmed down, now that he'd turned to begin walking back to the house, he was relishing the prospect of starting up a whole new game.

He was going to win Lydia back, even though he'd made a false start with her this time round by treat-ing her as though she had no morals and by giving rein to the anger that had simmered steadily for eight long years.

His manner might have given her pause for thought, but she hadn't been able to help herself—she'd said so! And that wonderful encounter last night—it had meant a great deal to her. She'd let that slip, too.

Striding back to the orangery, he felt as though he'd been reborn. The fog of bitterness had dissipated, he re-alised. The bitterness that had hung over him ever since he'd started to think Lydia had played him for a fool.

He *had* been a fool. But he'd managed to make a total mull of things without any help from Lydia. He'd been ignorant and selfish, and unaware of the value of anything. But what good would it do to dwell on what he'd lost, when he'd lost her? Hadn't he also gained much? The shock of hearing she'd married Colonel Morgan had given him a well-needed kick in the breeches. It had jolted him out of the complacency that would have made him just as bad a landlord as his father had been. He'd become a better man because of it. Besides, the past was gone. It was the future that mattered.

And the future looked bright.

The attraction between them was so fierce that it had broken through not only his own resentment, but also whatever barriers she'd felt she had to erect. In the night, when they were alone, she'd turned from the demure woman who was sitting primly chalking up the scores for a children's game, to a siren who'd flung her clothes aside, pinned him to the bed and had three orgasms in rapid succession.

It was a start. A foundation upon which he could build. Good God, he'd turned his practically bankrupt estates around, so there was no reason why applying the same energy and resources upon Lydia would not result in success.

He had a lot of ground to make up with her, what with one thing and another, but the point was, he had a second chance. Lydia was a widow now. They were already lovers. Even if it had only been sexual frustration that had driven her to his bed—and he didn't really think that was all there was to it—if he played his cards right she would never want to take another lover.

But there had to be more to their relationship than

just sex, even if it was spectacular sex. He was going to have to start courting her in earnest.

To start with, he was going to have to convince her that he had changed. The way he'd treated her the first time round, and the way he'd behaved at the outset of this affair was bound to make her think he would let her down.

He sauntered up to the refreshment table to take a much-needed glass of lemonade from Marigold, who complimented him on the number of runs he'd made.

So far, he hadn't bothered with the girl. He'd been too busy pursuing Lydia. But that would have to change. He was going to show Lydia that he could get on with her family, this family. Prove that he could fit in with them. Because they mattered to her.

And win their approval for his suit, while he was at it. Getting them on his side would be half the battle.

Lydia tried not to mind when he paused only to pick up his jacket, then made straight for the far end of the orangery and the tea table. They needed to be discreet. Of course they did.

And she might well have given her feelings away while she'd been watching him in bat. A curl of something positively primitive had sizzled inside her when he'd stripped off his jacket and rolled up his sleeves before taking the bat from Lieutenant Smollet. He'd stalked on to the lawn, swishing the bat as if he was striding on to a quarterdeck, preparing to repel boarders, rather than going to play a game invented to while away a sunny afternoon.

She hadn't been able to tear her eyes off him. She'd never seen him looking so very nearly…deadly. Such strong, dark emotion was something she found hard to equate with Lord Rothersthorpe. He had always been so easy-going in his youth.

Yet he defended his wicket against Lieutenant Tancred as though his very life depended on it. For the duration of their contest it was a no-holds-barred, edge-of-the seat spectacle of male pride and aggression.

She almost wondered whether she ought to get the children off the pitch and out of their way. But Robert was cheering Lord Rothersthorpe's hits and applauding his rapidly accumulating tally of runs. He was still in bat when Lieutenant Tancred finished his stint as bowler and handed the ball to Lord Beagle's sister.

She gave a quick frown. She really ought to try not to think of the girl by the name people had started to use after Cissy had made a mangled attempt to pronounce her brother's title. Especially since she was rather heavy jowled.

She got to her feet when Mr Bentley caught him out, half-wondering if the aggression would spill over in that direction.

But no. He'd sauntered back to the orangery with a cocky grin on his face, acknowledging the applause of his team with an airy salute.

Whatever mood had darkened his expression before he'd gone into bat had passed. Typical, she huffed, sitting back down and adding his score to the tally.

Nothing too deep, nothing too serious. A mood might darken his brow for a few minutes, but his propensity for making light of everything soon reasserted itself.

Just listen to him! Laughing and chatting to Marigold as she indulged in a fit of hero-worship over his prowess as a batsman, then turning his charm upon

Rose, casting the poor tongue-tied lieutenant completely in the shade by making her giggle and blush.

She ought not to have seen the blush. She ought to be keeping a close watch on the game. But she just could not help darting him thirsty little looks whenever there was a lull.

She couldn't blame the girls for hanging on his every word, she supposed, for he was putting on exactly the kind of display that had so enchanted her when she'd been their age. She had no right to feel searing pangs of jealousy, or wish she could be part of that golden circle glimmering around him.

It put her right back to her disastrous Season. Always on the outside looking in. Never part of the fashionable, self-assured, successful set.

Only now she felt old and tired as well as unappealing. And very aware of the fact that she was a widow. Not worth the effort of flattering and charming.

Especially not after he'd discovered how very easily he could get her into bed.

The fielding team had got the hang of things by now and got the remaining batsmen out in rapid succession.

She managed to smile and say all the right things as the players came inside, but half her attention was always with Lord Rothersthorpe. During the interval he moved from one group to another, congratulating Lord Beagle's sister for the throw that had resulted in his dismissal so gallantly that it brought a flush to her cheeks. Commiserating with Cynthia Lutterworth, with apparent sincerity, for her failure to hit a ball even once. Which was kind of him, going some way to ameliorate the damage her brother had done with the heavy scowl he'd bestowed on her when she'd returned to the orangery after all too brief an interval in bat.

This was how she remembered him. This was Rothersthorpe at his charming best. Dispelling gloom and spreading cheer.

And creating such a fierce yearning for him that she had never known quite how to handle it.

But it wasn't long before Michael ran out of patience with the adults, who would have stayed chatting and sipping lemonade in the orangery all afternoon if not reminded of the importance of finishing the match.

Which meant that Lord Rothersthorpe's team all went out to field.

He stripped off his jacket and rolled up his sleeves again. And her stomach swooped at the sight of the hair-roughened forearms.

He smiled at her as he went past. A slumberous, knowing sort of smile that made her heart beat faster. How did a man do that? Smile with perfect innocence, yet convey a message that was totally indecent, at the same time?

Still, it made up for the way he'd avoided her during the break. More than made up for it. Even though he'd not spoken one word to her since coming in from his turn in bat, he'd managed to convey his meaning.

He still wanted her.

She'd half-wondered if he'd had enough of her. After talking about her marriage, he'd seemed to withdraw from her. And he'd definitely been angry when he'd gone outside.

She sagged back into her chair, almost faint with relief. He wasn't angry any more. Whatever had provoked his mood had passed. If she had said something to annoy him he was over it now. And he was eager to continue with their liaison. She would never be able to explain to another living soul how she'd managed to deduce all that from one smile, but his meaning had been perfectly clear to her.

She recognised the look that came to a man's eyes when he wanted to take a woman to bed. Her husband had employed it, usually with an interrogative lift of one eyebrow when he wanted to know if he could visit her room at night. And of course, she'd always allowed him to have his way. It had been her duty.

It most certainly wouldn't be her duty to sneak up to Lord Rothersthorpe's room as soon as it was safe, but, oh, he only had to give her that slow smile and she could hardly wait to be alone with him. Preferably naked.

She watched him take to the field, all athletic grace, stripped down to his shirt sleeves. And what a treat for the eyes he was. He had the best body of any man on the field. He could afford better tailoring than either of the naval officers, he had broader shoulders than Mr Bentley and slimmer hips than Lord Abergele. All in all, he was utter masculine perfection. And having seen him unclothed, she could vouch for that in a court of law.

What woman wouldn't derive pleasure from feasting her eyes on him, on a sunny afternoon?

When he'd been batting, the energy and strength he'd applied to the game had made her breathless. The way his thighs had bunched when he'd been running had made her recall the delicious feel of those hair-roughened muscles on her own softer flesh.

But now the way his shirt moulded to his lean frame when he leapt to catch a ball gave a teasing hint at the perfect musculature she'd seen gilded by moonlight. And when he bent over to ruffle Slipper's ears, she recalled how those long, supple fingers had skilfully roused her to orgasm. He brought her pleasure just from watching him move, did her lover.

There, she'd formed the word in her own mind. Her lover.

She reached for her fan, plying it briskly in a vain attempt to cool down. He'd come here looking for an uncomplicated affair with a sophisticated woman. That was all. So she would have to play along and hope she could make him believe that was exactly what she was.

'What is the score?'

She jumped, startled to find that Rose had wandered away from the refreshment table and was peering down at the slate which lay in her lap. To her consternation, she saw that she'd smudged the chalk markings.

Rose grinned at her.

'Mama Lyddy,' she said, shaking her head in mock reproof. 'You do not seem to be concentrating this afternoon.'

'It is so hot,' she said lamely. 'And...'

'You simply cannot take your eyes off Lord Rotherthorpe, can you?'

'I...that is...' Her cheeks glowed with guilt and shame.

'I knew I was right to invite him along,' said Rose with satisfaction. 'You used to look so wistfully after him in town, whenever you thought he would not notice. And now he is here, you practically devour him with your eyes.'

'I do no such thing. I—' Did she? He'd accused her of more or less the same thing, before he'd thrown his insulting proposition at her.

And if she really had *devoured him with her eyes,* no wonder he'd thought she was casting out lures.

Rose was shaking her head again. 'You do. And I am glad. I want you to find someone. You deserve to find someone. And you may be surprised to know that, for once, Robert is in perfect agreement with me.'

'E-even if it is true, what you said,' she replied, stunned to hear that Robert was in league with Rose's matchmaking attempts, 'that does not mean that Lord Rothersthorpe returns my feelings.'

'Oh, I think he does,' said Rose. 'Else why would he spend so much time whispering into your ear and making you blush? If he didn't return your feelings, he would stay well away from you,' she ended on a note of triumph.

'He flirts with everyone,' she retorted. 'He was making you giggle and blush just now.'

'Ah, but he took great care to ensure that everyone else could hear what he said to make me laugh. When he flirts with you, he gets you on your own first. And he murmurs right into your ear.'

'Rose,' she replied slowly, choosing her words with great care, 'men of his class may admire a widow, may even flirt with her a little, but that sort of thing does not generally result in a proposal. Not a *marriage* proposal, at any rate.'

Rose looked crestfallen. 'Are you sure?'

When Lydia nodded, she sighed, then pursed her lips in a way that so nearly matched Marigold's pout it was hard not to smile.

'Well, I'm sorry I invited him down then, if all he is going to do is behave like a rake.'

'I am not,' she said with quiet certainty. She was actually relieved to have left her girlish hopes and dreams about him behind. That did not make her old and jaded. No, she preferred to think of herself as more mature and wiser.

When she'd been a girl, it was true she had needed

someone strong and dependable to rescue both her and Cissy. But she didn't need rescuing now. She'd gained her security. So it didn't matter that he wasn't the type of man upon whom a woman could depend. He pleased her eyes and thrilled her senses, and had made her poor frozen heart come roaring back to vibrant life.

This affair was turning out to be a bit like a firework. Spectacular while it lasted.

And when it was over…well, she would just have to get over him. She'd adapted to life without him before, and at least this time round she'd have a handful of utterly glorious memories to warm herself at in the long lonely nights that would follow.

'At my age, it is most flattering, I can tell you, to be on the receiving end of that kind of attention from a man of Lord Rothersthorpe's undeniable attraction. Yes, indeed,' she said, fanning herself and gazing at him across the width of the lawn.

Rose, to her great relief, broke into a giggle. 'Mama Lyddy, I declare, I never thought you would have such a wicked side.'

If only you knew, thought Lydia, *if only you knew.*

Chapter Twelve

'I still cannot believe you declared Slipper the winner,' grumbled Lieutenant Tancred at the dinner table that night.

Lydia blushed. It had been impossible to say who had actually scored the most runs, since she'd wiped the tally off the slate with her sleeve whilst daydreaming about Lord Rothersthorpe's prowess as a lover. And granting Slipper the victory had at least made everyone laugh.

'The game was only intended to amuse and entertain the children,' put in Robert in her defence.

'And some of you took it far too seriously,' said Rose, darting the lieutenant a teasing look.

Lieutenant Tancred shrugged. 'I play to win,' he said without trace of apology.

'And you—what have you to say for yourself, my lord?' said Rose to Lord Rothersthorpe with an engaging smile. 'What excuse do you have for looking so put out when Mama Lyddy did not grant your team the victory?'

Lydia's blush grew hotter. What was Rose doing? Well, she knew what she was doing. In spite of warning her that Lord Rothersthorpe didn't have any serious interest in her, she just would not relinquish her belief she could promote a match between them.

'I, too, believe that if a game is worth playing, a man should give it his all,' he said.

What fustian! Lord Rothersthorpe never took anything seriously. At least…well, she supposed she *had* noticed an intensity to him this afternoon she'd never seen before. And by all accounts, he *had* worked hard to halt, and then reverse, his family's declining fortunes.

And he himself had declared he had changed over the years. He'd told her that he was no longer content to *play the clown*.

Not that it made any difference to her. His very public hunt for a wife might be a signal to the world that he was now a man who did intend to take certain responsibilities seriously. But all she was to him was some kind of…temporary aberration. A last-ditch attempt, perhaps, to recapture something of his carefree youth before settling down.

Settling down with some innocent, young, wealthy girl of good breeding.

'Never seen a dog to match Slipper, though,' put in Mr Bentley. 'Remarkable animal. Seems to understand every word one says.'

'A great pity the same cannot be said for some of the people on the field,' remarked Lutterworth sourly.

'Words are strange things, though, are they not?' Lord Rothersthorpe was the first to break the rather shocked silence that followed his remark, a remark that had made Cynthia shrink into herself. 'For someone who writes poetry, for instance, finding just the right one requires a level of concentration that sometimes takes precedence over other things. Would you not agree, Miss Lutterworth?'

'You write poetry, Miss Lutterworth?' Lieutenant Smollet briefly tore his eyes away from Rose, to give the cringing, red-faced girl his attention.

'Y-yes,' she replied, darting Lord Rothersthorpe a look brimming with gratitude. 'And sometimes…well, like this afternoon. The grounds are so lovely and the way the shadows from the trees dappled the lawn, and the sound of the water just lapping on the edges of hearing…well, it all created such a tumult of images…and I wanted to find just the right phrases to capture the moment…'

'There is no need to make any excuses,' put in Robert, gently. 'It was just a game. But being able to write poetry is a gift.'

'If you can call, it poetry,' Lydia thought she heard George mutter. Cynthia must have heard him too, for after her brief foray into dinner-table conversation, she went right back into her shell. Throughout the rest of the meal she hardly said a word, apart from pleases and thank-yous as the dishes were passed round.

Though she did dart Lord Rothersthorpe soulful glances from time to time.

He'd done it again. Captured another poor girl's heart with his careless kindness. Had he any idea that he left a trail of hopelessly smitten females in his wake? Even Lord Beagle's sister was under his spell. Though she barely deigned to be polite to the naval officers, and positively turned her nose up at Mr Bentley, she…she *simpered* whenever he drew her into conversation.

And she was turning into a jealous cat. She lowered her eyes to her plate and concentrated on rearranging her features into a mask of calm serenity.

Though she supposed it would not matter all that much if people did see her cast Lord Rothersthorpe languourous looks. It was only what every other single female round this table was doing tonight. As long as nobody guessed they had become lovers, that was all that mattered. She did not want even the slightest whiff of scandal to spoil Rose's first grown-up house party.

She should be grateful nobody would be able to detect how intimate they'd been from the way *he* was acting.

Oh, stop it! She had to get this jealousy under control. Discretion was an *admirable* quality in a secret lover. It would be different if he truly was her suitor, as Rose so naïvely hoped. Then she might have a right to feel aggrieved.

But as things stood, he was behaving perfectly.

Yes, he was. Throwing dust in everyone's eyes, by spreading his charm indiscriminately, rather than attempting to corner her at every opportunity, the way he'd done the first day.

She just had to get through dinner, then put Michael to bed, then spend an hour or so in the music room amongst Rose's guests, then speak to both her stepdaughters, and then all she would have to do was wait until the house quietened down and she could go to him and they would be together in a way he would not be, could not be, with any other female sitting round this table…

She sighed and reached for her wine glass. It was going to be a very long evening.

But at last she was walking along the corridor to the bachelor guest rooms.

It would be different tonight, she promised herself.

She would not be nervous. Nor would she give way to the desperation that had her tearing off her nightgown and leaping on him.

Not that he'd seemed to mind, she reflected, a smile of feminine satisfaction playing round her lips.

But anyway, she'd crossed an immense hurdle last night, in taking a lover outside of wedlock.

Now she was…well, she was a sophisticated woman. A woman who made choices. *She* was not hastening to his room to try to recapture some youthful dream. This was about who she was now. What she wanted now.

And what she wanted was exactly what she had. A lover. A secret lover.

She slipped silently into his room, shut the door and leaned back against it for support. In spite of telling herself she wasn't nervous, her knees had not got the message. Besides, seeing Lord Rothersthorpe sitting up in bed, waiting for her, covered only with a sheet…oh, but now he wasn't even covered with a sheet. He'd tossed it aside and was stalking across the room to claim her, naked and proud and…totally magnificent, she sighed.

'You are not going to have it all your own way tonight,' he growled, sweeping her into his arms.

'I…I'm not?'

'No.' He bent his head and kissed her with such passion she could almost believe he'd been waiting for this moment with as much anticipation as she had.

Not that she needed to believe that. No.

Anyway, she'd already decided she wasn't going to appear so desperate tonight.

Although, in a way, she was. She'd been aroused all day, just watching him, remembering the feel of him, the strength of him. And then getting herself ready for bed had stoked the flames even higher. Undressing, washing herself, dabbing perfume on to significant pulse points, then sliding her silken nightgown over her head and letting it glide over her body, had been an erotically charged experience, rather than her usual relaxing exercise, designed to aid a restful night's sleep.

And having him clasp her in his arms, and kiss her so passionately, while naked and flagrantly aroused, was almost too much.

In spite of having decided she was not going to appear too eager tonight, two seconds into the kiss tremors of excitement were rippling through her entire body. Her legs were so shaky it was only his arm round her waist holding her up, yet her hips were grinding against him rhythmically.

And then, as though sensing just what she needed, he reached down between their two straining bodies and cupped her mound.

She bit down on her lower lip as sensation roared through her, sweeping aside all her resolutions. And when he bent to take one nipple between his teeth, she let her head fall back against the door, uttering a low moan.

She whimpered when he removed his hand from where she most wanted it. But she would not beg.

Anyway, he was still kissing her. On her throat. The valley between her breasts. Her shoulders. And it was all delicious. If only he would...

She gasped as he dropped to his knees and pressed his mouth there—right there. His lips were warm. His breath was hot.

And she was melting, flowing, exploding into searing pleasure.

Somehow he was on his feet and catching her as she sagged into a kind of blissful stupor.

He carried her over to the bed and laid her gently down, coming down next to her. He held her and stroked her hair, and kissed her brow while she floated softly back down to earth.

'This nightgown is very fetching,' he murmured, after a while. 'But it is time to dispense with it.'

She couldn't agree more.

But instead of stripping her of the gown with the determined haste she'd employed the night before, he kissed and stroked it away, so that her disrobing became an integral part of their lovemaking, rather than a prelude to the main event.

'Ah, Lydia,' he breathed when she was finally naked. 'You are so beautiful. I have been longing for this moment all day.'

She had not wanted him to talk the night before. But tonight, she decided, she didn't mind quite so much, so long as he said things like this.

'I have been longing for it, too,' she felt bold enough to admit. Then she rolled to her side, pressing her naked self against the full length of him. She ran her hand along his side as she pressed her breasts against his hair-roughened torso, creating a delightful friction.

But when she would have explored his body more intimately, he seized her hand.

'Not yet,' he said. 'It will be over too quickly if you do that.'

'We don't really have much time,' she protested, hooking one leg over his hip and flexing her pelvis against his.

'We have all night,' he countered.

'No,' she said firmly. 'I dare not be absent from my room too long. If Cissy has a nightmare, she will come looking for me. And there will be uproar if she doesn't find me.'

He frowned and was on the point of making an objection she was convinced would lead to an argument. So she stopped his mouth with a kiss that soon became so heated they almost rolled off the edge of the bed.

'That was a close call,' he chuckled. 'And a reminder.'

'A reminder?'

'Yes. Did I not promise you that I would spend the day thinking of ways to make the narrowness of this bed a positive pleasure, rather than a hindrance?'

He got out of bed, swung her up into his arms, then sat down on the edge and planted both feet firmly on the floor.

'I like a challenge,' he growled, arranging her limbs so that she straddled him.

'You are certainly rising to this one,' she said with a gasp as he tugged her so close his erection was nudging at her entrance.

'I would never have dreamed you capable of such naughty talk,' he said with a grin.

'I…I…'

His grin widened.

'Don't spoil it by making excuses, Lydia love. I like you like this.'

She liked him like this, too. Taking charge. Demonstrating his strength by picking her up and moving her about. Being inventive. And playful. She didn't think many men would have chosen to look upon a single bed as a challenge and rise to it with laughter on their lips.

'Now,' he growled, 'let me show you what *I'm* capable of.'

He tugged her closer still, penetrating her tantalisingly slowly.

When she would have flung her arms round his neck and snuggled close, he shook his head.

'Lean back,' he commanded her. 'I want to watch you.'

After only a moment's doubt, she decided she would not mind watching him watching her. And she got her reward almost at once. For the expression on his face was almost reverent as she leaned back against the steel band of his arm at her back. With his free hand, he cupped and stroked one breast, then ducked his head so that he could suckle at the other.

While she rode him.

It was an incredible sensation, having him hold and support her, feeling the strength of his arm keeping her in place, yet having the freedom of movement to bring herself pleasure as she wanted it.

It was sweeter than the night before—perhaps because it was less hurried.

Or perhaps it was because she'd accepted there could be no future for them. She had *now* and she wanted to savour each second, rather than grab at it in case it all faded away with the morning light.

So she didn't rush towards completion. She just revelled in the delicious sensations coursing through her body. Trusting that he could keep her here, on this pleasurable plateau, for as long as she wanted to stay there. She'd already learned he had remarkable self-control.

But eventually he reached down between them and deliberately began to take her higher.

'Come again for me, love,' he said. 'Let me see your face transformed with the ecstasy I can bring you.'

And the pace picked up. He rocked harder against her as he drove her to a peak of pleasure.

'Look into my eyes,' he said.

And when she did, the connection between them became more intense, more sensual, more heated. She could *see* his own need rising alongside her own, as well as hearing her gasps of pleasure wringing echoing groans from him.

And when she felt the first flutters of her climax, she saw the flare of triumph in his eyes before he began to thrust harder, and deeper, and faster.

'Lydia,' he groaned, his whole body shuddering at the exact same moment she exploded with pleasure. 'My love, my only…'

She collapsed forwards on to his chest, her heart pounding, her mind reeling. *His love? His only?* Where had that come from?

She supposed a man might shout anything at the moment of his release. She must not be deceived into thinking it was anything more by the way he was clasping her, nuzzling her earlobe, then pressing fevered kisses against her neck.

He was a generous lover. He'd paid her compliments the night before, when it was over.

But he didn't really mean it. Or perhaps he did, right at this moment. She would give him that much credit. But a week hence, when he'd left here, he could well be in another woman's bed, saying the same words, with the same fervour.

She wouldn't hold that against him. It was all part of his charm—wanting to make his current lover feel special.

She'd always, *always* know that as long as she didn't take him too seriously, he wouldn't be able to hurt her.

Having reached that conclusion, she hugged him round the waist. It would be safe enough to demonstrate her delight in him, physically, as long as she didn't say anything that would reveal the depth of her feelings.

He hugged her back, then lifted her and rearranged her so that they were both lying side by side on the narrow bed.

As soon as she got her breath back, she sat up.

'I wish you could stay with me all night,' he grumbled.

'Don't be silly,' she said with a smile as she went to retrieve her nightgown. She wasn't going to prolong the aftermath and risk getting into some squabble like they'd done the night before because of one careless comment that a truly sophisticated, experienced woman would have taken in her stride.

He raised himself up on to one elbow to watch her getting dressed.

'Would you not like to lie in my arms all night and wake up next to me? Share breakfast? A morning ride?'

He swung his legs out of bed and crossed the room to where her dressing gown lay. Picking it up, he helped her into it, then swept his arms round her waist and nuzzled her neck.

'I know you have to go now, I don't mean to annoy you by asking the impossible. But think about it, Lydia. Would it not be perfect if we could share more than just these stolen moments in the night time?'

Think about it, Lydia. Oh, how she wished he hadn't said those words. The very same words that had nearly caused her to make a grave error, once before.

'What is the point of even talking about it?' The moment ruined, she tried to pull out of his embrace.

But he held her even tighter.

'Because I want you, Lydia. More than I've ever wanted any other woman.'

He breathed the words into her neck. So passionately, so fervently, she could feel her resistance starting to melt.

'When we make love,' he continued, 'it feels…I have not the words to explain it. It is like coming home. Or being in heaven. Or finding a long-lost dream that turned out to be far better in reality than I could ever have imagined.'

She closed her eyes and swallowed back the response that sprang to her lips. She simply mustn't read more into his words than he meant. In all probability, he was trying to tell her that he was enjoying their liaison so much he would like it to continue beyond the duration of this house party.

'I'm flattered,' she therefore said, a little shakily. And she was. But could her heart really stand much more of him? The longer they were lovers, the harder it would be for her when they parted. She was already having to remind herself, over and over again, not to let him matter more than he should.

She turned in his arms and pushed away from him.

'I am glad you find me more than satisfactory in bed.' She smiled at him with all the nonchalance she could muster. 'But I would prefer you did not try to make more of this than it is. We both know that you will be leaving soon, while I will be staying here. There can be no waking up in each other's arms.' She reached up and stroked his cheek sadly. 'Please do not make me dream of it. That is not kind.'

He snatched her hand when she would have withdrawn it.

'Why should we not dream of being together, Lydia? Why could you not come with me when I leave?'

'D-don't be foolish,' she said sharply. 'I cannot just run off with my lover. Think of what the scandal would do to Rose and Marigold. And then there's Michael. Do you really think so highly of yourself that you imagine I would abandon my own son?'

'No. I would never ask you to abandon your son. You would bring him with you, of course.'

'What?' She backed away, horrified by what he seemed to be suggesting.

'He's a fine little chap,' he said, making a grab for both her hands this time. 'I would be only too glad to be a father to him.'

She kept right on retreating, slapping his hands away each time he tried to catch her.

'I would raise him as if he were my own son. In fact, I could not help thinking, today while we all played together, that he could have been mine if only I hadn't made such a mull of my proposal all those years ago...'

She stopped short, shock robbing her of breath.

'What are you saying?'

'Why, I'm asking you to marry me, of course!' He must have seen the shock on her face because he shook his head ruefully.

'I'm making a mull of it again, aren't I?'

'M-marriage? You are saying you want to m-marry me?'

Her back fetched up against the door.

'Yes, Lydia. More than anything. I don't think I've ever stopped wanting it, deep down. Even when I'd convinced myself I hated you for choosing Colonel Morgan, instead of me.'

She scrabbled for the latch and got the door open.

'I can see I've shocked you,' he said as she backed out into the corridor. 'Maybe I shouldn't have spoken so soon. But dammit, these past eight years have been sheer hell. I don't know how I'd survive if I let you slip through my fingers a second time. Not after tasting what our life together could be like...'

She didn't say a word. Just like last time, she gave him no answer.

Just like last time, he had to discern her response from her actions. And the fact that she was scurrying away from him, head bowed, should have been answer enough.

He pounded his fist against the doorframe. He'd suspected he might have trouble convincing her he was in earnest, but he'd never dreamed she might run from him, looking so...horrified.

Still, he wasn't beaten yet. The house party wouldn't break up for two more days. And even after that...a hard smile curved his lips. Well, he was no green boy, to slink away in the face of a little hostility. This time he was man enough to stand up and fight for what he wanted.

For her.

Lydia's stomach clenched into a ball of ice.

He'd wanted to marry her back then? He'd meant every word of that proposal?

Oh, dear God... She stumbled over an uneven floorboard. Or perhaps her knees had almost given way. She wasn't sure. She put her hand out to steady herself and carried on her way.

She hadn't believed him. She'd wanted to. For one whole night, she'd allowed herself to believe and had imagined what it would be like if for once, just once in her life, her wishes could all come true.

But in the cold light of day, hope had withered and died. When he hadn't come to visit she'd taken it as confirmation that she'd been clutching at straws. Day after day, he hadn't been there, but the colonel had.

And she'd recalled all the times he'd expressed his abhorrence at the prospect of marriage.

And weighed them against the one *hint* that *maybe* it wouldn't be such a dreadful chore if she was his wife against the colonel's rock-solid insistence that she was exactly what he wanted. No matter how she'd blushed and stammered, or how frail she'd been during the first few days. No, none of the things that had managed to repulse every other man who had shown an interest had dimmed the Colonel's enthusiasm for the match one bit.

Until in the end, she'd been convinced he was the only man who would ever actually put a ring on her finger.

But now Nicholas was saying *he'd* wanted to marry her back then, too.

A little sob escaped her throat. Pressing her hand to her mouth, she positively ran the last few yards to her bedroom door.

It had been the hardest thing she'd ever had to do—to stifle her revulsion at the prospect of having to allow a man of that age access to her body whenever the fancy took him.

And now he was telling her she needn't have done!

She stood on the threshold of her room, panting. If only he'd…convinced her that he was in earnest she needn't have gone through…any of this! With a strangled cry, she advanced on the bed, seized the filmy hangings and tore them from their moorings.

Then dropped to her knees on the mound of shredded silk and buried her face in her hands.

And remembered Cissy. What would have happened to Cissy if she'd put her own preferences first? She'd only just learned that Nicholas wouldn't have wanted to remove her from that asylum at all. Oh, yes, *she* might have had a young, handsome husband, and a roof over her head, but at what cost to her poor sister?

And then there was Michael. If she hadn't married Colonel Morgan, Michael would never have been born. Pain lanced through her so sharply she could hardly draw breath for a moment.

She could never wish for any kind of life in which Michael did not exist.

She lifted her head and gazed blindly round the room.

She'd made the right decision back then. Even though she hadn't really been aware there was a choice. Her life since then might not have been easy, but the alternative… She shook her head.

And as for marrying him now…oh, what was the use of even thinking about it? She could never marry a man who regarded Cissy as a burden. A distasteful burden.

It was no use, she told herself furiously, giving him credit for being willing to take on another man's son and vowing to be a father to him. Michael was the kind of boy it was easy to love—sunny tempered, intelligent and full of pluck.

She got unsteadily to her feet and flung herself face down on the bed.

Why had he had to go and ruin everything? She'd just about reconciled herself to the advantages of having a lover, had cast aside a lifetime's values to indulge herself in a pleasurable, *temporary* liaison with a man she couldn't help wanting even though she knew she could never really rely on him. She'd just wanted to enjoy what little they could have, for the short time they could have it. But she couldn't sleep with him ever again. Or it might encourage him to think she would accept his proposal.

And she couldn't. She didn't want to marry him! She didn't. She didn't.

And having come to that decision, she buried her face in the pillows and burst into tears.

Chapter Thirteen

The first person she saw at breakfast the next morning was Lord Rothersthorpe looking annoyingly cheerful as he tucked into a plate of sirloin.

She stalked across to the sideboard and picked up a plate. How could he look so disgustingly healthy, when she'd hardly had a wink of sleep after she'd left his room, reviewing a continuous parade of what-might-have beens, followed by a whole troop of if-onlys?

'Are you quite well, Mama Lyddy?' Robert was looking at her with concern. She knew her face was pale and her eyes red from weeping on and off all night. But she hadn't thought anyone would notice. Rose was the centre of attention, or ought to be.

'This house party isn't getting too much for you, is it?'

'I do wish you would stop treating me as though I am made of porcelain,' she snapped, slamming the lid down on the dish of scrambled eggs.

'I used to cater for more guests than this, at a moment's notice, for your father and he never questioned my capability. And they were more often than not plant collectors, trudging mud through the house.'

A silence fell as she shut her eyes and drew a deep breath. When she opened them, her family were gaping at her in astonishment, the guests looking determinedly anywhere else.

'I beg your pardon,' she said. 'I admit, I am feeling a little out of sorts this morning.'

'It is not like you to get so cross,' said Rose. 'I think Robert might be in the right of it—' she darted him a saucy look '—just this once. You might benefit from spending the morning quietly in your room.'

Lord Rothersthorpe looked up from his plate and gave her a searching frown.

Lydia gritted her teeth. If he made some clever remark about looking as though she wasn't sleeping very well, she might well launch the plate of eggs at his head. From the moment he'd come back into her life, she hadn't known whether she was on her head or her heels.

Why couldn't he have put off searching for a wife another year? Or three? Then their paths might never have crossed. She might not have abandoned every principle she'd ever lived by and taken him as a lover.

She might never have known the pain of having her first love held up to the light and discovered it was a threadbare thing, unable to withstand the scrutiny.

She could have...

'I think perhaps you are right, Rose,' she said, bowing her head. She could not face him this morning. She wasn't ready to tell him that, though it was going to break her heart all over again, she simply couldn't marry him. And she didn't have the energy to duck and weave and hide from confrontation the way she'd done yesterday. 'I think I shall return to my room.'

At least she would be safe from him there. He wouldn't dare trespass, not in broad daylight, surely?

* * *

She had had some breakfast sent up on a tray, which she ate at the writing desk under one of her windows. She didn't feel all that hungry, but she probably would later on. And it would be selfish to send for food when the staff were already stretched to the limit by the demands of this house party.

She had actually felt a little better after eating a slice of toast and downing an entire pot of tea, and begun to take notice of what was going on around her. From her window, she had observed Robert leading a party of the men out on horseback. Some time later, those who had not brought mounts began to drift into the garden in ones and twos.

Then she heard a soft knock on her door.

If he'd had the temerity to come here and pester her, she would…well, she didn't know what she would do. She strode across the room and yanked the door open, only to come face to face with three anxious faces. Michael, Cissy and Marigold had taken a detour on their way to the schoolroom to find out how she was.

'Have you got the headache, Lyddy?' Cissy's eyes were swimming with the start of tears.

Which she'd put there. That scene at the breakfast table must have worried her so much that both Michael and Marigold had brought her here to reassure her, for they were each of them holding one of her hands.

'No, I haven't got the headache,' she said, stepping forwards and sweeping her into a hug. She would never, ever, let Cissy suspect she wasn't completely happy to care for her. Any more than she could contemplate abandoning her. It just wasn't possible.

'You shouted at Robber.'

'Well, sometimes he deserves it,' she said, although

it had not been Robert who'd put her in a bad mood at all. Lord Rothersthorpe had been the one to make her feel as though she was being stretched out on a rack.

But how could she ever have chosen the man she'd once loved with her whole heart over her sister? Cissy *needed* her. He only wanted her.

And it wasn't Cissy's fault she was the way she was. If anyone was at fault in all this, it was Lord Rothersthorpe, for not being the man she needed him to be.

Yes, that was better. If she couldn't completely stifle her resentment, she could at least aim it squarely in his direction, which wouldn't hurt him anyway, because once she explained about Cissy, he would show a clean pair of heels. Just as he would have done if she'd garnered the courage to put his so-called proposal to the test last time.

'Come in, you three,' she said, standing aside and waving her hand to her room.

With a whoop, Michael charged in and bounced on to the bed, swiftly followed by Cissy.

'Where have your curtains gone, Lyddy?'

Lydia gave the puzzled Cissy the same reply she'd already had to give Betsy earlier. 'I decided it was time for a change.'

Marigold meanwhile had slouched across the room and flung herself down on the window seat.

'It isn't fair.' She sighed, gazing longingly out of the window. 'Everyone else is outside enjoying themselves, while we are condemned to another morning with Mr Thomsett and his abominable grammar books.'

'We cannot always have what we want,' Lydia began, then realised that she was doing more or less exactly what her stepdaughter was doing—pouting and sulking because life wasn't giving her exactly what she wanted.

'Oh, dear, how strict I sound.' If she wasn't careful, she was going to end up turning into a bitter and twisted old harridan, making everyone else's lives a misery because she was nursing her own disappointment.

It was the height of irony that at that very moment, she caught a glimpse of Lord Rothersthorpe strolling along one of the gravelled walks with Rose on his arm. Rose was looking particularly fetching as she laughed up into his face. She could not see the expression on his, as he was bending his head to speak right into her ear, but she could imagine it. It would be the one he'd shown yesterday, when he'd been flirting with everyone left, right and centre. When she'd thought that if he was really her suitor, she would have reason to feel aggrieved.

Lord, what an awful husband he would make, if she were stupid enough to accept his proposal! In fact, she really couldn't understand why she was in such a dither about turning him down. Or why she should still yearn for him, even when she knew how bad he would be for her.

For she did. She craved him, just like an addict craved opium.

Her only hope would be to break the habit now, before it got its claws into her too deeply. She must never go to his room again, that was certain. Not even to tell him it was over. For she didn't think she was strong enough to resist the temptation to make love with him, one last time. Which would make her hate herself.

She whirled back to the room, a determined smile fixed to her lips.

'Do you know, I think it would do us all good to take a nice brisk walk.' Sitting around doing nothing was only making things worse. She needed some distraction from thinking about him and how bad he was for her, how he tempted her to be utterly selfish and how he was making her hate him, and herself, more with every passing day.

Marigold brightened up at once. Michael cheered and Cissy, sensing something good was about to happen, smiled too.

Slipper's ears had pricked up at the word *walk*. He trotted over to the door and lifted a paw to scratch at it.

'Marigold,' said Lydia, 'would you mind going up to the schoolroom and telling Mr Thomsett he may have a holiday today? I should think he will be only too glad to get back to the vicarage and resume studying for his own examinations.'

Marigold did not need telling twice. For once, she shot off on her errand without uttering a single complaint.

It took a matter of only minutes to get them all ready for their impromptu outing. Soon they were strolling across the lawn, but not in the same direction she'd seen Rose and Lord Rothersthorpe take. The last thing she wanted was to come across them and have him suspect she was pursuing him, or checking up on what he was doing with Rose.

Instead, they skirted the formal Persian Pools, heading for the woodland terraces that led right down to the river. It was deliciously cool in the shade of the trees. In spite of saying she did not have a headache, she had no intention of wandering about in the kind of glaring light that would induce one.

They saw that some of Rose's guests were already seeking shade in the pavilion. Lord Beagle's sister was sitting on one of the stone benches gently fanning herself, while Lieutenant Tancred and the Prince of Pickles stood by the balustrade, making desultory attempts to engage her in conversation.

Both Marigold and Cissy pulled faces, letting her know the last thing they wanted was to stop and exchange pleasantries, even though, given half a chance, Lieutenant Tancred would have joined them.

So, as quietly as they could, given there was a dog and a six-year-old boy in their party, they ducked into the woodland and out of sight.

Because they'd veered from the main path and wanted to avoid being spotted by anyone in the temple, they ended up squeezing round the back of the grotto—a small cave Colonel Morgan had constructed to conceal some of the machinery required to keep the fountains and waterfalls going.

Suddenly Lydia heard the sound of Rose, giggling, with a slight echo that told her she was inside the grotto.

Then a man's voice, though the words were indistinct.

And then silence.

No footfall, no sign they had just peeped in and were emerging.

'Is that Rose?' Marigold came to a halt next to her and only then did she realise she'd frozen in place. 'Whatever can she be doing in the grotto? It's so cold and damp in there.'

And dark. And utterly private.

There was a low murmur. The distinctive sound of a man…groaning with pleasure.

Marigold gasped, then clapped her hands over her mouth to stifle her own giggles.

'Oh! She's with a man. Which of them do you think it is?'

She knew exactly who it was. She'd seen her walk this way with Lord Rothersthorpe not an hour since.

'What's the matter, Mama?' Michael had come panting back up the hill to see why she'd stopped. 'You've gone white.'

It was hardly surprising. She was chilled to the marrow. There was a numbness about her lips and a roaring sound in her ears.

She took a deep breath. She was not going to faint. Because then she wouldn't be able to give that lying, cheating…toad a piece of her mind!

How could he speak of marrying her, then turn round and start making love to her stepdaughter?

Her wealthy, beautiful, *young* stepdaughter.

She'd known, deep down, that he hadn't meant what he'd said last night. That he would move on to some other woman without a qualm when she turned him down. But she hadn't thought it would be this soon. Or this woman.

Or before she'd had a chance to inform him she wouldn't marry him if he was the last man on earth.

'Uh-oh,' said Marigold, looking down at her hands. And she discovered she'd clenched her fists. 'Rose is in big trouble, isn't she?'

'Marigold,' she said grimly. 'I would like you to take charge of Michael and Cissy, if you please.'

'Yes, of course,' she said, backing away hastily. Lydia watched until she and Michael reached the steps that led back to the main path, where Cissy was waiting, before making her way round to the edge of the temple pool and the concealed entrance to the grotto.

'Why is Lyddy so cross?' she heard Cissy asking.

'Because Rose is being very naughty,' she heard

Marigold answer. 'She's kissing some man in the grotto...'

Their voices trailed away as Lydia ducked under the overhanging boulders, pushing aside the trailing ferns and creepers as she went.

They knew she would want them to make themselves scarce. She had made a point of never scolding any of them in public. It was bad enough for them when the Colonel lost his temper and gave them a savage dressing down no matter who was watching. So she'd done her reprimanding in private and with as much calm as she could muster.

Calm. She had to calm down. She couldn't go storming into the grotto and tear rose from Lord Rothersthorpe's arms.

And it wasn't because it would be undignified to give in to jealous rage.

It wasn't. If she actually saw them, Rose would be effectively compromised. She would *have* to marry Lord Rothersthorpe.

She took a step back, biting down on her lower lip.

In some ways it would be better to pretend she didn't know this was happening. Once she confronted them, Rose would have no option but to marry Lord Rothersthorpe.

And she couldn't bear to see Rose married to him. Because...

Well, what kind of scoundrel seduced the stepmother into bed, made her think he had marriage in mind, only to callously lure an innocent young girl into the grotto so that he could toy with her as well?

Then something else occurred to her. He'd talked about how the last eight years had been hell because she'd chosen Colonel Morgan. Was this his idea of getting revenge? Proposing to her again, only to cast her aside this time, the way he'd thought she'd cast him aside, to marry a wealthy, more appealing person?

He was…he was… Something inside her shattered. It felt as though all her emotions were draining out through the gaping wound in her chest, leaving her dead on her feet.

He was the worst sort of villain.

But the way he'd used and deceived her didn't matter. She had to do what she could to extricate Rose from his schemes. She couldn't permit Rose to be condemned to a lifetime of misery with a man who was…

Oh, God…

She couldn't stand here all day. She *had* to put a stop to whatever was going on in the grotto right now, before it went too far. The giggles had stopped. All she could hear now was heavy breathing and the rustling of fabric. The sound of two people straining together…

'Rose!'

There was a shocked gasp, a muttered imprecation. Then stillness.

'Rose, I know you're in there,' she said, stepping up to the entrance, so they would be able to see her silhouette. 'And that you're not alone. Come out, the pair of you, right this minute!'

There was some more muttering, some scuffling, then Rose emerged, red-faced and with her hair and clothing somewhat disordered.

And right behind her…

'Lieutenant Smollet!'

Grim-faced, he was buttoning up his jacket.

Rose stretched out her hands as though imploring her to understand. 'Mama Lyddy, please, do not be cross—'

Lieutenant Smollet cut her off. 'Of course she is angry, Rose.'

But she wasn't angry any more. She was relieved.

'And shocked.'

Yes, she was definitely shocked. She had not though Lieutenant Smollet was the kind of man to sneak around like this. But then what had she really learned about him? About any of Rose's suitors? She had been so wrapped up in Lord Rothersthorpe she had taken hardly any notice of any of them.

A wave of guilt almost swamped her. What kind of chaperon was she? She ought to have been watching her stepdaughter like a hawk, not allowing her to run amok in grottoes with any Tom, Dick or Harry.

Or Rothersthorpe.

'I have behaved disgracefully,' said the Lieutenant. 'I should never have—' He broke off, running his fingers through his already rather disordered blond locks. 'Of course, I will go and speak to Morgan at once and explain myself. I hope both you and he will forgive me when I tell you that Rose has agreed to be my wife.'

Rose whirled towards him, her face lighting up.

In unmistakable triumph.

'I will come with you,' she said eagerly, 'and help you explain.'

'Oh, no, you don't,' said Lydia, suddenly starting to question just exactly who had been seducing whom just now. Between the Lieutenant's hangdog expression, and Rose's triumphant one, she was beginning to draw her own conclusions.

'You will stay here, Rose,' she said firmly. 'You have a deal of explaining to do.'

'Please, do not be angry with her, Mrs Morgan,' interposed the Lieutenant. 'The fault is entirely mine.'

'That I very much doubt,' muttered Lydia. Rose was looking at her with her most wide-eyed expression of innocence. It was an expression with which Lydia was all too familiar: the one Rose always adopted when she'd been caught in some enterprise red-handed.

When he turned and marched off, Rose made as though to follow him. Lydia's hand shot out and stayed her.

'For goodness' sake, let him have the illusion of thinking that at least he is in control of the proposal,' she said in an urgent undertone, since he was not yet out of earshot. 'Though I am quite sure he will soon discover he will never be in control of any aspect of his life again.'

'Why, Mama Lyddy,' said Rose, her eyes widening even further. 'Whatever can you mean?'

'Do not take me for a fool. He could not have found his way into the grotto unless you showed it to him, which you must have done quite deliberately and not for any good reason. Unless you expect me to believe you and he were discussing the irrigation methods your father put in place and both felt a burning desire to inspect the pumping mechanism.'

She coloured at the unfortunate connotations her choice of words had conjured up, but at least it caused Rose to drop her air of injured innocence. Her eyes dancing with mischief, she broke into a peal of giggles.

'How could you, Rose? Have you no shame?'

Rose grasped her hand. 'I had to do something. Or he might have left without ever plucking up the courage to propose.'

It was only when Rose took her hand that she realised it was trembling. In fact, she was trembling all over. Her mistaken belief it had been Rothersthorpe in

there with Rose, her anguish, her fury, her subsequent
relief, all of it had taken a heavy toll after her sleepless
night. 'Rose,' she said faintly, 'I thought I had taught
you better than that. Whatever were you thinking?'

'But I love him,' Rose cried.

And she hadn't the heart to give Rose any sort of
lecture. She had no right to take the moral high ground,
when she'd only just learned how badly astray a woman
could go, for the sake of being with the man she loved.

Loved.

Lydia turned away, stumbled to one of the stone
benches encircling the grotto pool and sat down heavily.

She loved Lord Rothersthorpe.

In spite of everything. Even when she'd thought him
the worst sort of villain, her heart was deaf to reason,
and logic, and even common sense.

'Why him?'

'Because I have never met anyone like him,' said
Rose, thinking she had been questioning her about
Lieutenant Smollet.

When Lydia hadn't even been aware she had spoken out loud.

'What about Lieutenant Tancred?' After all, she'd always had trouble telling the pair of naval officers apart.
And she had to say something that sounded sensible,
instead of sitting there reeling with shock.

'Oh, him,' said Rose dismissively, sinking to the
grass at her feet. 'Cissy had the measure of him the
very first night, when she spoke of him polishing up
his buttons.'

At Lydia's puzzled frown, she went on, 'Have you
never noticed the way he cannot resist inspecting his
reflection every time he passes a mirror? Everything
he does is for effect. Although I am grateful to him,

in a way. If not for him, and the rivalry that exists between him and my Toby, they would never have both started courting me.'

'And you do not object to being the…the object of some sort of competition between them?'

'Well, it only started out that way. And back in town, I knew very well they were more interested in besting each other than actually winning me, but since we've come down here…' She sighed. 'It is the way he looks at me. Well, you know…' she sent her a conspiratorial smile '…exactly the same way Lord Rothersthorpe looks at you.'

When Lydia made a dismissive gesture with her hand, Rose plunged on. 'Oh, I know you say he doesn't truly love you, but I just know Toby really does care for me. Only…he's got this ridiculous notion into his head that he isn't worthy of me. And he's been growing more and more tormented at the thought I would favour someone else. Well, don't you see? I had to put him out of his misery!'

Rose knelt up and clasped Lydia's hands, her whole face alight.

'He is so good with Cissy. And Cissy adores him. She couldn't trust him if he wasn't a good man. And he is such a brave man, too. I have heard about life on board ship and what it is like for a naval officer during a sea battle.'

'From him?'

'Oh, no. He is far too modest to puff himself up the way Lieutenant Tancred does, trying to impress me. Only when *he* goes on about how heroic *he* is, and Toby just glares at him, I know the truth, you see.'

'You do?'

Rose nodded her head vigorously.

'He is a far better man than any of the others.'

'Really?'

'Well, surely you must have noticed the way Lord Beagle looks at the house, at the furnishings and the choice of dishes on the table, and compels his sister to swallow their dislike of my lineage, in the hopes of getting his hands on some of my wealth. And Mr Lutterworth is perfectly beastly to Cynthia whenever he gets the chance.'

'And…what has poor Mr Bentley done to disqualify himself?'

She wrinkled her nose. 'Oh, pooh. Mr Bentley is just a boy. I do not dislike him. But he is not really a man. Not like Toby. There is not another man like him in the world,' she sighed.

'I hate to mention this, but…well, are you sure he is as wonderful as all that? After all, he did not appear to have noticed that you…press-ganged him into marriage.'

'Well, that is because we planned it so carefully. Lord Rothersthorpe and I.'

'Lord Rothersthorpe?'

'Yes. I do like him, Mama Lyddy. He is so clever and so understanding. I knew he would be just the person to help me give Toby a nudge.'

'You did?'

'Oh, yes. It was the way he kept looking at Toby yesterday, during the match, then shooting me sympathetic glances. Toby was glowering at everyone else when they flirted with me, but couldn't think of a word to say himself. He gets so tongue-tied at times and it infuriates him.'

'Was it…was it Lord Rothersthorpe's idea…?' She gestured towards the grotto.

'Oh, please! Give me some credit for being able to think up my own stratagems.'

Lydia squeezed her eyes shut for a few moments. How could Rose be proud of having deliberately entrapped the poor man?

But then it hit her. 'I saw you leaving the house with Lord Rothersthorpe, earlier. *This* was what you were discussing?'

'Yes. I could tell he is just the sort for engaging in such a lark. Nothing stuffy about him, is there?'

'No,' she said faintly.

'And as soon as we saw the others in the pavilion of Suraya, he seemed to know instinctively what to do. He made straight for Cynthia, poor dear, who was drooping over one of the railings gazing into the water and being totally ignored by the others, and told her he was dying to hear more about her poetry. Begged my forgiveness for cutting our walk short, but was sure one of the other gentlemen would be only too pleased to escort me and then practically pushed me into Toby's arms...'

Lydia couldn't help wondering why he'd been so helpful. If he genuinely wanted to help Rose get married, there had to be a reason.

'And then I just sort of steered Toby down to this pool. When we got here, I told him about the grotto and what a magical place it was, and darted inside. He followed, of course. Only I forgot to warn him to duck his head as he came in,' she admitted, with the first sign of contrition since being discovered.

And Lydia went cold inside as it all became clear. If Lord Rothersthorpe could help Rose marry the one man that Cissy plainly adored, too, he would think she would be content to let her go and live with them. He'd seen how attached Rose was to Cissy, how dependant

Cissy was on her, and had hoped that if he could get her out of the way, she would have no reason for turning down his proposal.

'And because it suddenly gets so dark just there, he bumped his head, quite hard. But that,' said Rose, brightening up, 'gave me just the excuse I needed to get close to him. I made him sit on the bench, got out my handkerchief and dipped it in the spring at the back, then leaned in very close as I dabbed at his forehead.'

'So, in effect, you kidnapped him, bashed him over the head and then stole a kiss under the pretext of tending to his hurts?'

Rose hung her head. 'I suppose if you put it like that, it does sound rather bad. But I didn't make him do anything he didn't want to do, I promise. In fact, it was not I who kissed him first,' she said with a smile of triumph. 'I only had to sigh and look into his eyes, and he…well, he finally forgot all about his stupid principles and the fact that he's only a half-pay officer from an ordinary family.'

'Yes, but why, Rose? Why go to such lengths to wrest a proposal from him?'

'Because we were running out of time. Everyone will be leaving in a day or so and I might never have seen him again. He could get orders from the Admiralty any day. Once he sets sail, I might not see him for years and years, and he would forget all about me!'

Lydia only just managed to refrain from pointing out that if he really could forget all about her, just because he was at sea, he couldn't really be all that much in love with her.

She didn't want Rose to face that kind of disillusion, just yet.

No more than she wanted her to have to spend years pining for the man she thought she loved.

Not that Rose was the type of girl to pine. She was very much like her father in that respect. When they saw something they wanted, they just reached out and grabbed it.

Rose had decided she couldn't live without her lieutenant, so she'd done what she had to, to ensure he couldn't get away from her.

She looked at her stepdaughter with something approaching awe. At her age, she would never have dared compromise a man.

Although she'd thought about it. She'd had umpteen opportunities, had she been brazen enough to take them. But she'd drawn the line at trapping Lord Rothersthorpe into a marriage she'd been convinced he hadn't wanted. There had been too much at stake.

Although…now he was saying he might not have minded after all.

Though he would surely have changed his mind again once he'd found out about Cissy.

She pressed her hand to her forehead as her mind started veering to and fro all over again.

'What is it? Oh, Mama Lyddy, please do not say you are disappointed in me?'

'No, no, of course not…well, perhaps I was at first. But now, to be truthful, mostly I…I envy you your confidence. Though I am a little worried, too. I do hope you will not regret this day's work.'

'Well, if I do, you may be sure I will not blame Toby. It was all my doing. I know that. I will be a good wife to him, no matter what.' She nodded her head decisively.

Lydia felt another wave of pity for the hapless lieutenant, envisioning Rose managing him ruthlessly if he did not take her in hand right from the start.

'May we go back to the house now?'

Rose was hardly able to sit still in her eagerness to find out how Lieutenant Smollet's interview with her brother had gone.

'No. We must give them time to talk it out. If he's even back from his ride yet. And knowing you,' she put in quickly, when Rose made as though to object, 'if they are still closeted in Robert's study, I won't be able to stop you listening at the keyhole.'

Rose grinned at her, acknowledging the hit.

'And I feel I ought to prevent him from discovering what a ruthless baggage you are, just until after the wedding ceremony.'

'Oh, then you are on my side after all? You mean to help me?'

'Yes. I can see that you have your heart set on him. And I understand,' she said slowly, 'that when you fall in love, it grows very hard to hang on to your principles, especially when you fear losing the object of your affection.'

What was more, she'd learned that when you did hang on to your principles, and did the right thing, it felt as though you were going to die from grief. She'd only survived those first months of marriage because the Colonel had been so patient with her and so good with Cissy.

Rose had no reason to suffer, the way she'd done.

So why should she?

Chapter Fourteen

Somewhat to Lydia's surprise, Robert drew her aside, just before dinner, to talk about Rose and Lieutenant Smollet.

'I gave him my blessing,' he said with a frown. 'And then I wondered whether I'd done the right thing.'

Naturally, he hadn't asked her opinion *before* he'd made his decision, but then he was Rose's legal guardian, after all. It was for him to say whom she could marry.

'Given the scene he described in the grotto, I felt I had no choice,' he said. 'And if Rose didn't want to marry him, she would have come flying into my study after him, vowing nothing could make her do so.'

He looked at her searchingly.

'Have you not worked out yet that she arranged the whole thing?'

Robert looked relieved. 'I had wondered…it all sounded so far-fetched. And I'd always thought of him as a man of integrity, not the sort to lure innocent girls into secluded nooks and make free with them.'

'Secluded nooks that nobody outside our family, and the gardeners, know anything about,' she said drily.

'Good lord,' he said. 'Do you think he really is the man for her, if she's managed to run rings round him like this?'

'Well, according to Rose, he loves her to distraction. And the only thing that stopped him from proposing off his own bat was the fear that she was too good for him.'

Robert let out a shocked bark of laughter. 'Quite. And although I am a little concerned by the haste with which she has fixed upon him, he does appear to genuinely care for her, rather than her wealth. Which was what we wanted for her in a husband, was it not?

'And...' Robert tugged at his earlobe thoughtfully '...he is used to maintaining discipline on board ship. Perhaps he will be able to keep Rose in line.'

The trouble with that train of thought was that Lieutenant Smollet probably wouldn't give tuppence for any of the crew he had to discipline, whereas he loved Rose.

But Rose had sworn she would be a good wife to him. She wouldn't want to forfeit his good opinion. *That* would be what kept her in check.

Robert announced the engagement during dinner, though anyone with eyes in their head could already tell that something momentous had happened to Lieutenant Smollet. And it wasn't just the enormous bump on his forehead and the bruise which was already discolouring his skin that brought the dazed look to his eyes. It was Rose. He kept looking at her as if he couldn't believe his luck.

None of his rivals could possibly harbour any ill feeling towards a man who was so clearly besotted. Lieutenant Tancred even went so far as to shake his hand and declare that the best man had won.

The atmosphere in the music room after dinner was

positively festive. Which probably had something to do with the copious amounts of champagne with which Robert had toasted his sister and her intended.

Lord Rothersthorpe took advantage of the rather noisy gathering to lean and speak right into her ear.

'Will Robert be making another announcement before this house party breaks up?'

She tensed. She could not give him her answer here. A simple no would not suffice and the explanation he deserved was one she could not risk anyone else overhearing. But she'd already decided it was far too dangerous to go to his room again, even though it would give them the necessary privacy.

'Come and meet me in the pavilion,' she said, 'when things begin to quieten down. You will find some lanterns by the garden door of the orangery, which will help to light your way.'

When the ladies began to yawn, Lydia sent Rothersthorpe a look before quitting the music room. He gave an imperceptible nod. It wouldn't be very difficult for him to break away from the other men when they started making for the billiard room.

She arrived at the pavilion first, and sat down on the bench where earlier that day Lord Abergele's sister had granted audience to Lieutenant Tancred and the Prince of Pickles. She set her lantern on the ground at her feet. The pavilion could not be seen from the house, but the light might attract attention if anyone decided to take a stroll through the grounds which looked almost magical on moonlit nights like this. And were bound to tempt the newly engaged couple outside, for one last kiss... if Rose had her way.

She had not long to muse on exactly what her enter-

prising stepdaughter might not attempt to entice her besotted Toby into doing, when she saw a lantern bobbing
along the path. Seconds later, she made out the unmistakable form of Lord Rothersthorpe, striding along so
swiftly he was making his lantern swing wildly.

He would not be in such a hurry to get here if he had
any idea what she was about to say.

Nerves sent her leaping to her feet as he mounted the
steps. She couldn't quite see his face, but, immediately
after putting his own lantern on the floor just inside the
doorway, he strode across and caught her in his arms.

Before she could manage to utter a protest, he was
kissing her passionately.

And, oh, but she couldn't deny herself the sheer bliss
of being in his arms, this one last time. Flinging her
arms round his neck, she kissed him back with all the
desperation that had been building in her ever since he'd
asked her to do the impossible: to marry him.

He was the one to draw back and break the kiss to
ask a question.

'What do you have in mind for me tonight?'

He looked eager, excited, just as though he expected
her to have some sexual treat for him. As though she'd
asked him out here to indulge in a little alfresco lovemaking.

Why should she be surprised? It was what he'd suggested the very first day he'd arrived, when he'd treated
her as though she was the kind of woman he'd only consider good enough to be his mistress.

Though if he now assumed she was sexually ad-
venturous, she supposed she should take some share
of the blame. She'd been utterly brazen with him in
the bedroom.

No wonder he was so sure of her that he couldn't

imagine her saying anything but 'yes' to his proposal, even though he'd treated her shabbily.

Something about the look on her face as she thought about where to start explaining why she couldn't marry him must have got through to him, because his smile faded.

'What is it? Tell me. Is it Rose?'

He plunged on without giving her a chance to say a word.

'The timing of her betrothal is a bit awkward for us, is that what you think? I know you wouldn't want to do anything to spoil her wedding plans, or take the attention away from her. We can put off making an announcement until after she's married, if you like. I have already waited eight years for you. A few more weeks won't kill me. Though my preference would be to marry as soon as we can. By special licence, if needs be, so that nothing need part us again. Now that we've found each other...'

'No. You don't understand. It isn't Rose. It's...it's Cissy.'

'Lydia.' He shook his head. 'I can see that you have grown to love those girls dearly. But...'

'Please, let me explain...'

'It doesn't matter what it is,' he said fervently, 'we can work it out. Marrying me won't mean you have to cut any of them out of your life completely. And I have already told you, I would be only too pleased if Michael could come to look upon me as a father.'

She gave him a hard look.

'Yes, but what would you arrange for Cissy?'

'Arrange? What do you mean? She will either stay here, or go and live with Rose, won't she? That's the beauty of her picking Smollet. The man is so solid he makes her feel safe. She adores him. She'll be fine, Lydia, you'll see.'

'No, she won't, she—'

'Lydia, listen to me.' He took her by the shoulders, his expression becoming serious.

'Your first husband should never have let her grow so dependent on you that you cannot have any life of your own. I suppose I should have foreseen it would upset you to think of hurting that poor creature, but I am thinking of you. Of us. She is not your responsibility. She is Robert's.'

'That's just where you're wrong,' she said, pulling out of his grasp. 'She is not Robert's responsibility at all. She is mine. She is *my* sister. Mine. I brought her into this family when I married Colonel Morgan.'

A frown flickered across his face. 'But I thought…'

'Yes.' She flung up her chin and glared at him. 'I let you think it, so you would show your true colours. And you did. You said it would be better to palm her off into the so-called care of some professional person!'

'Only because I thought you were being used by the Morgans. I did not think it was fair of them to expect you to be a full-time nursemaid, on top of running their household and so forth. Had I known from the first she was your sister…'

'You might never have had anything to do with me at all,' she said vehemently. 'You might have feared that kind of weakness runs in the family and shunned me altogether.'

He glanced at her stomach.

'Yes, now you are worried about what I might be carrying in my womb, too, are you not?'

'No, I—'

'Well, you need not worry. For one thing, Cissy was

perfectly normal when she was born. And for another, the Colonel taught me how to take measures to prevent a further pregnancy after I bore him Michael. He did not want to take any risks with my health.'

'You took…precautions…to avoid having my child?'

'Yes. For I have no intention of bringing an illegitimate child into the world.'

He reeled back as though she had struck him.

'You…you have been using me,' he gasped. 'You thought I was good enough for a fling, but not to become the father of your child.'

Mounting anger turned him into another man, right before her eyes.

'You *never* had any intention of marrying me, did you? All these years, I've been right!'

The shadows cast by the lanterns on the floor made gave his face an almost demonic cast.

'It's all falling into place now. You were just as secretive when we first knew each other, weren't you? You could have told me all about your sister and how you needed to get married to provide her with a home—I take it that was the pressing reason you sought security?'

She nodded.

'But I could not have spoken to you about such things then.'

'You said you thought of me as a *friend*. Friends don't deliberately hide things from each other.'

'You are not being fair,' she protested. 'A single lady cannot really think of a single gentleman in that way…'

'You didn't trust me one bit. You never really opened your mind or your heart to me. Did you?' He seized her by the upper arms. 'Did you? You never gave me a chance. Not back then.'

'I could not! I—'

'Not then and not now, either. You knew I thought Cissy was Robert's sister. Instead of telling me the truth, you led me on a merry dance. Setting me tests I didn't even know I was failing. Inventing reasons not to trust me!'

'It wasn't like that...'

'Have you ever trusted anyone, Lydia? Ever given anyone the benefit of the doubt?'

He flung her from him and gave her a cold look.

'You have to do it all on your own, don't you? You won't share responsibility for Cissy with me, or anyone. We could have carried the burden together. I could have helped you. Instead you have deliberately shut me out of your life. Just like last time, you've written me off as useless without even giving me a chance to prove myself. I suppose I should consider myself lucky you at least deigned to give me any sort of answer this time. You didn't think it worth bothering with before. I had to find out I'd been rejected from your newly acquired stepson. I should have known how you really felt about me from the way you came into my room and helped yourself to my body that first night. No sharing. No giving. You just took what you wanted from me and then left.'

'No. I didn't! I mean, I didn't mean to...'

'Don't try to make me feel sorry for you by putting on that woebegone look,' he said with disgust. 'It won't work on me any more. You are responsible for your own actions, Lydia. You, and nobody else. You made your own choices. Nobody made you do any of it. Nobody made you marry your colonel. Knowing you as I do now,' he said with a look of utter contempt, 'I dare say you preferred the cold, business-like arrangement you had with him. An arrangement that allowed you to keep your heart intact. You will never risk it, will you? You…you share out tiny portions of yourself, but you keep most of it back. You are incapable of trusting, or sharing, or seeing the best in others. You always look for the worst and so you find it.'

He spun round and stalked away. But just as he reached the doorway, he turned back and sneered, 'I cannot believe that I allowed you to dupe me all over again. All day, I've been thinking about the future I thought I would have with you. I pictured you at my side, helping me care for my tenants, travelling up to the manufactories I will inherit one day and working out ways we can improve the lot of the workers. And you know, even though I believed Cissy was Robert's sister, I was already wondering if I would have to make a place for her in our home so that you would not be distressed at the prospect of abandoning her.'

He would have what? No. He could not mean that. He was just saying it to hurt her.

Once again, he must have read from her face what she was thinking, because he said, 'I would have done it for you, Lydia. But what do you care for all of that now? Why am I even telling you? You've already made up your mind.'

He bent down and picked up his lantern. Then he stood quite still for a moment, holding it high as he stared at her coldly.

'I cannot believe that, even now, I find you beautiful. Just look at you,' he sneered. 'You look so frail, still, as though you are made of clouds and moonlight, and the slightest breeze could waft you away. And in a way,' he laughed bitterly, 'that is true. You have no substance. No heart. You look like a lovely woman, but you are not. You are just an empty shell, Lydia. Perhaps I should be grateful I found out in time that you are incapable of really loving a man.'

With that, he turned away and stalked off.

Lydia sat down with a thud on the nearest bench, his condemnatory words ringing in her ears.

She was *not* incapable of love. She had loved *him* for years. Against her better judgement...

Which was a kind of lack of trust.

But then she hadn't ever dared believe he might change his mind about marriage, back then, and want to marry her. So she hadn't spoiled what precious few moments they shared with her problems. She hadn't thought he would be interested...

Lack of trust.

But how could she have trusted him? He'd made it so plain that he didn't want to get married.

Except...last night he'd said he *had* meant that proposal. That he'd wanted her *more than anything.* That he'd never stopped wanting her, even when he thought he hated her for *choosing Colonel Morgan, instead of me*...

She went cold inside.

He was right. She had misjudged him. First as a youth, and now as a man.

She'd blamed everyone around her for her predicament and borne it like some kind of martyr. But it had been her own fault. She hadn't trusted him.

Well, she hadn't trusted *anyone.* She had thought she had to rescue Cissy all on her own. She had been terrified of having to find a husband during her Season, because she hadn't believed the man existed who would take both her and her unfortunate sister. Her guardian had been so strident about what society thought about people like her. He said that everyone thought they should be locked away from normal people and the fact that her father hadn't done so was just another example of his poor judgement. Which in turn had led to the mountain of debt and chaos he'd left in his wake.

She'd believed him and that was what had made her Season so horrific. There were so many prettier, wealthier, more accomplished girls in town and such a dearth of eligible men, let alone the kind of men who exhibited the slightest symptom of being amenable to a plea for clemency for her poor unfortunate sister.

Nicholas had accused her of preferring the Colonel's bargain to real love back then…but she hadn't *known* she'd had a choice! At least, she hadn't dared to believe she had a choice. And the Colonel had been so concerned when he'd found her ill on his sofa, and so taken by what he termed her fragile beauty, that she'd felt the first flicker of hope that he might be the one…

The one who would give Cissy a home.

The only one she could believe might really do so.

And now…well, she hadn't dared let herself think of ever marrying again, because she hadn't thought there was a man alive who would agree to her terms.

And it wasn't that nobody measured up to the Colonel. The Colonel hadn't seen Cissy when he agreed to become responsible for her. Besides, her limitations were far more obvious now she was in her early twenties than they had been at fourteen. He'd been able to think of her as a child. And accept her as a child. She'd fitted into the schoolroom quite well at first. Only when his own daughters had overtaken her, while she'd stayed exactly the same, had he truly seen how deep the damage had gone. But by then Cissy had won him over with her total hero-worship.

But now Lord Rothersthorpe was saying that he would have been prepared to have Cissy living with them. For her sake.

She bent double for the pain that gripped her stomach. She'd let her guardian's attitude sink into her and take root like a poisonous weed. She'd believed all men would be like him, deep down.

But it hadn't been true. It had never been true.

The Colonel had never shown the slightest sign of revulsion for Cissy, nor had Robert. On the contrary—they'd both gone out of their way to protect her.

And all the men who'd come here courting Rose had been tolerant of her, to varying degrees. Lieutenant Smollet was strict with her, but not unkind—rather like the Colonel had been. He could calm her down when she grew boisterous. And she felt safe with him—that was why she adored him.

Mr Bentley made a fuss of her dog and treated her as though she was in truth the same age as Michael.

Lieutenant Tancred had made a game out of the way she mispronounced everyone's names, encouraging everyone to call Lord Abergele 'Lord Beagle' to his face.

And Lord Beagle himself had never appeared shocked or embarrassed by her. In fact, the pair of them had reached a kind of rapport when Cissy discovered he could always produce edible treats from his pockets between meals.

Even George Lutterworth treated her no worse than he did his own sister.

All week, she'd been denying the evidence of her own eyes and kept right on believing what her guardian had told her.

By doing so, she'd wrecked any chance for happiness with Lord Rothersthorpe. Twice over.

She had misjudged him.

And she had hurt him.

She hated what he'd forced her to see about herself. She'd thought she'd always striven to do the right thing, but she'd really just been a coward when it came to love. She'd always played it safe. Been too timid to take risks.

Was he right? Was she incapable of trusting anyone? Or really loving a man?

She'd certainly never had to risk her heart with her first husband. He hadn't been interested in it. Only in her body and her capabilities as a housekeeper.

It had been a *safe* arrangement. For her heart.

And ever since Lord Rothersthorpe had come back into her life she'd been talking herself out of loving him. Putting the worst possible interpretation on all his behaviour, to give herself an excuse for doing so. Looking for the worst, she'd found it. Even this afternoon, she'd assumed he'd been attempting to seduce Rose. And even when it had turned out not to be the case, she'd then condemned him for 'helping' her for nefarious reasons.

What was she to do? Could she let him leave tomorrow, thinking she was as cold and shallow as he'd just accused her of being?

Admittedly, she'd made a mess of things with him, but she'd had her reasons.

But…why should he listen to anything she had to say? Now?

Oh, what was the point of even attempting to make him listen? It was over.

She buried her face in her hands.

Why couldn't she be more like Rose, who'd been courageous enough to fight for what—no—who she wanted? She'd never fought for Lord Rothersthorpe.

She'd always talked herself out of hoping she had a chance with him. Even now, she was just…just sitting here, bemoaning her fate!

Could she dare take a leaf out of Rose's book?

Rather shakily, she got to her feet.

It probably wouldn't work, but then what did she have to lose? He couldn't think any less of her than he already did. And if she achieved nothing else, she could not let him leave thinking she hadn't *wanted* to marry him when she'd been younger. It was too cruel to let him carry on thinking she'd discounted him out of hand, or considered him unworthy of a reply.

Her hands trembled as she picked up the lantern. In spite of telling herself she couldn't make things worse by going to him and trying to explain, doubts and fears rose up in legions as she made her way across the lawn. The grotesque shadows cast by her bobbing lantern were like goblins leaping and whirling round her in a mocking dance. Silently taunting her with her many, many faults. She was cowardly. She didn't trust anyone. She was hollow. She was heartless.

And she was probably about to make a colossal fool of herself.

Even if he let her into his room, why would he listen to a word she had to say?

But she was done with sitting back, and thinking the worst, and only half living. How would she find out if there was any chance he might have it in him to forgive her, unless she went and asked?

To paraphrase what Rose had said that afternoon, there was only one Lord Rothersthorpe. She would never find another man like him. She would never feel about another man the way she felt about him. And if she didn't stand up and, just for once, fight for what they could have, she didn't deserve him.

When she reached his room she did not knock. In the mood he'd left her, he was unlikely to let her in. She just opened the door and walked in.

He was standing, shirtless, by his washstand, looking as though he'd just tipped the entire contents of the jug over his head. Water dripped from his hair, trickled down his chest and dripped from his chin into the basin over which he was leaning. He whirled round, glared at her, then reached for a towel and began mopping at his face and chest. 'What do you want?' He raked her body with an insolent appraisal. 'I am in no mood to satisfy your desires tonight. You should leave.'

He looked dangerously angry. But she stood her ground. She had learned something from Rose today. If you loved a man, then it was worth fighting for him.

'I am not going to leave,' she declared. 'Not until I have...apologised.'

'You think an apology will make it all better? I am not a child.' He flung the wet towel on to the wash stand and planted his hands on his hips.

'No. I do not think an apology will make it better.' She put her lantern on the floor. 'But at least an explanation might help you to understand.'

'I very much doubt it.' He took a pace towards her. 'Get out of here, Lydia,' he growled. 'Before I pick you up and throw you out.'

'If you do that, I will scream. And everyone will know that I have been in your room. There will be a scandal.'

'You think I care?' He advanced another step, a look of cold purpose on his face. 'You think a man who has just had his hopes and dreams shattered, had his heart broken for the second time by the same deceitful, treacherous, self-centred woman, will really care about dragging her name through the mud?'

'I never meant to break your heart.'

He placed his hands round her waist.

'I never even suspected you loved me.'

He lifted her off the floor and began to walk her towards the door.

If she didn't think of something, fast, she was going to be out on the corridor with the door bolted in her face.

Chapter Fifteen

'Nicholas, please, listen to me! It wasn't *all* my fault! You swore you didn't want to get married. *You* made me believe we could never be more than friends!'

He came to a standstill, his jaw working.

'And I couldn't tell you about Cissy. My guardian said he didn't want me bringing shame to the family by admitting we had someone like that in it. He made me promise never to speak about her to *any* man, until *after* I'd got a proposal from him.'

'You didn't tell me about her. And I proposed.'

'I would have told you if you'd given me a chance. But you ran from the room the minute the words left your lips. And you didn't come back, Nicholas. You didn't come back.'

His fingers were digging into her flesh. He wouldn't look at her, but at least he'd stopped his inexorable march to the door.

'I…I concede that it would have been difficult for you to break your word,' he grated, lowering her to the floor.

'Yes.'

He still looked grim, but at least he was listening.

'I dared not tell *anyone*. He had made me agree to so many restrictions in return for funding me for that Season. And I dared not break any of them, for fear of what he might do to Cissy. He'd already sent her away from home. He wouldn't tell me where he'd sent her. He said it was none of my business. That he was her guardian and it was for him to dictate her fate. Especially since he was obliged to pay for it.'

'The man sounds like a complete bastard,' he said grimly.

'N-no, to be fair, my father had left his affairs in rather a mess. And the poor man, coming into what he thought was going to be a handsome estate, found only debts and dependants when he came to take possession.'

'Still, he had no need to be so unkind…'

'I don't think he saw what he did as being unkind. He funded me out of his own pocket, you know. And I think he genuinely believed that Cissy would be better off being…*looked after by professionals.*'

He winced as she used the very same phrase he'd used himself. It was hard to deliver such a cruel reminder of the things he'd said, but she had to make her point.

'Maybe there are places where the warders are kind to the inmates, but that was not the case at the place she was in. They…' She shuddered. 'They…they tried to… cure her. She was upset and confused when she first got there, because our father had just died and then this stranger walked into our house and told us our home was no longer ours, but his.'

'Stranger?'

'Yes. We had never met him before. He was some cousin of my father's, I think. I can't really recall. That time was so upsetting. The estate was entailed and, because my brother had died, it passed to the nearest—'

'Male relative, yes, I understand all about entails.'

'And then he sent her away to a place where they just locked her in her room, saying she was being difficult and had to learn to behave. Then they did other things to her, too. Barbaric things. All in the name of treatment. So that by the time we found out where she was, Colonel Morgan and I, she was…an absolute mess. That scene, the day you arrived…well it was as nothing compared to the state she was in then.'

He hitched in an affronted breath.

'Do you seriously believe that I am the kind of man who would condemn any fellow human to such suffering…?'

'No! No—not deliberately. But I don't suppose my guardian knew what that place was really like either. He just took advice from some medical man he knew and packed her off there without even looking at it. He had a horror of that kind of infirmity and never set foot in the place, to my knowledge. But anyway, no matter what kind of place it is, or how pleasant the staff might be, I *promised* Cissy that I would never send her away from home again. And I never will. I couldn't be so cruel!'

'I see,' he said, his face bleak. 'And I would have seen much sooner, had you deigned to tell me.'

He stared at her grimly, folding his arms across his naked chest.

She wasn't reaching him.

'How could I Nicholas? You didn't c-come back,' she hiccuped, as a tear ran down her cheek. 'I…I suppose you are going to say I should have waited for you. That I should have believed that you would return…that I… should have trusted you. But…you are right about me.

I do find it hard to trust anyone. I compare myself to Rose at that age…' She shook her head, furiously swiping at the tears which were running down both cheeks now. 'She is so strong. So confident. But then she has always been sheltered, and loved…not like…m-me.'

'Oh, please…'

'No. No, you have to listen. My whole family started to fall apart when I was only ten. When my brother brought the measles home from school, we both, Cissy and I, took it from him. T-Thomas had never been all that strong and died quite quickly. Cissy seemed as if she was getting better, only to relapse into some sort of brain fever. Mama and Papa were distraught. Mama seemed to just…give up. She died not long after we buried Thomas. And then Papa buried himself…in a bottle. He knew that Cissy became almost deaf, but I don't think he ever grasped the full extent of her problems. But I took care of her from then on. So I knew…'

She paused, grappling for the right words. 'It was as though her mind stopped growing. As though her ability to grow up was destroyed, somehow, during that brain fever. B-but that was not all. I didn't see it before you challenged me tonight, but I think I was damaged, too. You see…' she gulped '…my parents were devastated by losing their son, the heir. And Papa was also upset by Cissy's hearing loss. But the fact that I made a full recovery didn't seem to mean anything. I was no consolation to anyone. And though I tried and tried to make things better for him, and for Cissy, nothing worked.

'I think I got so used to not mattering, that when I came to London for my Season, I just couldn't believe anyone could love me. Let alone a man like you…'

She caught at her lower lip and hung her head. She felt his arm go round her shoulders.

'Come,' he said, leading her to the bed and sitting her down on it. 'I can see that my attitude didn't help you to place your faith in me back then. You were going through a kind of hell, and I was…'

He took his arm away and clasped his hands between his knees.

'One by one, all the adults around you, all the people you should have been able to rely on, had all let you down.'

'Not deliberately.'

'But they did it just the same.'

He stared at the floorboards between his feet. 'You learned you had only yourself to rely on, even before that guardian came along and taught you that men could be selfish and cruel, as well as unreliable.'

She nodded.

'He saw straight away that Cissy was not behaving like a normal fourteen-year-old. It was more obvious to him than Papa, who…had not been looking at anything clearly for a long time.'

'No wonder,' he said grimly, 'you developed a will of iron. You hid it under a façade of meekness, but underneath that gentle demeanour you displayed during your Season, you were determined to find a husband. And not just any husband, but one you could persuade to let you have Cissy back. And all this time I thought… well, even after you told me, just yesterday, that you'd driven a hard bargain with your Colonel, I assumed it was because you were too delicate to go out and work for a living.'

She pulled herself up straight.

'People are always making that mistake about me and I hate it! Everyone thinks I am some fragile blos-

som that needs protecting, a silly chit with no brain in
my head…' She drew in a shuddering great breath, her
tears evaporating in the heat of anger.

'I could have tolerated having to work for a living,
if it had only been me. But if I had become a governess, or a teacher, how would I ever have had either the
freedom, or the means, to find her, rescue her and give
her a home? Perhaps I should have defied my guardian and broken my promise, and told you all about her.
Perhaps I should have listened to my heart and taken a
chance on being able to change your mind about marriage, but I loved you. How could I trap you into a relationship you claimed never to want and burden you
with a dependant that I'd been given to believe most
people would abhor? I couldn't do that to you. Besides,
I…I wasn't brave enough.'

Her strength ebbed as her fury dimmed, leaving
her tired, weak and shaky. 'I am not surprised, not really, that you have changed your mind about wanting
to marry me.' She got up. 'I understand. But I hope
that at least you can forgive me. That in future, when
you think of me, it won't be with too much bitterness.
I know I let you down, badly…'

She walked to the door, but paused with her hand
on the latch.

'Above all, though, I don't want you to go away believing that I was using you just for sexual gratification.
It wasn't like that between us. When we met up again,
you acted as though you hated me. But when you offered me an affair, I snatched at it, just as I snatched at
your offer of friendship when we were younger. Both
times I truly believed it was all I could ever have of
you. I thought when you married, it would be to a nice

young virgin. Not a widow with a son. Not to mention a sister who will hardly let her out of her sight.'

She leaned her forehead against the door, completely unable to turn round and look at him.

'I hope you find someone who will be all the things I cannot be for you. I truly do. I want you to be happy.'

He got to his feet, uttering an oath. 'Would you be happy with any other man?'

She froze and closed her eyes tight shut. She already knew she couldn't. Oh, she'd found a kind of contentment with Colonel Morgan, but it had taken time and a good deal of resolve.

She shook her head.

'Then, dammit,' he said, striding across the room, seizing her by her elbow and tugging her round to face him. 'How the devil can you expect me to be happy with any other woman?'

'B-but you said that I was hollow. Not a real woman at all. That...'

'Do you mean to fling every stupid word I've uttered, when I was so angry I hardly even knew what I was saying, back in my face? Lydia, I love you. You, you...you foolish woman.'

With that, he hauled her into his arms and crushed her to his chest.

'But how can you?' Her words came out somewhat muffled, but he heard her.

'Well, if it comes to that, how can you love me?' He leaned back and lifted her chin with one hand, so that he could see her face.

'When we first met I was a callow, selfish boy. When I began to suspect I was falling in love with you I deliberately distanced myself from you, several times, only to get drawn back like a moth to a flame.'

He cupped her cheek with one hand. 'I accused you of not trusting me, but was it any wonder? I've got to take my share of the blame. I'd already seen that it wasn't surprising that you found it hard to believe I really meant that proposal. I kept on blowing hot, then cold, didn't I? And in part, it was because I didn't dare start to think seriously about you. You see, I had the devil of a reputation, which wasn't just down to the way I behaved, but stemmed from what my family has been like. The number of times I heard chaperons warning their charges about my "bad blood".'

She had a sudden searing memory of him talking about unmarriageable people sticking together. She'd thought he'd meant her. But he included himself in that description. It wasn't so much that he hadn't wanted to marry, but that he thought no decent girl would have him.

'I was hardly the kind of man any girl would take seriously back then, let alone one who needed so much more from marriage than most.'

Oh—then her apparent refusal must have hurt him so very much more than she'd ever imagined.

'Nicholas…I never thought you were as bad as they said. You were so kind to me. So patient. Oh, if only I had waited for you to come back and told you about Cissy, you would have found a way to rescue her, w-wouldn't you? You are the man who turned his fortunes round, and made everyone who's ever said bad things about you eat their words… Oh, why didn't I just…hang on to hope?'

Tears poured down her cheeks as she saw what damage her lack of trust had done. What needless misery she'd wrought…

'Stop right there,' he said sternly. 'I won't have you

blaming yourself. The truth is that neither of us had the confidence to fight for our love. I realise now that I should have told Mrs Westerly, straight away, that I'd proposed. And that I intended to turn my life round and prove I was worth you taking a chance on. Only… I thought I'd stand a better chance of vanquishing the old dragon, and of impressing you, if I could produce a marriage licence and a stash of money from my pockets.'

'Oh, Nicholas. I thought you'd just…'

He folded her into his arms. 'Shh…I know what you must have thought. And I'm sorry I acted in such a way that led you to think so poorly of me.'

'But if only I'd trusted you more, and told you about Cissy, and explained how desperate I was to get married…even as just a friend, not expecting anything more, then…'

He shook his head. 'How could you have broken a promise? I would not love you so much if you were the kind of woman who could so easily go back on her word.'

His face swam as even more tears gathered in her eyes.

'You still love me? You really mean it?'

'I don't blame you for finding it hard to believe. I was horrid to you when we first met up again, wasn't I? I was still carrying a weight of bitterness.'

She hugged him hard. 'Rose guessed at once. She said you would not have been so bitter if I had not hurt you.'

'Well, if you did it was my own stupid fault for blowing hot and cold. For not speaking up when I had a chance to win you. I knew you loved me. I… God, that makes me sound such a coxcomb, doesn't it?'

'No. You are not a coxcomb. I did love you. I tried to hide it from you…'

He shook his head. 'You used to look at me with your heart in your eyes. It scared the hell out of me.'

'I'm sorry.'

'No. I am the one who should be sorry. For being—'

'Young? And a bit insecure underneath all that bravado? You were no worse than I was.'

'You put me to shame, Lydia. You are so ready to understand and forgive. Even when we met again, you never uttered one word of reproach for the way things turned out between us. When I spent all these years…'

'Hush,' she said. 'We were both too young to know any better.'

'Yes.' He leaned his forehead against hers for a moment. 'And do you know what? In a way…no, let me be completely honest. The pain of losing you set my whole life on a different course. I would have ended up just like my father if losing you hadn't caused me to stop in my tracks and take stock of my life.'

'Yes, Robert told me how much you have accomplished at Hemingford Priory. I'm proud of you.'

He set her back from him a little, so that he could look into her eyes.

'I shouldn't have been so angry with you when we first met. I had no right to speak so harshly to you, but I'd spent years blaming you for the empty, lonely years we spent apart. And then when I saw you, you didn't look at me the way you'd done when you were a girl. It was as if I was just…anyone, when I'd spent years missing you. I couldn't stand it. I had to provoke a reaction from you, even if it was anger. I could tolerate anything but your indifference.'

'I was not indifferent to you. But over the years I had learned to guard my expression more. I could not afford to be an open book. Not in this house. Too many people's happiness depended on me putting on a calm front.'

'My God,' he breathed, clasping her to his chest again. 'Was it hell, being married to that old man? I cannot bear to think of you having to allow him to—'

She reached up and put one finger over his mouth, silencing him.

'Then don't think about it. It is past. He was fair in his dealings with me. And after a while I grew fond of him, but I was never…that is, I never…' She blushed. 'The way I was with you, in that bed there.' She nodded in the direction of the narrow bed they'd shared twice now. 'I cannot imagine getting so…carried away with any other man. Truly, I rather shocked myself. I just wanted you so much. You, not just your body. Only, it was all I thought you would allow me to have. When I came to you, I still thought you despised me…'

He groaned and kissed her.

At last! She clung to him and kissed him back, with feverish relief.

'And now?' he murmured into her ear, when eventually he paused for breath. 'Now that you know I love you. Adore you. Want you to be my wife. Do you still want me?'

'More than ever.' She sighed.

'Then come,' he said, leading her back to the bed. 'Let us make love. Truly make love. For the first time.'

They sat side by side on the bed and just looked at each other. He had one arm round her shoulder. She had both of hers round his waist.

'The other times were tainted by bitterness,' he said, kissing her brow gently. 'And lack of trust,' he said, stroking her cheek. 'And fear of rejection. But I'd like,' he said, looking unusually sombre, 'to make this a new beginning. For us both.'

They undressed each other this time, pausing often to kiss and caress whatever they'd uncovered. Every time he touched her, it felt as though he was touching her soul, not just her body. He no longer acted as though he had anything to prove. And she'd lost that edge of desperation that had made her snatch at what little she thought she was going to get from the encounters.

When they were both completely naked, they stretched out side by side on the narrow bed, gazing into each other's eyes as their touches became more urgent. She hooked her leg over his hip when he entered her and he held her tight round the waist as they pressed together, rocking each other to an orgasm that came to them both at exactly the same moment. They truly had reached paradise together.

Until, suddenly, he jolted, jerked back and looked down into her face with a troubled expression.

'You are going to marry me, now, aren't you? I took it for granted when you said you loved me. But I've suddenly realised you haven't actually said yes.'

'Yes.' She sighed, sliding her arms up and round his neck. 'Yes,' she repeated solemnly, looking deep into his eyes. 'Yes,' she said, reaching up to kiss him. 'And I shall keep on saying yes, every day for the rest of my life, just to remind you, if you like.'

'Oh, I like,' he growled, pressing her back into the pillows with the ardour of his kiss. 'And I especially like the sound of having a wife who is going to say yes every day for the rest of my life. Though I wonder,' he said with a troubled frown, 'how on earth I am going to survive your insatiable demands.'

For a moment, she thought he was serious, until she caught the twinkle in his eye.

'Oh, you need not worry about that,' she said with false solemnity. 'After all, you know very well that if you are not up to it, I am quite capable of, um, helping myself.'

He flung back his head and barked with laughter, then, with a roguish smile, flipped on to his back, carrying her with him so that she draped over him in a tangle of sprawling limbs.

'I am feeling just a touch fatigued now, to tell you the truth,' he said, stretching his arms above his head and feigning a yawn. 'Perhaps you had better just remind me how adept you can be at helping yourself.'

She raised herself up on her hands and knees and, looking straight into his eyes, slowly took into her the part of him that demonstrated he was very far from being spent.

'I warn you,' she said with mock severity, 'that this could take a very, very long time.'

'Nooo…' he groaned, flexing his hips as she rotated hers.

'Yes,' she countered, bending down to kiss his lips. 'At least fifty years, I should think.'

He let go of the bedpost and placed his hands round her waist. 'In fifty years' time, I shall remind you of that,' he warned her.

'I will be here,' she vowed.

'Thank God.' He sighed, stroking his way up her sides, until he very gently cupped her breasts. 'For I could not survive another day like today. When I thought I'd lost you…'

'You have not lost me,' she said. 'You never did. I have always been yours. And I always will be.'

* * * * *

Author Note

As I began to research the treatment and possible care of those classified with mental problems, I was shocked to discover just how vulnerable they were to the most cruel forms of abuse. There was no public health system in place, as we know it today.

Although there were some public asylums for those with mental health issues, many wealthy people preferred to have their family members cared for privately. Private asylums were run according to the theories of whoever set them up and the proprietors did not have to have any medical experience at all. Instead, they might claim experience, handed down from parents. One of Jane Austen's brothers, George, was sent to live in a village several miles away from the rest of the family, in such an establishment. It is uncertain what his condition was, but he was referred to as 'poor George' in correspondence and steps were taken to make sure financial provision was made for his care because there was not '…the least hopes of his being able to assist himself'.

The one advantage of these private asylums was that

if satisfaction was not given, the inmates might well be removed. Public asylums, however, were generally populated by people who had no wealthy relatives to come rescue them.

The first public asylum intended for mental patients was the notorious Bethlehem Hospital in Moorfields. Because it was known to house the largest collection of mad people in the country, it became a favourite resort for sightseers. Provincials visiting London would put it on their itinerary, along with the lions in the Tower and Bartholomew Fair. It quickly became a byword of man's inhumanity to man.

By the Regency era there were public asylums in many cities. The one in York became the centre of a scandal which resulted in a Parliamentary committee being set up, in 1815, to investigate the running of such institutions. It all started with the death of one Hannah Mills, a Quaker. The members of her congregation had become concerned in the first place because she wasn't allowed to have any visitors once she became an inmate. After she died, they didn't let go, but very deliberately bought places on the board of trustees, so they could have the right to inspect the asylum and question the physician in charge, Dr Best. He and his staff—known as the Bestials—were suspected of profiteering, ill treatment, embezzlement and the covering up of up to 144 untimely deaths. Then the asylum burnt down, destroying what might have been vital evidence, as well as resulting in the deaths of several more patients.

After 1815 it was not so easy for corrupt physicians to feather their own nests at the expense of their patients.

Sources:

Madmen—A Social History of Madhouses, Mad Doctors and Lunatics, by Roy Porter.
Quacks—Fakers and Charlatans in Medicine, by Roy Porter.

THE COWBOY WHO CAUGHT HER EYE
Lauri Robinson

Pregnant and unmarried, Molly Thorson knows her livelihood is under threat. The last thing she needs is a distracting cowboy swaggering into view. *Especially* one who knows she has a secret and still looks at her with desire in his eyes. Carter Buchanan knows all about secrets. It's his job to know. And Molly sure has something to hide....

(Western)

HER HIGHLAND PROTECTOR
The Gilvrys of Dunross
Ann Lethbridge

Lady Jenna Aleyne must marry well if she is to claim her lands...only there is a complete lack of eligible suitors in the Highlands! But then Niall Gilvry is assigned to watch over Jenna, and there's no denying she finds this handsome Scot *most* distracting!

(Regency)

A LADY RISKS ALL
Ladies of Impropriety
Bronwyn Scott

It would be unwise to mistake me for an innocent debutante—for years I have graced the smoky gloom of many a billiards club and honed my skills at my father's side. But now he has a new protégé—Captain Greer Barrington. While my father would see me attract the attentions of an eligible lord, I, Mercedes Lockhart, have other ambitions...even if that means seducing the captain to earn back my father's favor!

(Victorian)

MISTRESS TO THE MARQUIS
Gentlemen of Disrepute
Margaret McPhee

They whisper her name in the ballroom's shadows—*the marquis's mistress!* It will take all of Alice Sweetly's renowned acting skills to play this part: *smile until it no longer hurts, until they believe your lie, until you believe. Pretend he means nothing.* But if the Marquis of Razeby thinks he can let his mistress go easily, he is so very wrong.

(Regency)

You can find more information on upcoming Harlequin® titles, free excerpts and more at www.Harlequin.com.

REQUEST YOUR
FREE BOOKS!

 HARLEQUIN® HISTORICAL:
Where love is timeless

2 FREE NOVELS PLUS 2 **FREE GIFTS!**

YES! Please send me 2 FREE Harlequin® Historical novels and my 2 FREE gifts (gifts are worth about $10). After receiving them, if I don't wish to receive any more books, I can return the shipping statement marked "cancel." If I don't cancel, I will receive 6 brand-new novels every month and be billed just $5.44 per book in the U.S. or $5.74 per book in Canada. That's a savings of at least 16% off the cover price! It's quite a bargain! Shipping and handling is just 50¢ per book in the U.S. and 75¢ per book in Canada.* I understand that accepting the 2 free books and gifts places me under no obligation to buy anything. I can always return a shipment and cancel at any time. Even if I never buy another book, the two free books and gifts are mine to keep forever.

246/349 HDN F4ZY

Name _____ (PLEASE PRINT)

Address _____ Apt. #

City _____ State/Prov. _____ Zip/Postal Code

Signature (if under 18, a parent or guardian must sign) _____

Mail to the **Harlequin® Reader Service:**
IN U.S.A.: P.O. Box 1867, Buffalo, NY 14240-1867
IN CANADA: P.O. Box 609, Fort Erie, Ontario L2A 5X3

Want to try two free books from another line?
Call 1-800-873-8635 or visit www.ReaderService.com.

* Terms and prices subject to change without notice. Prices do not include applicable taxes. Sales tax applicable in N.Y. Canadian residents will be charged applicable taxes. Offer not valid in Quebec. This offer is limited to one order per household. Not valid for current subscribers to Harlequin Historical books. All orders subject to credit approval. Credit or debit balances in a customer's account(s) may be offset by any other outstanding balance owed by or to the customer. Please allow 4 to 6 weeks for delivery. Offer available while quantities last.

Your Privacy—The Harlequin® Reader Service is committed to protecting your privacy. Our Privacy Policy is available online at www.ReaderService.com or upon request from the Harlequin Reader Service.

We make a portion of our mailing list available to reputable third parties that offer products we believe may interest you. If you prefer that we not exchange your name with third parties, or if you wish to clarify or modify your communication preferences, please visit us at www.ReaderService.com/consumerschoice or write to us at Harlequin Reader Service Preference Service, P.O. Box 9062, Buffalo, NY 14269. Include your complete name and address.

HHI3R

*Lauri Robinson's THE COWBOY WHO CAUGHT HER EYE
will make you fall in love with the Wild West and its cowboy
heroes all over again!*

"What's your dream, Molly?"

Having been stuck in the past for so long, she struggled to offer the truth. "I've so many regrets, wishing I could change things… I can't say I have a dream."

He ran a single finger down the side of her face. "That's not right, Molly. A person needs to have dreams."

Her insides atremble, she had to close her eyes for a moment. "Have you always had them?"

"Yes. I'd have never gotten here without dreaming of how better things could be."

Molly didn't want to be this hopeless, but the truth was very little could compare to what was in her future. "What if they can't?" she asked.

"Everything can always get better, Molly."

She knew the opposite. And she didn't need to drag him down with her. Dredging up what she hoped resembled a smile, she said, "I better get back to the store."

Carter frowned and his features turned hard. His hand slid from the side of her face to grasp her chin firmly. "I won't let anyone hurt you, Molly."

She did know that, but she couldn't ask him to stay, to right her wrongs, to give up his dreams. The things that made him who he was. A truly remarkable man. "Thank you, Carter. For all you have done. It's made a world of difference." She broke from his hold then, started walking away.

"I'll take you to Montana," he said from behind her. "You and Ivy and Karleen, if that's what you want."

The struggle within her was fierce. Half an hour ago that had been exactly what she'd wanted him to say. She even contemplated it for a moment as she stood, staring toward the big house with its storefront and the outbuildings surrounding it. But she had more than many people had, and she wouldn't give it up, wouldn't make her sisters give it up. "Thank you, but no. That's your dream, Carter, and I don't expect you to share it with me."

It's Carter Buchanan's job to know about secrets and Molly has something to hide. But she touches a place he thought long ago dead, and those eyes have got this cowboy considering exchanging his pistol for a band of gold.

Look for Lauri Robinson's
THE COWBOY WHO CAUGHT HER EYE,
coming July 2013 from Harlequin® Historical.

SADDLE UP AND READ 'EM!

This summer, get your fix of Western reads and pick up a cowboy from some of your favorite authors!

In July, look for:

ZANE by Brenda Jackson
The Westmorelands
Harlequin Desire

THE HEART WON'T LIE by Vicki Lewis Thompson
Sons of Chance
Harlequin Blaze

OUTLAW LAWMAN by Delores Fossen
The Marshals of Maverick County
Harlequin Intrigue

BRANDED BY A CALLAHAN by Tina Leonard
Callahan Cowboys
Harlequin American Romance

Look for these great Western reads and more, available wherever books are sold or visit
www.Harlequin.com/Westerns

HARLEQUIN® HISTORICAL:
Where love is timeless

LADY JENNA ALEYNE MUST MARRY WELL IF SHE IS TO CLAIM HER LANDS...

Only there is a complete lack of eligible suitors in the Highlands! But then Niall Gilvry is assigned to watch over Jenna, and there's no denying she finds this handsome Scot *most* distracting!

Niall knows Jenna is too fine a lady for the likes of him—after all, high society has little time for a lowly third son—but he takes his duty seriously. With danger lurking in the shadows, Niall stays close. It would just be oh, so easy to pull her into his arms....

THE GILVRYS OF DUNROSS
Capturing ladies' hearts across the Highlands

Look for

Her Highland Protector

by Ann Lethbridge in July 2013.

Available wherever books are sold.